"You took a nasty tumble," he said. "I think you slipped on ¹⁰/₁₇
an oil slick."

I looked at his handsome face and nodded. "Probably," I mumbled.

"Hey," he said. "Aren't you . . ." He snapped his fingers. "Didn't we meet last summer? Aren't you related to Chloe? I think we met at LuLu's when you were having lunch there."

I looked at him more closely. He was right. Chloe had introduced us. He had even given me his business card, telling me if I did decide to relocate to give him a call because he owned a real estate agency.

"Yes. You're Chadwick Price. I remember meeting you."

"Right, and you're Isabelle. So I take it you did move here?"

"Yeah. About a week ago. I'm staying at Koi House with my daughter till we find our own place." All of a sudden I recalled the way Chloe had met him the year before and I started laughing. "Do you make a habit of rescuing damsels in distress in the rain?"

Also by Terri DuLong

In the Cedar Key series
Spinning Forward
"A Cedar Key Christmas" in Holiday Magic
Casting About
Sunrise on Cedar Key
Secrets on Cedar Key
Postcards from Cedar Key
Farewell to Cedar Key

In the Ormond Beach series
Patterns of Change

Stitches in Time

Terri DuLong

LYRICAL SHINE
Kensington Publishing Corp.
www.kensingtonbooks.com

LYRICAL SHINE BOOKS are published by

Kensington Publishing Corp.
119 West 40th Street
New York, NY 10018

All Kensington titles, imprints, and distributed lines are available at special quantity discounts for bulk purchases for sales promotion, premiums, fund-raising, educational, or institutional use.

Special book excerpts or customized printings can also be created to fit specific needs. For details, write or phone the office of the Kensington Sales Manager: Kensington Publishing Corp., 119 West 40th Street, New York, NY 10018. Attn. Sales Department. Phone: 1-800-221-2647.

Lyrical Shine and Lyrical Shine logo Reg. US Pat. & TM Off.

First Electronic Edition: June 2016
eISBN-13: 978-1-60183-553-6
eISBN-10: 1-60183-553-1

First Print Edition: June 2016
ISBN-13: 978-1-60183-554-3
ISBN-10: 1-60183-554-X

Printed in the United States of America

For Bill Bonner
My first reader, my writing partner, but most of
all . . . my friend.

ACKNOWLEDGMENTS

For Deborah Sorensen and Tatiana Castano, thank you for sharing with me your love and devotion for the sea turtle program. Your work at the Sea Turtle Oversight Protection organization was my inspiration for Isabelle and her mother to share this worthy cause with my readers. And an extra thank you to Deborah for answering my multitude of questions concerning the process.

Another thank you to April Reis for your design of Isabelle's Challenge. I have no doubt that my readers will enjoy knitting the scarf mentioned in my story.

And to my readers . . . Thank you for the reviews you write for my books, for your comments on Facebook, for your emails, but most of all for the strong support you have shown for my stories. Your loyalty is deeply appreciated.

Chapter 1

I had been toying with the idea of relocating to Ormond Beach since I'd visited my friend Chloe last summer. But I didn't think it would take a fire in my house to force the move—a fire caused by my smoldering cigarette. To take up the habit of smoking at age forty-five had been stupid at best and dangerous at worst: it had caused the near destruction of my home.

I rolled over in bed and saw sunshine streaming through the windows as the aroma of Petra's coffee drifted into the bedroom. Petra. The meaning of her name was *the rock* and she had been my rock since we'd become best friends at age five on the first day of kindergarten. Through the joys of childhood, the emotions of teen years, and the reality of adulthood. For forty years she had been there for me through good and bad, and once again she had extended her friendship by insisting that Haley and I spend some time at her home in Jacksonville before driving down to Ormond Beach.

I let out a yawn and glanced at the bedside clock to see that it was going on seven. After the five-hour drive from Atlanta the day before, Haley and I had arrived at Petra's home in late afternoon. By nine I was ready for bed and now realized I'd slept straight through the night.

After hitting the bathroom, I wandered out to the kitchen to find it empty, but I noticed a note on the counter near the coffeemaker. *Gone to take Lotte for her walk. Help yourself to coffee. Be back soon*, it read.

I glanced around the designer kitchen and smiled. Petra had done very well for herself. Never married, no children, she had a top job with a software company and she never failed to admit that the bonus of her job was being able to work from her home. She'd had men in her life over the years but never any serious enough to consider marriage. Unlike me, who only ever wanted a husband and family, Petra was content lavishing all of her love on various dogs she'd had over the years; Lotte was the current recipient of that love.

I poured myself a mug of the strong coffee and headed out to the pool area. It was a beautiful late January morning and I was grateful to be spending some time with Petra. Just as I sat down, my cell phone rang. I looked at the caller ID to see that it was my mother calling. Again. I let it go to voice mail and let out a sigh. Our mother-daughter relationship had been going downhill ever since I was thirteen, and by the time I was fifteen and she left my father and me, it was pretty much nonexistent. When my dad passed away two years ago, my mother began a continuous effort to renew that relationship—to no avail.

"We're back," I heard Petra call from the kitchen.

"Out here," I called back.

Lotte scampered over to me and I laughed when I saw she was dressed in a pink-and-white outfit and wearing a pink sun visor. She was an adorable Yorkie, but I did think Petra went a bit overboard on the pampering.

Petra joined me with a mug of coffee. Placing it on the table, she scooped up Lotte before sitting down. "Sleep okay?"

"Yeah, I sure did. All night. Which hasn't happened in a while."

"Good. Well, I'm sure you were tired from your drive, and polishing off almost a bottle of wine probably helped."

Was that a tinge of reproach I heard in her tone?

"Haley still sleeping?" she asked.

"Yup. We might not see her till noon."

"Hey, she's a teenager. We did the same thing at her age."

"Do you ever wonder where all the years went?" I let out a deep sigh as I rested my head on the back of the chair, letting the sun warm my face.

"Not really." Petra took a sip of coffee. "I won't lie. They do seem to be going faster. And when I think back to our days at Penn State, it seems like ages ago, but we've both done a lot of living since then. You got married, had Haley . . ."

"Right," I interrupted. "That's about all I did. While you traveled the world, relocated here, bought this gorgeous home, and built a good career for yourself."

"True," she said, nodding her head. "But like I've always said, we all make our choices."

Petra was a no-nonsense type person.

"You've had a rough two years, Isabelle. Your father passed away, Roger left you, and you still haven't made an effort with your mom. Don't be so hard on yourself. You're taking the first step to a new start by moving to Ormond Beach. Who knows what's ahead for you?"

I knew she was right and I also knew I was feeling sorry for myself. Losing my father suddenly to a heart attack had rocked my world. When my mother left thirty years ago and my parents were divorced, my father and I became even closer, making the loss of him more difficult. And a few months later, when Roger informed me that he no longer loved me and was leaving me for somebody else, I felt like my life was being ripped away from me. Roger wasn't the most passionate of men, but I thought the love we shared was mutual and would continue. I came to understand how wrong I was. Looking back, I now realized that if not for Petra and Chloe, I wasn't sure I would have walked through that dark time to the other side.

"You're right," I told her, making an attempt at being optimistic. "And I'm very grateful to Chloe for insisting that Haley and I come to Koi House. There she is in the middle of planning her wedding to Henry, running the new yarn shop in town and everything else she does, and yet she finds the time to worry about me." I sniffed as I felt moisture stinging my eyes.

Petra reached over and gave my hand a squeeze. "You're worth worrying about, Isabelle Wainwright, and don't you ever think different. And besides, I think Chloe and her friends are just as grateful that you'll be there. Chloe was thrilled that you agreed to look after Mavis Anne while her brother is in Italy. And how about that delivery service her niece wants to set up? I'm sure she's very happy that you'll be doing that for her."

I smiled. Once again Petra was right and had cheered me up. Mavis Anne Overby was the owner of Koi House, where Chloe lived and where Haley and I would be staying until we found our own home. She was also part owner with Chloe of the yarn shop, Dreamweavers. Mavis's niece Yarrow owned the tea shop where Dreamweavers was located and had been wanting to set up a morning delivery service for offices and merchants who wanted coffee and baked goods to start their workday. Yarrow was unable to leave the shop during this busy time and therefore needed somebody willing to work part-time making the deliveries. And Mavis Anne would have had to resort to hiring a stranger to look after her while her brother, David, and his partner, Clive, were on holiday.

"Yeah, maybe you're right."

Petra's smile matched mine. "Of course I'm right. It's obvious that they love you, and Haley and I know they're very happy that you're going to be staying with them for a while. Come on," she said, getting up. "Time for a coffee refill and then I'll make breakfast for us."

"You still make the best French toast in town," I told her as I took the final sip of my coffee. I looked up to see my fourteen-year-old daughter walk into the kitchen. Haley was tall and slim now, proof of how quickly the years had passed. Not for the first time I wished we could recapture the closeness we had shared a few years ago. But, like me, she'd had to endure losses in her life as well as being a victim of bullying the previous school year. My hope was that our relocation to Ormond Beach would enable the sulky, unhappy teen to morph into the well-adjusted daughter I'd once had.

"Good morning, sunshine," I said.

"Hmm," was the response I got.

"How about a batch of French toast?" Petra asked her.

"No. But thanks. Just some juice, please. And I'm going for a run."

"Juice it is," Petra told her.

I knew I sounded like the nagging mom, but I couldn't refrain from saying, "Maybe you should have something to eat before you exercise?"

Haley shook her head. "No, Mom. It's not good to eat first. I'll have something when I come back."

She gulped down the juice, scooped Lotte up for a hug, and headed toward the front door. "I'll be back in about an hour," she hollered over her shoulder.

I let out a sigh and shrugged. "I don't know which is worse—her being overweight or being borderline fanatic with her food and exercise."

I recalled the year before and the misery that Haley had endured after she'd packed on too many pounds. It had been Chloe who had somehow gotten Haley on a healthy eating plan and walking routine. When we returned home two weeks later, I thought perhaps Haley would resume her old ways of eating and lack of exercise, but I was wrong. Instead, she asked to join the local gym and pretty much existed on salad and protein. Now I was concerned that maybe she was going too much in the opposite direction.

"Oh, God, you don't think she's anorexic, do you? I did notice last evening at dinner that she seemed to move more food around her plate than she put in her mouth."

"I honestly don't know, but I plan to keep an eye on it." Just then my cell phone went off on the table beside me. Once again the caller ID read *Iris Brunell*. My mother.

"Why the hell does she keep calling me?" Annoyance tinged my voice.

"Your mother?" Petra questioned.

"Yup."

"Geez, Isabelle. I think she's just concerned about you and Haley. She knows about the fire and she knows you're moving to Ormond Beach. She probably just wants to know if you got here okay."

"What? How did she even know we were coming here? You've been talking to her, haven't you?"

Petra raised a palm in the air. "Hey, don't get me involved in this. You know damn well your mother has always been like an aunt to me. You have your differences with her. I don't."

A sense of betrayal shot through me. "Yeah, well, it wasn't *you* she left to take off to Oregon with a lover when you were fifteen," I retorted as I headed to the bedroom.

Chapter 2

An hour later I came out of the bedroom to find another note on the kitchen counter. *I'm holed up in my office working for a few hours. Help yourself to whatever you need. Haley has gone to the mall with the girl across the street*, Petra had written.

I looked around the kitchen and decided a glass of wine was in order. The saying that it has to be five o'clock somewhere had become my mantra over the past year. I found a bottle of chardonnay in the wine rack, uncorked it, poured myself a glass, and walked out to the pool area.

Another gorgeous day in paradise. No wonder so many people vacationed and retired to this state. I curled up on the lounge and gazed at the aqua water. It was then that I recalled I'd done the very same thing the day of the fire.

I took a sip of wine, closed my eyes, and leaned my head back. That morning had started like any other. Haley had left for school and once again I gave thanks for that. At least the fire hadn't happened during the night with both of us asleep and our lives possibly at risk. I had wandered around the house aimlessly, hating the long day that stretched ahead. No job. Nowhere to go. Nothing that required my attention. By eleven, I had poured myself a glass of wine, took the bottle with me, and sat staring at the pool, wondering how my life had unraveled so completely. I was having a difficult time adjusting to the death of my father and the breakup of my marriage. Each day seemed to blend into another with no prospect of change. Chloe and Haley had repeatedly tried to convince me to relocate to Ormond Beach, but I felt my energy had been sapped. Petra was convinced I was depressed, and she was probably right, because it seemed that drinking had become my only comfort.

I now recalled sitting there by the pool feeling sorry for myself as I consumed a few glasses of wine. I must have dozed off, because the next thing I knew, I woke to the shrill sound of a fire alarm and saw smoke billowing out of the downstairs windows. By the time the fire department arrived, there had been moderate damage to the family room and kitchen. If there was anything good about the fire, it was the fact that the cigarette that started it was my last.

"Ready for lunch?" I heard Petra say.

I shielded my eyes from the sun with my arm and looked up. "Sure."

"Grilled cheese and tomato soup?"

I smiled. Ever since we were kids, that had been our comfort lunch. No matter how bad things were at school or home or with our other friends, a grilled cheese and tomato soup was the solution.

Petra turned around and headed back inside. I finished my last sip of wine and followed her.

"I'm sorry I snapped at you," I said.

"I know you are. But geez, Isabelle, maybe you should cut your mom some slack. She really is trying."

"It's not that easy, Pet. You, of all people, should know that. You were there when she left. You know how tough it was for me."

I watched as she slathered butter onto slices of sourdough bread, placed a slice of Monterey Jack in between, and put the sandwiches on the sizzling grill.

"I know it was hard for you, but just remember it wasn't all about *you*. You know yourself you used to complain about your parents not getting along. They didn't have major fights, but I still remember the tension in that house. They weren't happy together anymore, Isabelle. This happens. As you now know."

"Right. But she left us for somebody else. Imagine how my poor father felt. God, they worked at the same university together. He must have been so embarrassed that his wife left him and he had to face their colleagues every day at work."

"But that was their problem, as I've told you a million times. It shouldn't have affected your relationship with your mom. Iris is a kindhearted person. She really tried over the years. It was you who always rejected her. When was the last time you even saw her?"

It had been when I was pregnant with Haley. Fourteen years ago.

She had flown back to Atlanta, stayed in a hotel for a few days, met with my dad over some financial matters, begged me to have dinner with her, and then returned to Oregon. I did have dinner with her, but it was strained and uncomfortable for me. And in the years since then, our relationship could be described as out of sight, out of mind.

When I remained silent, Petra said, "Yeah, when you were pregnant with Haley. Believe me, I remember. You have effectively pushed her out of your life. The only thing I can give you credit for is not taking Haley away from her, but even with that you could have tried harder and allowed them to see much more of each other over the years. She *is* Haley's grandmother, but you've made very little effort to let Iris be part of Haley's life."

She was right and I knew it. When Haley turned twelve, I finally let her fly to Oregon for a week during summer vacation, and when Haley returned I pretty much ignored anything she had to relate about the visit.

"You just don't understand," I said, wanting to drop the subject.

"I do understand and you know that. Okay, enough. Let's enjoy our lunch."

I reached for the two bowls of soup and placed them on the table while Petra brought the sandwiches.

"Ice water with lemon?" she asked.

I had a feeling wine wasn't on the menu. "Sure."

I took a bite of the sandwich and groaned. "Delicious. I swear that the problems of the world could be solved with these sandwiches."

Petra laughed. "If only. Hey, I need to go to the yarn shop later to get some sock yarn. You'll come with me, right? I think Haley also wants to go."

Over the past year, I had actually made more of an attempt to become a knitter. While I wasn't nearly as proficient as my daughter, I had to admit that I did enjoy the hobby, and could now brag that I'd actually completed a few scarves and was working on a cowl.

"Sure. That sounds like fun. A new yarn shop to explore. Knitting really is addictive."

"I'm jealous, you know. You're so fortunate you'll be staying at Koi House with Dreamweavers right out back. Talk about a knitter's fantasy."

I let out a chuckle and nodded. "Yeah, probably true. I haven't seen the completed shop since it opened last September, but Chloe says it's just beautiful and business is doing very well. I think more and more women are either learning to knit or returning to it after many years."

"Well, no doubt about it. I'm a confirmed knitter. I always found it odd that when your mom offered to teach both of us as kids, you showed little interest. Your mom is still an expert knitter, you know."

"I'm not surprised. She's always been a creative person. That's why she teaches art at the university."

"Taught," Petra said.

My head snapped up to stare at her. "What do you mean, *taught*?"

We were interrupted by Haley walking into the kitchen—with stripes of pink streaking her thick, gorgeous, honey-colored hair.

I jumped up from my chair. "What the hell did you do, Haley?"

I saw her smirk as she said, "Oh, Mom. Chill out. I went with Liz to the hair salon. She had blue put in her hair. It'll grow out."

"What were you thinking? You've ruined your beautiful hair! How could you do such a stupid thing?"

She shrugged. "We didn't think it was stupid. Liz's mom was fine with it. She drove us there."

I shook my head. "Well, I'm not fine with it. It looks . . . it looks . . ." I found I had no words to adequately describe what I thought it looked like.

"Cool?" was my daughter's reply.

"Oh, God, Haley. No, not cool." I blew out a breath and wondered if I'd survive my daughter's teen years.

"Yes, well . . ." Petra said, standing up and clearing the table. "How about some lunch, sweetie?"

"I'm not—"

Before she could finish, I said, "You *will* eat lunch before we go to the yarn shop."

As if not daring to assert any more of her independence, she said, "Do you have any yogurt and fruit?"

"I do," Petra said. "In the fridge. Help yourself."

The drive to the yarn shop was fairly quiet, with Petra making small attempts at conversation. We pulled up to a strip mall and I saw a sign that said "A Piece of Ewe."

"Cute name for a yarn shop," I said, getting out of the car and following Petra inside.

I'll never understand how walking into a yarn shop surrounded by shelves and tables of fiber can suddenly make stress and concerns slip away. But I think any knitter can attest to the fact that this is exactly what happens. So for the next hour the three of us touched and exclaimed over various yarn fibers and colors.

By the time we checked out, we each had a filled shopping bag. I had found some Bamboo Pop by Universal Yarns that had me drooling over the gorgeous colorways. Petra felt it was time for me to move on from scarves to make myself a short-sleeved top. She found a pattern with twisty cables and said she'd teach me that evening.

Haley got some Ultra Pima cotton in various shades of pink—no doubt to match her hair—and was going to make herself a pullover sweater.

And Petra found some funky colors in fingering weight sock yarn, claiming she never wore store-bought socks anymore, only her hand-knitted ones.

We returned home and I helped Petra prepare dinner. I wanted a glass of wine before we ate but I was hesitant to ask and felt guilty just helping myself.

Petra put lemon chicken into the oven while I prepared a salad.

"Okay," she said. "All I have to do is the rice pilaf. How about a glass of wine by the pool?"

"Sounds good."

We took the wine out to the patio table. Haley was already curled up in the family room casting on the stitches for her new sweater.

I took a sip of wine and then remembered our interrupted conversation earlier.

"Oh," I said. "What did you mean about my mother and that she used to teach art?"

"When was the last time you talked to her?"

I honestly wasn't sure. "Maybe November. A few months ago. Why?"

"Well . . . she's retired."

"Retired? Since when?"

"Since last month. Early December."

"She never said a word to me about that."

Petra took a sip of wine. "Maybe she thought you wouldn't be interested."

I ignored this comment. "Well, she's always been a bit of a hippie. Maybe now she can go retire on a commune."

"Oh, she's not retiring to a commune."

"So where is she planning to retire?"

"To Florida," Petra informed me.

Chapter 3

Out of all the states in this country, why did my mother have to choose the one I was moving to for her retirement?

I had attempted to pump Haley for information the night before, but I didn't get very far.

"So you knew she was moving here to Florida?" I had asked her.

"Yes."

"Why didn't you tell me?"

"Maybe because I didn't think you'd be interested?"

She had a point. I had never hidden from my daughter the fact that my mother and I weren't close. Well, Florida was a fairly large state. "Where in Florida? Do you know?" I had asked.

"She still isn't sure, but she does want to go to Ormond Beach so she can visit with me for a little while."

Haley continued to focus on her knitting and I dropped the subject, but when I woke this morning the annoyance I'd felt the evening before had returned.

Petra was working in her office and Haley had taken off with Liz—with strict instructions from me not to even *think* about coming back with a body piercing or tattoo.

I took my coffee and walked out to the patio area. This would be our final day in Jacksonville. I had decided we'd drive to Ormond Beach the following day.

I had just removed my knitting from the tote bag when my cell phone rang. I saw it was my mother again and thought it best to answer this time. It would probably be the only way I'd get any details.

"Yes, Mom. How are you?"

"I'm well, Isabelle. How are you doing?"

"Okay. Haley and I are heading to Ormond Beach tomorrow."

"Oh, good. I know Haley is excited about moving there."

"Right. And speaking of moving, I hear you're now retired and planning to move to Florida also."

"Yes, and so far I love this retirement life. At sixty-eight I'm ready to move aside and make room for the younger teachers. And yes, I made the decision to live my retirement years in Florida. With the great weather and so many social activities, it seemed like the ideal location. It won't be a problem, will it?"

I answered her question with another question. "Where exactly in Florida are you planning to live?"

"Well, I'm not quite sure yet. I've been doing some research and the west coast looks good. Around Naples and that area; however, during the summer it's about ten degrees hotter there than other parts of Florida."

I did a quick calculation in my head and was pretty sure Naples was about a four and a half hour drive from Ormond Beach. Probably far enough to prevent frequent visits.

"I know there are a lot of retirement communities there," I told her.

"Yeah, but I'm also considering the east coast. I might be happier not living surrounded by only retirees. Having neighbors of various ages might be more to my liking. At any rate, I've made plans to fly to Orlando on March twenty-eighth; I'm renting a car at the airport and I've booked a hotel in Ormond Beach for a week. I really want to spend some quality time with Haley. I hope that's okay with you."

I knew I'd been stingy over the years with the time I allowed my daughter to spend with her grandmother. And I also knew that Haley was now at an age at which she spoke up about this fact.

"Yeah. Fine," I mumbled.

"Good. While I'm there, I plan to check out that area and see what's available for housing. I'd also like to find a part-time position. Something to do with the arts. Lord knows I've got plenty of experience. Well, I won't keep you, Isabelle. Have a good trip tomorrow and give my love to Haley and Petra."

We hung up and I realized that she hadn't sent any love my way. Not surprising. I'd learned over the years not to expect warm and fuzzy exchanges with my mother. I might not be mother of the year, but I did know there was no way that I would suddenly decide to leave Haley, move across the country, and build a new life for myself. It just wasn't possible. Especially not just to be with a lover. Somebody my mother had put above me.

I picked up my knitting and began working on the top while I pushed thoughts of thirty years ago out of my head.

Petra emerged from her office around one and found me still sitting on the patio knitting.

"Well, look at you," she said. "That top is working up very nicely. I love the color."

I looked up and nodded. "I really do enjoy knitting." I removed the earbuds from my ears. "And listening to music at the same time makes it especially relaxing."

"That it does. But I'm starved. Ready for lunch?"

"Sounds good," I said, getting up to follow her inside.

I helped Petra prepare a crabmeat salad plate and we settled down at the table.

I took a sip of iced tea. "My mother called," I told her.

Petra looked at me with arched eyebrows. "Oh. And?"

"And she's flying down here late March. Already arranged for a rental car and booked a hotel in Ormond Beach for a week. So she can see Haley, that's what she said."

"Makes sense to me. She has all the time in the world now. Where is she planning to actually live?"

"She's still not sure. Possibly the west coast, but it could also be the east coast."

"Hmm."

"What's that mean?" I took a bite of salad.

"It means you'd prefer she stay right where she is. Hey, be honest. You don't want her living in your area."

"No. I really don't. There are plenty of places for her to go."

"Maybe she doesn't want to be alone."

I let out an exaggerated chuckle. "She should have thought about that thirty years ago. What ever happened to her lover? Obviously, he's gone and not in her life anymore. So now she's ready to coming crawling back to her long-lost daughter. Life doesn't work that way."

Petra blew out a breath.

"What? You don't agree?" I said.

"Isabelle, I love you dearly. I've loved you like a sister since we were kids. But . . . you are *the* most stubborn person I know. People make mistakes. People have flaws. We all do. But holding on to so much anger and resentment doesn't make life easier. It makes you a bitter and unhappy person. Cut her some slack. She only wants to be a small part of your life. Just remember . . . she's not getting younger."

I stabbed a piece of tomato. "Oh, so now you're making me feel guilty because she's getting older. Should I just forget that she *chose* to leave my father and me?"

"I hate fighting with you over this. I really do. I'm just saying maybe the time has come to take a deep breath, try to get along with her, and see where it all goes."

I knew I was being difficult. But I also knew that the way I felt was a result of many years of hurt, and I wasn't sure our relationship could ever be fixed.

Chapter 4

Petra and I were having coffee the following morning when Haley wandered into the kitchen. It was only nine, so I was surprised to see that she was already showered and dressed.

"You're up early," I said. "Eager to get to Ormond Beach?"

"I was out running at six," was all she said as she headed to the fridge for juice.

Sometimes I found it hard to believe that she was no longer the toddler who had been so attached to me, sharing all her thoughts, and looking to me for guidance and advice. My daughter had grown into a very attractive young woman who at fourteen was already showing signs of the independent adult she would become. The pink streaks in her hair were proof of that.

"Are we still leaving at ten?" she asked.

"Yes. It's a ninety-minute drive, and I told Chloe we'd be there in time for lunch."

Haley finished the juice and reached for a peach from the fruit bowl on the counter.

"Okay, well, I'm going across the street to say good-bye to Liz. Did you mean it when you said she can come visit us in Ormond Beach?"

"Yes, of course," I assured her. "Petra has promised to come and visit when we get our own place and maybe she'll bring Liz with her."

"Okay. I'll be back in a little while."

I saw the smile on Petra's face.

"What?" I questioned.

"I just can't get over how fast she's growing. It seems like yesterday I was visiting you in the hospital after she was born."

"Yup. I was just thinking how close we were when she was younger. But everything changed a couple years ago when her grandfather died and her father left."

"It's been a tough time for her, but she's a good kid, Isabelle. I think moving to Ormond Beach will be good for both of you. She likes Chloe a lot and she loved visiting there last summer. Most teenage girls go through trying to separate from their moms. It's almost a rite of passage, to prove we're our own person and not an extension of our mothers."

"Hmm, well, I didn't have the opportunity to do that, so I'm not familiar with this particular phase." I heard the sarcasm that tinged my words. "My mother did that for me. She was the one who chose to separate from me."

"Any word from Roger?" Petra asked, clearly wanting to change the subject.

"He called last week. Wanted to wish us well on the move and to be sure I was okay financially."

"Be grateful for that. At least you won't be struggling to pay for a new house. Roger always did look out for you and Haley."

She was right, but being rejected for somebody else had a way of creating bitterness that wasn't always buffered by money.

Shortly after ten, the three of us stood in Petra's driveway exchanging hugs and weepy good-byes. I loved spending time with her and was glad we'd now be living much closer.

I backed out of the driveway, and looked back to see Petra waving and then lifting her hand to her ear, reminding me to call when I arrived at Chloe's house. I nodded, gave a final wave, and headed toward I-95 south.

We had been driving about thirty minutes in silence. Haley had earbuds in her ears as she listened to music on her phone and stared out the window.

I reached over to pat her knee. "Excited?" I asked in a voice louder than normal, hoping she heard me.

To my surprise, Haley removed the earbuds and nodded. "Yeah, I am. I think it will be good for us. I love Chloe and I can't wait to see Basil."

Haley had formed a close attachment to my father's mixed terrier, Basil. When my dad died, there was the question of what to do with the dog. Haley had begged for us to take him, but I wasn't crazy about that idea. The added responsibility of a dog was just too much for me at that time. When I suggested maybe he should go to the pound, Chloe, my father's girlfriend, refused to allow that and she took Basil home with her. I had to admit when I saw them together last summer I knew that was the right decision.

"Would you like a dog?" I blurted. I had no idea where that thought had come from.

Haley swiveled in her seat to face me. "Seriously?"

I focused on the highway in front of me. "Well . . . yeah . . . maybe. So you'd like that?"

"Oh, Mom, I've always wanted a dog. Always. I would love to have my own dog. And I'm not a kid anymore. I'd be the one to feed it and walk it and take care of it."

She might not be a kid, but the exuberance I heard in her voice reminded me of the twelve-year-old who had disappeared.

"I think you're right. You're at an age where you're responsible and could care for a dog. You were excellent with Basil last summer."

"So I can? I can get a dog?"

I nodded. "Here's the deal. When we get our own house and we're settled in, yes, you can have your own dog."

Haley leaned over as much as the seat belt would allow and gave me a hug. "I love you, Mom! I love you so much. And thank you."

I wasn't quite sure what caused me to agree to this, but I did know that hearing the joy in Haley's voice telling me she loved me made me positive I'd done the right thing.

We pulled up in the driveway of Koi House shortly after our expected arrival time. I thought back to last summer when Haley and I had driven down from Atlanta. My daughter had been overweight, miserable, and a victim of bullying at school. I glanced at her and smiled. Maybe this move truly would be good. For both of us.

The front door flew open and I saw Chloe on the porch with Basil close at her heels. Haley jumped out while I flipped the lid on the trunk.

"Hey, welcome," Chloe called.

I raised a hand in greeting. "Thanks. I'm just going to get a couple bags. I'll be right there. Haley, come help."

I removed a piece of luggage and a tote bag filled with knitting from the trunk and glanced at the house. It was a beautiful old-fashioned Victorian complete with a turret jutting out from the second story. I knew Koi House had become Chloe's oasis when she relocated here from Cedar Key the year before. Mavis Anne Overby was the official owner but now resided next door with her brother and his partner. Chloe had been fortunate to meet this woman and her niece when she'd visited Yarrow's original tea shop. An instant connection had formed among the three of them, and they now shared both a friendship and a business relationship.

"I'll take these," Haley said, reaching into the trunk and removing more luggage.

I walked onto the porch and into Chloe's embrace.

"I'm so glad you're here," she said. "All of us have missed you. Come on in and get settled."

I followed her into the foyer. She pointed to the staircase.

"I hope you don't mind, Isabelle, but I've taken the larger bedroom in back that used to be Mavis Anne's. So I've put you in the front one, if that's okay. Go on up and put your things away while I get our lunch together."

"That's fine," I told her. "Not a problem."

As Haley and I climbed the stairs, I recalled our visit from the previous summer. Chloe had been very gracious when she'd invited Haley and me to spend two weeks with her. She was also going through the grieving process of losing my father and realizing that everything they had planned had ended when my father died. They had expected to purchase a home in Ormond Beach, where my dad would raise alpacas and both of them would run a yarn shop together downtown. But that wasn't to be. Chloe's life had taken another direction, which now included Henry Wagner, the man she'd be marrying in a few months.

I looked around the room and smiled. Everything felt so welcoming. The beautiful furnishings and décor had an old-fashioned, cozy feel. I opened my luggage and began putting clothes away in the closet and bureau drawers. Buffered around the items in my leather tote were four bottles of wine. I had brought two to give to Chloe, but the other two I slipped into one of my drawers. I liked knowing they were there to enjoy at night before I went to sleep.

I placed the empty luggage in the closet and looked around. This bedroom at the front was the one with the turret; it had belonged to

Mavis Anne's sister, Emmalyn, Yarrow's mother. She had died at age twenty-eight in a tragic car crash that had been tinged with scandal, according to Chloe. It was eerie, but this room was definitely much cooler than the rest of the house. Chloe had hinted that Emmalyn's ghost still lingered. I had no belief in such things, and smiled as I headed out to the hallway to check on Haley.

"Need any help?" I asked.

"No, thanks. I'm fine. I'll see you downstairs."

I walked to the back of the house and found Chloe in the gorgeous designer kitchen putting the final touches on salad plates.

She came over to give me a hug. "I'm so glad you're here, Isabelle, and even happier that you'll be staying in the area permanently."

"I am too and I know Haley is excited."

I saw a look of concern cross her face. "I can't believe the weight she's lost since last summer. She isn't sick, is she?"

I laughed. "No, not at all. Just very serious about her exercise and food plan."

"Gosh, I'd hate to see her go the other way. She's borderline skinny now. I hope she's not overdoing it."

Despite my own concerns, I brushed her words aside. "No. Really. She's fine," I said. My gaze went to the French doors leading out to the patio and garden area. "Oh, Dreamweavers. I'm dying to see it. It wasn't even open when I was here last. Is that where Mavis Anne and Yarrow are?"

Haley walked into the kitchen followed by Basil. "Oh, the yarn shop. Can I go out there?"

"After lunch," I told her.

"Yes," Chloe said. "Let's eat and then we'll go. Have a seat. Water, iced tea, wine?"

"Water, please," Haley said.

"I'll have a glass of wine," I told her with no hesitation as I walked to the beautiful blue-and-yellow breakfast nook area.

"This is such a pretty spot," I said, sitting down at the lemon yellow wooden table.

"It is," Chloe agreed as she placed plates of quiche and salad in front of us. "Compliments of Marta, who said to say hello. She'll see you tomorrow."

Marta was a Polish immigrant who had been the right hand of Mavis Anne for ten years and now continued to work for Chloe as housekeeper and cook. I knew they adored her and valued her exceptional work ethic, and there was no doubt that Marta was devoted to Mavis Anne, David, and now Chloe.

"This is delicious," Haley said as she nibbled on the salad.

I was happy to see her eating, but her quiche remained untouched.

"We have so much catching up to do," Chloe said.

I took a sip of wine and nodded. "I know. I'm dying to hear all about your wedding plans. How *is* Henry?"

Chloe smiled and I saw the look of pure love on her face. "Oh, he's great. He'll be over later. And yes, I'll fill you in on all the wedding plans, but it's just going to be a small gathering out there by the fishpond with my sister and her husband and some friends."

"I'm so glad we'll be here for your wedding," Haley said.

"I am too." Chloe shot her a smile. "So . . . what's going on in your lives?"

"My nana is retiring to Florida," Haley informed her.

I looked up to see the look of total surprise that crossed Chloe's face.

"Oh. Really? Well . . . that sounds . . . interesting?"

I laughed. "Hmm, yeah. *Interesting* is a good word for it. I'll fill you in later tonight when we have our evening gabfest."

I took a gulp of wine and realized that my mother's moving to Florida might have more implications than I could begin to think about.

Chapter 5

Following lunch Chloe, Haley, and I walked out to the patio area. I took in a deep breath. It was a beautiful, warm afternoon and I could smell salt air from the Atlantic. I looked over to the stone wall and archway where I knew the fishpond was located; then my gaze fell on the beautiful honey stone building that reminded me of a thatched cottage in England, complete with oval-shaped wooden door. Dreamweavers. The name was Chloe's inspiration. A wooden sign dangled from a post with the etched words "Dreamweaver Yarn Shop & Nirvana Tea and Coffee." Yarrow had also chosen the perfect name for her business.

"I'm dying to see the yarn shop," Haley said, walking in that direction.

We followed her to the wooden door and stepped inside. It had been an empty shell when I'd seen it last summer, but now it had been transformed into an enticing yarn shop. My gaze took in the cubbyholes filling the wall to my left, each one displaying various colors and fibers. Tables held baskets of yarn, and knitted items had been placed to catch the eye of a knitter. Mavis Anne Overby looked up from the cherrywood desk at the front of the shop when we walked in.

Clapping her hands together, she reached for her cane and walked toward us, a huge smile covering her face. "Welcome, welcome," she exclaimed, as she hugged Haley and then me. "I'm so glad you're here. Did you have a good drive? How about lunch? Have you eaten?"

I laughed and nodded. Mavis Anne had one of those big personalities that made you feel good just being in her presence. "The drive was good and yes, Chloe had lunch ready when we arrived."

"Hey, you're here," I heard Yarrow call from the back, where her tea shop was located. She joined us and more hugs were exchanged. I waved my hand around the shop. "This is just gorgeous. I can't believe what you've done with it." I now saw the large rectangular wooden table to my right and knew that it was used for the instruction sessions and knit-alongs the shop had. And behind the display tables were a couple of cushy sofas and chairs, which I knew visitors and regulars to the shop couldn't resist using to chill out and socialize while they knitted.

Haley was already fingering various yarns on display. "Oh, I know. This place looks so great. How lucky am I to stay right next door to a yarn shop," she said, and all of us laughed.

"Thank you," Mavis Anne said. "I think I can speak for the three of us when I say it's been a labor of love. And so far, it's proving to be very successful."

All of us looked down at Basil, who had begun whining and dancing in circles as he repeatedly ran to the French doors at the side of the shop.

"What's up with him?" Haley asked.

Yarrow laughed. "I think he might want to introduce you to his buddy. Come on outside."

We followed her out to the patio area. A canopy of trees provided shade over the cushy chairs arranged around a fire pit. Curled up in one of the chairs was a gorgeous black-and-white cat snoozing.

Haley walked directly toward the chair. "Oh, wow. Who's this?"

Yarrow smiled. "This is Merino, my cat, but he also claims the title of the shop mascot. Actually, it was Basil who found him last fall cowering in the bushes. Just a tiny kitten and I couldn't resist him. So I took him to the vet, got his shots, and decided that for the first time in my life I'd become a pet owner."

I laughed and watched as Haley gushed over him. Merino opened one eye, then the other, gave a huge yawn, stood up, stretched and then proceeded to lie back down to resume his nap.

"Does he stay here all the time?" Haley questioned.

"No. I take him home with me each evening and bring him back in the morning. He sometimes wanders into the yarn shop but so far he hasn't touched any of the yarn. For the most part, he prefers to be out here. Who'd like some coffee or tea?"

We followed Yarrow back inside and while she headed to the back to prepare the drinks, I settled on a sofa with Chloe.

"So are you doing classes and knit-alongs?" I asked.

Mavis Anne nodded. "Yes, we have my friend Louise teaching a class on entrelac once a week and our current knit-along is a sampler afghan. A few more weeks and that will be finished. Are you keeping up with your knitting?"

I nodded. "Yes, actually, Petra took us to a yarn shop in Jacksonville yesterday and I got some Bamboo Pop to make myself a top."

"Oh, I love that yarn," Chloe said and pointed to a gorgeous mint green pullover displayed on a manikin. "I made that last month for our display."

"I'm so glad you decided to relocate here," Mavis Anne said. "And it means so much to me that you're willing to look after me when David and Clive leave for Italy."

"It's my pleasure. And I'm very grateful you've invited Haley and me to stay here."

I couldn't help but wonder again why it was necessary for Mavis Anne to have a caregiver while her brother and his partner were away. Especially with Chloe right next door. But I did know that many nights Chloe and Basil stayed over at Henry's condo on the beach. I also knew that Mavis Anne Overby could be a prima donna. She adored being waited on and spoiled.

I smiled as I heard her say, "Oh, honey, it's Koi House and I that are grateful. The house was ever so happy when Chloe moved in, but now with you and Haley here . . . well . . . my goodness, I have no doubt Koi House is filled with joy."

I caught the wink and smile Chloe sent my way and recalled what she'd shared with me the year before. Koi House had been the childhood home of Mavis Anne, David, and their deceased sister, Emmalyn. According to Chloe, Mavis Anne fully believed that her sister's spirit still lingered and also that the house had a soul that was happiest when people resided within its walls. She claimed it had energy and enveloped those who lived there with love. I wasn't sure if Chloe actually believed all of this, but she did indulge Mavis Anne in her beliefs.

"Here we go," Yarrow said, placing a tray with mugs of tea on the table in front of us.

"Thanks," I said and took a sip of the lemon ginger tea. "Hmm, very good." I wasn't much of a tea drinker but had to admit that Yarrow's brews were exceptional. "So when do you want me to begin working?"

"Well, I thought you should take the next few days to just settle in. So I told all of our new customers you'd begin next Monday, the first. Would that be okay?"

I nodded. "Yes, fine. That'll give us time for you to go over the routes with me too."

"Right. But I don't think you'll have much of a problem. Everyone is located right here in Ormond Beach, so it's pretty easy to get around."

A few of the regulars dropped into the shop throughout the afternoon, and a fair number of customers came in to make purchases. I was surprised when I heard Chloe say, "I'll go put the closed sign on the gate." I looked at the clock on the wall and saw it was just after five. The afternoon had flown by as I sat there knitting and conversing, and I was happy to discover that I now had about eight inches done on my top. I was reminded of my days in Atlanta when sometimes an hour felt like a week. Maybe moving here would prove to be a good thing for me.

The three of us walked into the kitchen of Koi House to find Henry preparing dinner.

"Hey," he said, coming to give me a hug. "Welcome to Ormond Beach. And you too, Haley."

I saw my daughter's smile as he also pulled her into an embrace. "Obviously, I'm Henry," he said.

Chloe had only started dating him the previous September, so this was our first time meeting him. She had rented his condo on the beach for a month when she first came here from Cedar Key. And when they actually met in person it appeared to be a case of love at first sight; now their wedding was just a few months away.

I saw him pull Chloe into his arms and without a trace of shyness he kissed her lips. "Have a good day, sweetie?" he asked.

"I did," she told him. "And thank you so much for coming over to get dinner started."

"My pleasure," he told her, and held up a bottle of red wine. "Shall we toast Isabelle and Haley's arrival?"

"That would be nice," Chloe said, reaching for wineglasses in the cabinet.

"Oh, who's this?" I heard Haley say. I turned around to see a large golden retriever wander into the kitchen, followed by Basil.

Henry laughed. "Oh, this is my dog, Delilah. Delilah, meet Haley and Isabelle."

"She's just gorgeous," Haley said, kneeling down to let the dog sniff her hand and then accepting her paw. "What a beautiful girl."

"Thank you. She and Basil are best of friends, which makes it nice."

I smiled as Chloe passed me a wineglass. I could already see that my daughter was in her glory with the yarn shop, Chloe, and two dogs to fawn over. I also had a feeling she had taken an instant liking to Henry, and this made me feel coming here was the right thing to do.

Henry held up his glass. "Here's to Isabelle and Haley. Welcome to your new home. May you have much happiness here."

"Thank you," I said, before I took a sip and realized this was the first time in a long while that I hadn't already had two or three glasses of wine before five o'clock.

Following a delicious dinner of shrimp stir-fry and rice, Haley and I pitched in with the cleanup.

"Well," Henry said, "I'm going to take the dogs for a walk on the beach. This will give you gals some more time to catch up. Haley, would you like to join me?"

"Oh, yes," she said, jumping up.

Chloe and I took our herbal tea out to the patio with our knitting.

"I like Henry," I told her. "A lot." And I did. He'd kept us laughing throughout dinner with humorous stories of some of his travels as a photographer for *National Geographic*. He was a kind and friendly man, not to mention very good looking and completely besotted with Chloe.

She nodded. "Yeah, he *is* pretty special. I guess I knew it the moment I met him."

"You were fortunate," I told her. "Many women go through life never having that kind of love."

"That's true, but, Isabelle, don't ever give up on love. If somebody had told me a year ago when I lost your dad that not only would I meet somebody like Henry Wagner, but that I'd fall utterly in love with him and he would return that love, and that we'd be getting married on May first, I would have said that's nuts. But believe me, sometimes love happens when we least expect it."

I very much doubted this, but allowed Chloe her fantasies. "Hmm," was all I said.

She took a sip of her tea. "So tell me, what's this about your mother retiring to Florida? I didn't realize you had a relationship with her."

"I don't. Not really. But I allowed Haley to begin seeing her now and then, and the next thing I know . . . she's moving to Florida. I'd prefer it to be any other state, but obviously I have no control over where she chooses to retire."

"Yes, that's true. Well, maybe it's just conversation at this point."

I shook my head. "Ah, no, I don't think so. She informed me that she's booked a flight for March twenty-eight, booked a hotel here in Ormond Beach, and is coming to the area to check things out."

"Oh. Yeah, that sounds like she's made a decision to consider this area. Will that be awkward for you?"

"Me?" I let out a deep sigh. "I don't know. I have no idea what will happen. She claims she wants to get to know Haley better."

Chloe smiled. "I can certainly understand that. In five months I'm becoming a grandmother for the first time and you have no idea how excited I am. Thank God Eli and Treva live in Jacksonville now and not Boston. I can't even imagine being separated from my grandchild."

Maybe Chloe was right. Maybe this wasn't about me at all. Maybe my mother really only wanted a relationship with her granddaughter—not her daughter.

"Will it be awkward for you if you meet her?" I asked.

"Me? Why would I feel awkward?"

"Well, because you dated my father, and, well . . ."

Chloe shook her head. "Oh, gosh, no. It'll be fine. Actually, I hope I do have the chance to meet her while she's here."

Well, at least somebody besides her granddaughter was anticipating the arrival of Iris Brunell at Ormond Beach.

Chapter 6

I woke the following Monday morning and couldn't identify at first the shrill sound disturbing my sleep. I opened one eye and then the other before I groaned. My alarm clock. I slammed my hand on top of the clock to silence it and saw it was five a.m. The first delivery of muffins and coffee was scheduled for seven thirty.

I showered, applied my makeup, and got dressed. Pulling a Nirvana T-shirt over my head, I smiled. Yarrow had ordered a bunch of them for me to wear—black with a white steaming cup and Nirvana Tea and Coffee logo in the upper corner. I put on a pair of white cropped pants to complete my uniform.

Walking toward the kitchen, where the aroma of brewed coffee filled the air, I was surprised to see Chloe up so early. Basil came running to greet me.

"You didn't get up this early because of me, did you?" I asked.

"Well, I wanted to make sure you had a good breakfast before setting off for your first day on the road."

I accepted the mug she handed me. "Thanks, but you shouldn't have."

"How about a ham and cheese omelet and grits?"

"Sounds wonderful. Can I help?"

"Just enjoy your coffee. I'm all set. What time did Yarrow say she'd arrive with the muffins?"

"A little past six thirty. That'll give us time to fill the baskets and get the coffee brewed."

"How will you keep the coffee hot between your drops?"

"Oh, Yarrow got some thermos dispensers. So I'll fill the Styrofoam cups before taking them in."

"Sounds like a plan. How many stops do you have to make?"

"Well, she worked it out that the last customer will have their coffee and muffins by ten thirty. So that's three hours of deliveries, but if traffic is light it might go faster. Also, a few of the deliveries are either in the same office building or a few doors away from each other in the same complex. Yarrow did a good job with the logistics."

"I'm not surprised. She's good at that. I hope you'll enjoy doing this. I know she really appreciates your help getting the delivery service off the ground."

"Actually, I'm looking forward to it. I think it'll be fun meeting different people and getting to know them a little each day. She did say if it works out well, she plans to hire a couple more people and increase her route."

"Are you delivering on Saturdays too?"

I shook my head. "No, but I told her I wouldn't mind. She insisted she wanted me to have the weekends off. However, I think if this works out and she expands her route, she'll hire somebody to do Saturdays and a few days during the week."

"So do you see yourself doing this permanently or do you plan to look for other work?"

I let out a sigh before swallowing my last sip of coffee. "I'm not really sure. As much as I appreciate staying here, I'd love to get a place for Haley and me. So having a full-time job makes sense."

Chloe nodded.

"How about you?" I asked. "What are your plans after you and Henry get married? Will you still be staying here?"

I watched her spoon grits into a small bowl before placing my omelet onto a plate and bringing it to the table.

"Well, I think for a while, we'll continue what we've been doing. A few nights here, a few nights at Henry's condo. I think it would break Mavis Anne's heart to have this house empty."

"Hmm, true." I took a bite of my omelet. "Oh, this is delicious. Thanks, Chloe."

"Well, you gals are up early."

I looked up to see Henry walk into the kitchen, followed by Delilah. He went directly to Chloe and kissed her.

"Good morning," she said. "Yeah, I wanted to send Isabelle off to work with a good breakfast on her first day."

"You're a good mom," he said, giving me a wink.

"It was very nice of her to do this, but from now on, please get up at your normal time."

I finished up my breakfast while listening to them discuss plans for their day. The yarn shop was closed on Mondays and so was the florist shop where Chloe's friend Maddie worked.

"Maddie will be here at ten with books so we can choose the flowers for the wedding," Chloe said. "Even though it's a small wedding, there seem to be a million things to do."

I laughed. "Oh, yeah. Weddings have a way of growing out of control. It'll be so pretty having the ceremony outside by the fishpond. Are you having a reception here?"

Chloe nodded. "Yes, the ceremony is at five, followed by dinner. David and Clive insisted on helping Henry with that part of it, so they're booking a caterer and getting a canopy for the garden area."

"And have you decided on a dress yet?"

"Not yet. It's on the list along with those million other things."

I laughed as I got up to put my plate into the dishwasher. "Well, you know I'd love to help with anything that I can."

"And I'll hold you to that."

I glanced at my watch and saw it was just past six thirty. "Well, I'm heading over to the tea shop. You guys have a good morning and I'll see you when I get back."

I walked into the side door of the tea shop to see Yarrow already busy at work.

"Hey, good morning," she said, looking up.

"Good morning. What can I do?"

"Take the coffee carafes and begin filling those dispensers. Then make two more pots—that should be enough for the orders."

"Okay," I said as she continued filling baskets with plastic-wrapped muffins. She then added small napkins, creamers, sugar packets, and a typed list of items and prices.

Baskets and coffee dispensers were all filled just after seven.

She let out a deep sigh and nodded. "Okay. I'd say you're ready to hit the road. Here's the order of the deliveries. As you know, some are in the same building or complex. The addresses are listed on here too," she said, passing me a typed piece of paper. "Got your cell phone?"

I nodded.

"Okay, if you have any problems just call me here. Any questions?"

I shook my head. "None."

"Great. Okay, come on. I'll help you load up the car with these baskets and coffee."

I backed out of the driveway ten minutes later as Yarrow gave me a wave and a thumbs-up.

I headed up Granada and took a left on Williamson Boulevard, my first stop, which was a medical office building next door to the hospital.

I was glad Yarrow had come up with the idea of a folding cart to use when I had multiple deliveries at one location. I filled the cart with baskets and coffee dispensers and headed to the door.

"Good morning," I said, walking into the first office with my basket. I felt a bit like Little Red Riding Hood. "I'm Isabelle and I have your coffee and muffins."

The girl behind the desk jumped up to help me unload the goodies. "Nice to meet you. I'm Rochelle, and you're going to be our new best friend."

A nurse and two office workers came from the back of the office and laughed.

"She's right," one of them said. "This is such a great idea. I'm Carol and this is Ann and Pat. And we really look forward to your morning visits."

The one named Carol laughed. "Yeah, even if our scales might not."

Rochelle waved her hand in the air. "Hey, come on, girl. We'll have salads for lunch."

This caused more laughter. "Right," Pat said. "Like that's gonna happen."

I joined their laughter. I could easily see they worked well together. Each one paid; I placed the money into a zippered bag and headed to the other offices. I encountered more friendly workers, and the same warm welcome from all of them.

Heading back down Granada, I felt a smile cross my face. This *was* fun. And after months of being secluded in my Atlanta house, this was good for me. Being out and being productive. Accomplishment was always the first step in bumping up one's self-esteem. I hadn't given much thought to it before, but I could now see that when Roger left me for somebody else, it didn't just break up a marriage. It had broken my confidence.

I turned the car radio on and hummed along to a Madonna song as I headed to my next stop, a yoga studio. I received the same warm reception and even an invitation to join one of their classes.

The rest of my deliveries brought more friendly people who welcomed me. Food was the universal ice breaker and since I was the one supplying that food, I was also part of their happiness. I returned to the tea shop just after ten thirty to find a nervous Yarrow waiting in the patio area.

I got out of the car and asked, "Everything okay?"

"Yes, fine here. But how did it go for *you*?"

I walked to the patio, petted Merino between his ears, and gave her a huge smile. "It went fantastic!"

"Really?"

"Really," I assured her. "I felt like the candy man dispensing love and happiness with those muffins. The customers couldn't have been friendlier, and I enjoyed meeting them and getting to chat for a few minutes. You had a brainstorm of an idea, Yarrow. You really did."

She collapsed into a chair and whooshed out a breath of air. "Thank God."

"Did you really have doubts? I thought you were pretty confident about this business venture."

"I've always been a good actress. Yeah, I was concerned people would change their minds, think it was silly to have muffins and coffee delivered every morning, that you'd run into problems and not want to continue doing this or—"

I grabbed her hand and squeezed it before she could continue. "None of that happened. It went perfectly, so congratulations to you. It was a brilliant idea."

Yarrow jumped up and hugged me. "Thank you and thank you for your help. Come on, we both earned ourselves a cup of tea *and* a pastry."

Chapter 7

Haley and I had spent the previous afternoon getting her registered and set up to begin classes at her new school. She seemed to be enthusiastic, and my fingers were crossed that she'd be much happier and make new friends.

I looked up from my coffee and newspaper as Haley came into the kitchen. Wearing a pullover sweater and jeans, hair pulled back in a ponytail and nails painted a bright blue, she looked like the quintessential fourteen-year-old girl.

"You look great," I told her. "All set for your first day?"

She nodded as she reached into the fridge and removed a container of yogurt. "Yeah. I think I'm going to like the kids at this school much better."

I had noticed that while we were being shown around by one of the volunteers, many of the girls flashed Haley a smile and welcome greetings. It didn't escape my notice that a fair number of the fellows also gave my daughter appreciative glances.

"That's good, Haley," I said. "I really want you to be happy here and that means enjoying school and being involved."

"How about you?" she questioned.

"Me?"

"Are you happy here?"

I hadn't really thought about being happy. It seemed for the past couple of years I had been on autopilot. Getting through my days doing what was required of me, attempting to make a life for Haley, and pretty much just existing.

"Well, yeah . . . I guess I'm happy. I think moving here will be good for both of us."

"I think so too, but I want you to also be happy. You know, meet new friends, go out, do things. Maybe even have a new guy in your life eventually."

I smiled and thought my daughter sounded like Dr. Phil. "I'm fine, Haley. Except for the new guy, I plan to get involved doing things too. I just don't think I need a man complicating my life again."

"It isn't always that way. Look at Chloe and Henry."

I certainly didn't want to sour my daughter on love. "You could have a point," was all I said.

Haley tossed the yogurt container in the trash. "Oh, did you see the signs all around the school yesterday? About the spring musical they're having in May? It said that sign-ups would begin today. I'm hoping maybe they'll need somebody to help out with the costumes."

"Oh, that would be great. Be sure to check that out. Not only would you be good at something like that, but I know you'd enjoy it."

"I would. Well, I have to head to the bus stop." She leaned over to place a kiss on my cheek. "Have a good day, Mom, and I'll see you this afternoon."

"You too," I told her, and watched my mature daughter head to the front door, but not before bending over to pat Basil good-bye.

This reminded me of my promise to her about getting a dog. But I still had a reprieve on that because the deal was it would happen when we got our own place. We'd only been here five days, so plenty of time to think about a dog later.

My morning deliveries had gone well and I returned to find the yarn shop more crowded than usual.

"Tuesday is knitting for charity," Yarrow explained. "Want some tea or coffee?"

"Yeah, coffee would be great. So the women gather on Tuesdays to knit items and then donate them?"

Yarrow nodded as she filled a mug and passed it to me. "Yeah, they knit chemo caps and some make baby items to donate to the local organizations for mothers who need them. I'm working on a baby blanket at the moment."

I took a sip of coffee. "That's a nice thing to do. I'm not a great knitter, but . . . maybe I could make a blanket too."

"That would be great," Yarrow said. "Go speak to Fay. She's the one who handles all of it."

I had met many of the regulars the previous summer and I knew that Fay was the woman with white hair sitting beside Chloe.

"Hey, Isabelle," Chloe said as I walked to the table. "Did your deliveries go well?"

"They did. I'm really enjoying this little part-time job."

"That's great," Mavis Anne said, looking up from a baby bootie she was knitting. "And Haley got off okay for her first day of school?"

"Yeah, I think she was actually excited. She liked it there when we got her registered yesterday."

"That's wonderful." Mavis Anne nodded. "She's such a sweet girl."

"I was thinking about . . . is there any chance you could use another baby blanket, Fay?"

A smile covered her face. "Oh, definitely. So many of these women have very little. That would be great. Would you like to join our group on Tuesdays?"

"Yeah, I would," I said. "I need to get some yarn, a pattern, and needles."

Chloe jumped up. "Right this way." She headed to a bookshelf filled with various books and pamphlets. "Everything on the first two shelves is baby related. So browse through those and see what you'd like to make."

I pored through various books and finally decided on a blanket that looked fairly easy.

"How's this?" I brought the book over to Chloe. "But those pretty holes along the edges. I'm not sure I can do that."

"Of course you can. Those are simple yarn overs. I'll show you how to do them, and the rest of it is basic knit and purl." She pointed to an area of the wall where the cubbyholes held various skeins of yarn. "The baby yarn is down there at the end. So choose what you'd like and I'll get your needles."

I gazed at the pretty colors and found myself reaching out to touch each one. They were so soft and the colors so appealing that I began to get excited about working on the blanket. I had previously made a half-hearted attempt to make a couple of scarves and my knitted top was close to being completed, so my knitting ability was growing. It wasn't easy choosing, but I finally decided on Plymouth Dreambaby in the Egg Cream colorway. Since I wasn't sure if it would be for a girl or boy baby, this was a nice neutral color.

"Perfect," Chloe said, when I returned to the table. "And I have size six needles here for you. So pull up a chair, cast on, and join us."

It was really such a simple invitation, but it made me feel like I belonged. I took an empty chair next to Mavis Anne and followed Chloe's instructions, casted on and looked back at the pattern.

"This says to knit three and then *yo*? I guess that means yarn over?"

"Exactly," Mavis Anne said as she leaned over to explain the stitch. "See, simply wrap the yarn around the needle to the front, and knit the next stitch as the pattern says."

I did as she said. "That's it?"

She laughed. "That's it, honey. You did your first yarn over. I think sometimes knitters make the stitches sound more intimidating than they are. So you'll follow the pattern across the row and do the same thing at the end, just like the pattern says."

I worked along quietly as I listened to the conversation around the table. June was telling a humorous story about her grandson, Charlie, that brought forth laughter. Maddie told us how she dreaded the following week because Valentine's Day would be on a Sunday this year, which meant Friday and Saturday would be exceptionally busy for her.

"I really have to hire a helper," she said. "But the thing is, I really don't need anybody permanently. I can usually handle the business, except during a holiday."

"Yeah," Chloe said. "Unfortunately, most people looking for a job want something permanent even if it's only part-time."

I had no idea why, but Haley popped into my head. "You know," I said, looking up from my knitting, "I think Haley would be more than happy to help you out. She doesn't have florist experience, but she's very good at following directions, and she's reliable."

"Really?" A smile crossed Maddie's face. "Gosh, what I need doesn't really require florist skills. It would be more like answering the phone and taking down the orders. Separating flowers, putting bows on, which I could teach her to do. Do you really think she'd be interested? Of course I'd pay her. She's such a nice girl. I'd love to have her in the shop."

"I bet Haley would really enjoy that," Chloe said.

"I'll definitely ask her when she gets home from school and I'll have her call you if she's interested."

* * *

The knitting group broke up around one and I went back to Koi House to have lunch. I had just finished a tuna sandwich and was pouring myself a glass of iced tea when my cell phone rang. I saw Petra's name and smiled.

"Hey, girlfriend. What's going on?" I said.

"That's what I was calling you to find out. Haven't heard from you since you got there last week. Everything okay?"

"Yes, everything's going really well. I'm sorry. We were busy unpacking and settling in over the weekend."

I brought her up to date on my delivery job, Haley starting school, and me joining the charity knitting group.

"Oh, Isabelle. I'm really happy for you. It sure sounds like you made a great decision moving there. I haven't heard your voice sound this happy in ages."

I recalled what Haley had asked me that morning about being happy, and I smiled. Maybe I was happy after all.

"Yeah," I told her. "Yeah, I think both Haley and I are happy here. So what's up with you?"

"Nothing new here. Have you heard from your mother?"

"No, but I think Haley has. I think they call each other but Haley is careful mentioning her name, which is fine with me."

When there was silence on the line, I said, "What? You know I'd rather avoid talking to her if I don't have to."

"Yeah, I know. I just wish it could be different for the two of you. But I won't hound you about it. So the plans are coming along well for the wedding?"

"Yes, and I wanted to give you a heads-up. Chloe mentioned the other day she'd love to meet you, so she hopes you'll come visit before, but she's definitely sending you an invitation."

"Oh, how nice. I never turn down a chance to get glammed up and attend a wedding. I'll circle the date on my calendar. May first, right?"

"Right. That's a Sunday. Maybe you could come down on Friday and spend a few days here."

"Sounds great, but I will try to get down there sooner."

After another ten minutes of conversation, we hung up. I got my tea and headed outside to the patio to work on my blanket. I was so engrossed in knitting, I was surprised to look up when I heard Basil barking and see Haley had returned from school. She scooped him up in her arms, showering him with kisses.

"So how was your first day?" I asked.

"Really good," she said, and I saw the smile on her face. "I made a new friend. Well, I think I made a few new friends, but one in particular I really liked. We just clicked. Her name is Tina and we have all the same classes together. Plus, she's going to be in the spring musical. She likes to sing and she's trying out for a solo and she got me to go with her and I signed up for costume and design. We'll find out on Friday if we got accepted."

Just seeing my daughter so happy made *me* happy. It had been a while since I'd seen her so excited. Especially about anything related to school.

"Oh, Haley. That's super. I have no doubt that you'll both be accepted. And . . . I just might have some more good news to finish off your day for you."

I explained about Maddie and her request for assistance at the florist shop.

"Really? She'd like to have me helping her out? Oh, wow, yes. I'd love to. You know I love flowers, and she's so creative with her arrangements. It might even give me ideas for some of my designs."

I passed her Maddie's business card. "Well, she said to give her a call."

Haley jumped up to go inside and do just that.

"Yarrow made a nice fruit salad for you," I said. "It's in the fridge, so help yourself."

"I will," she called back as she ran into the house with Basil at her heels.

Chapter 8

Before I opened my eyes I could hear the rain pelting on the roof and windows. I let out a groan as I realized that making my deliveries this morning might not be quite as pleasant as the previous days with sunshine.

I headed downstairs to get my coffee and peeked out the front door. Rain was sluicing down from the sky and creating large puddles in the driveway. The perfect day to curl up with knitting, but that would have to wait until later.

Yarrow was already in the tea shop filling the orders when I walked in.

"Nasty day out there," I said.

"I know. I feel bad that you have to be out driving around in it."

I waved a hand in the air. "Not a big deal. I have my umbrella."

I set off with windshield wipers on high and listening to a CD of Bruce Springsteen to brighten up the day.

Choosing to wear sneakers rather than my usual flip-flops had been smart. Huge puddles filled the parking lots, but I managed to complete my first few deliveries with no incident. By the time I pulled up to the yoga studio, the rain had increased even more and I could hear thunder in the distance. That was one thing I noticed about rain in Florida. It didn't come down in a shower; most of the time it was a deluge.

I had managed to get out of the car and was juggling my basket of muffins and coffee while trying to adjust my umbrella when my feet shot out from under me, the basket went flying, and I found myself smack down on my butt in a puddle. I must have tried to break my fall with my right arm because it was scraped from the pavement and my wrist was aching.

As if out of nowhere I heard a male voice say, "Are you okay? Here, let me help you."

I saw a hand outstretched and looked up into gorgeous blue eyes that looked vaguely familiar.

"I think . . . I think I'm okay," I said, reaching for his hand as I stood up. I was engulfed with embarrassment. That's when I noticed that the coffee and muffins were a total loss. I burst into tears.

"It's okay," the man assured me as he went to retrieve the empty basket and then proceeded to lead me to the passenger side of his car. "Here, get in and dry off a little bit."

He slid in beside me as I continued to cry. I couldn't even do a simple delivery job without screwing up.

Passing me a box of tissues from the backseat, he said, "I did salvage the basket for you."

I wiped my tears and sniffed as I inspected the laceration on my arm. "Thanks," I said. But now what? I had no coffee or muffins for the delivery, I was soaking wet, and I wasn't sure which was bruised more: my arm or my pride.

"You took a nasty tumble," he said. "I think you slipped on an oil slick."

I looked at his handsome face and nodded. "Probably," I mumbled.

"Hey," he said. "Aren't you . . ." He snapped his fingers. "Didn't we meet last summer? Aren't you related to Chloe? I think we met at LuLu's when you were having lunch there."

I looked at him more closely. He was right. Chloe had introduced us. He had even given me his business card, telling me if I did decide to relocate to give him a call because he owned a real estate agency.

"Yes. You're Chadwick Price. I remember meeting you."

"Right. And you're Isabelle. So I take it you did move here?"

"Yeah. About a week ago. I'm staying at Koi House with my daughter till we find our own place." All of a sudden I recalled the way Chloe had met him the year before and started laughing. "Do you make a habit of rescuing damsels in distress in the rain?"

He threw his head back, laughing. "Hmm, I do seem to have a knack for that, don't I? That's how I met Chloe with her flat tire."

I looked at the basket in my lap and let out a sigh. "God, what am I going to do? I ruined my delivery."

"What were you doing with the coffee and muffins?" he asked.

I explained about my job and working for Yarrow. "And now the yoga studio won't get their delivery," I moaned.

"Well, we can fix that. Let me run in and tell them it will only be delayed. I'll be right back."

He jumped out of the car before I could question what his solution was.

A couple of minutes later, he was back. "Okay," he said, starting the ignition. "We're good."

"We are?"

"Yup. I'm driving you to Biggby Coffee just up Granada. We're going to get the order there and bring it back. Coffee and some muffins."

"Really? They said that was okay?"

"They were fine with the idea and mostly concerned about you. You *are* okay, aren't you?"

All of a sudden, I was feeling decidedly better. "Yes, I'm fine. And thanks so much. This is really nice of you."

He pulled into a spot in front of Biggby's and ran in to get the items. It was then I realized I must look like a drowned rat. Water was still dripping from my hair, my pants were wet and stained, and my top was sticking to my skin.

Chadwick had been drenched too, but somehow it looked better on him. He was wearing jeans and a polo jersey. He was quite a handsome guy. I wondered why it had not gone beyond a platonic relationship with him and Chloe. With curly dark hair tinged with gray, I thought he was probably eight to ten years older than I was, but the gray in his hair only enhanced his good looks.

He jumped back into the car a few minutes later holding a coffee container and a bag. "Here," he said, passing it to me. "Hold this and we'll have that delivery there in no time."

He headed back down Granada and I thanked him again. "Gosh, you really didn't have to do this, but it's very nice of you."

"Not a problem. So do you do these deliveries every day?"

"Yeah. Monday through Friday. This was just my first week and I'm really enjoying it. Well, except for this morning."

"I'm glad I could be there to help. I had a dentist appointment a few doors down from the yoga studio."

"Oh, no! Have I kept you from an appointment?"

"No, not at all. I was finished and on my way out when I saw you fall. Are you sure your arm is okay?"

I looked at the scrape on my elbow and moved my wrist. "My wrist still aches a little, but I'm fine."

"Do you think you need an x-ray?"

I wiggled it again. "No, it's not broken. Maybe a slight sprain but nothing more."

He pulled into the parking lot of the yoga studio. "Here, let me take that in for you."

I passed the container and bag to him. "Tell them I'm so sorry and I'll see them on Monday morning."

He returned a few minutes later. "They thanked you for getting the order to them and said to take care."

"Oh, I owe you for the coffee and muffins." That was when I realized my purse was still in my car. With the keys. Thank God I hadn't locked the door.

"No, no. Really. But I was thinking, since you live here now, maybe we could get together sometime. Would you be free for dinner?"

A dinner date? I hadn't been out with a guy on a date since before I met Roger. And a woman could certainly do much worse than Chadwick Price.

"Oh . . . yeah. Thanks. That would be nice."

"Great." He reached for his cell phone. "Give me your number and I'll give you a call. Tomorrow morning I'm flying to Atlanta for a few days, but can I call you next week?"

"Yes, that would be fine," I said, shooting him a smile and telling him my cell number. "Well, again, I don't know how to thank you for all of your help. But I'd better get back to the tea shop or Yarrow will be worried."

"Okay, you take care of that arm and I'll talk to you next week."

I walked over to my car and was about to get in when I heard his car horn and looked up to see him wave good-bye.

I started the ignition and heard Springsteen singing "Hungry Heart." As the lyrics said, I *had* gone out for a ride, and who knew where this morning would lead?

* * *

Yarrow glanced up from the counter when I entered the tea shop.

"Oh, God! What happened to you? Are you okay?" She ran toward me and inspected my arm.

"Yeah, I'm fine," I told her and went on to explain my ordeal.

Chloe heard us and came from the yarn shop to check out my arm too.

"Are you serious?" she said and started laughing. "Oh, I'm not laughing at *you*, but really? Chadwick Price? He rescued you in the rain just like he did me last year?"

I grinned and nodded. "Ah, yup. It would seem that way. When I mentioned it to him, he laughed and said he did have a knack for rescuing damsels in distress."

"Wow," Yarrow said.

"Interesting," Chloe added.

"What do you mean?" I questioned.

"I bet he remembered you from last summer at LuLu's, didn't he?"

"Yeah, actually, he did, why?"

"Oh, nothing . . ." she said in a way that begged me to question her more.

"Come on," I demanded. "What do you mean?"

"Well . . . it's just that I remember when I introduced you. He seemed quite interested that day and I remember thinking there was some chemistry going on there."

I waved my hand in the air, but I wondered if Chloe was right, because I recalled how I'd felt the moment I met him. "Don't be silly. He's just a nice guy. *You* know that. Look how he helped you with that flat tire and then took you for dinner. So he did the same for me."

"He asked you for dinner?"

"Well, he said he'd call me next week."

Chloe nodded her head and grinned. "Hmm, right. Nothing to it at all."

Chapter 9

Haley flew in the back door that afternoon followed by her new friend, Tina, both of them consumed with excitement.

"Guess what? Guess what?" she yelled, jumping up and down as Basil danced around her feet.

I looked up from the mug of coffee I'd just poured and laughed. It seemed this was proving to be a banner day for both of us.

I raised both arms in the air and said, "I don't have a clue. What?"

"I got chosen to assist with the designs for the costumes in the musical and Tina was chosen to do two solos."

"Oh, wow," I said, sharing their excitement. "That *is* great news. I'm so happy for both of you."

"I know," Haley said, reaching down to pick up Basil and give him a hug. "This is going to be so much fun. I was wondering... would it be okay if Tina spent the night? There's no school tomorrow and we wanted to talk about the musical."

"Of course she can. I was hoping the twin beds in your room would get used for sleepovers. But do you have your parents' permission?" I asked.

"Oh, well... I don't have a dad. It's just my mom, and I called her earlier. She said it was fine."

"And rather than go back to her house for pajamas, she can borrow some of mine," Haley added. "Would that be okay?"

"Sure," I said. "Would you girls like to celebrate with some muffins and hot chocolate? I know it's not cold out, but with all this dreariness and rain, it feels like a hot chocolate kind of day."

I was surprised to hear Haley say, "That would be great," since she seldom indulged in sweets.

They both pulled up stools as I began to prepare the hot chocolate and they chattered away. I felt good that my daughter was settling in so well at school. It was time for her to be happy and enjoy what most teens did: socializing and friendship and a sense of belonging.

When they finished their snack and went upstairs, I took my knitting into the living room to work on the blanket for a while. I had a few rows done when my cell phone rang, showing my mother's name on the caller ID. I debated whether to let it go to voice mail, but ended up answering.

"What's up?" I said.

"Oh, Isabelle, I was hoping you'd answer. Well, I have some news about my trip to Florida."

"Did you change your mind?" One could only hope.

But instead, she surprised me by saying, "Not at all. Actually, I'm coming in a few weeks, a month earlier than I'd planned."

"Oh." My good mood was quickly evaporating. "So you had to change your flight and hotel reservations? Why would you do that?"

"Well, I'm pretty positive that your area is where I want to retire. So I thought it was silly to stay in a hotel and I began doing some research to find a more permanent place."

"And you found one?"

There was a pause on the line before she said, "Yes, I did. A townhouse in The Trails. Maybe you're familiar with it?"

I was. And I knew it was a mere five-minute drive from Koi House.

"Yeah, I know where it is. What about your furniture and belongings?"

"I've arranged for movers and they'll be here next week. I've been pretty busy packing and giving things away. I fly down on the twenty-fifth and will spend that night at the hotel. The movers arrive the next day. So it's all worked out perfectly."

For who? I thought. *You or me?*

I remained silent.

"Isabelle? Are you still there?"

"I'm here," I mumbled.

I heard a deep sigh come across the line. "Isabelle, I'd really like for us to make amends and work at having a relationship. It's never too late. You just have to be willing, and I can't do it from across the country."

"Whatever," I said, feeling the old hurts resurfacing. "I certainly can't stop you from moving here and I know Haley will be happy to hear this news."

I heard another sigh. "Right. And I'm hoping that in time you'll be happy too. Okay, I won't keep you. Tell Haley I love her and I'll call her over the weekend. And Isabelle . . . I love you too."

"Bye," was all I said.

Great. Just great. I flung my knitting aside and headed to the kitchen. I had planned to make a casserole for supper but figured the kids would be just as happy with a pizza delivery. Opening the fridge, I removed a new bottle of pinot grigio and poured myself a glass.

I returned to the living room, plunked down on the sofa, and took a sip. My intake of wine had been at a minimum during the past week and the cold, fruity taste was like welcoming an old friend.

I thought back to the first few years after my mother had left and recalled how much I'd missed having that one special person in my life. That person to offer advice on fashion, hairstyles, and makeup. The woman who most daughters seek out for guidance on dating and all the dilemmas that the teen years bring. I didn't have that. My father tried, but it wasn't the same.

I found myself turning to Petra yet again to help me along. I picked up my phone and dialed her number.

"Hey," she said. "I've been thinking about you. How's everything going?"

"Okay," was all I had to say, and she instantly knew it wasn't.

"What's going on?" she asked.

I told her about my mother's call and change of plans.

"Hmm, okay. Yeah, I can see this news wouldn't make you happy. But you have to admit, Isabelle, she *is* trying. Isn't there any chance you can meet her halfway?"

"I seriously doubt that. I feel it's too little, too late. Why did she have to wait till my father was gone to make any attempt?"

"I don't know, but maybe she had her reasons. And the bottom line is there isn't much you can do about her moving there."

"No, but I can do plenty to avoid her." I knew I sounded like a petulant child, but I felt the need to strike back. "I can avoid her like she avoided me for so many years."

"Yeah, you could do that."

"You don't agree, do you?"

"Look, I do *not* want to get into the middle of this. You know very well how I feel. Yes, she was probably wrong to leave and yes, she should have made more of an attempt to stay in touch over the years, but Isabelle ... sometimes people simply don't do what *we* think they should. That's just the way it is."

I took a gulp of wine and remained silent.

"So what else is going on? How's your delivery job going? And how's Haley doing?"

I realized that I was allowing my mother to overshadow my happy news. "Good," I said. "Yeah, Haley has a new friend here to spend the night. She got chosen to design costumes for the spring musical and my job is going well. I might even have a date soon."

I heard Petra laugh. "Now that *is* good news. All of it, but especially the date part. So who's the lucky guy?"

I told her about Chadwick Price and our chance encounter. "So he said he'll call next week when he gets back from Atlanta."

"That's really great. See, things really are starting to turn around. Don't allow your mom to dampen your spirits. Any update from Roger?"

"Not since I first got here last week. He did call to check and make sure we arrived safely. I get the feeling he'd like to be friends."

"He probably does. Just because he has somebody else in his life doesn't mean he wants you completely out of it. You're the mother of his daughter. You'll always have that connection."

"Yeah, true. Well, thanks for listening to me. I'll let you go. I miss you and can't wait for you to come down here for a visit."

"I miss you too. I'm aiming to get down there late March or early April."

"Oh, that would be great, Petra. And you know you can bring Lotte. Mavis and Chloe said that wouldn't be a problem at all."

"Okay. Now go relax and enjoy your evening. Think happy thoughts. Love you."

"Love you too," I said and hung up with a smile on my face. Petra never failed to lift my spirits.

By the time the pizza had been delivered I realized I'd managed to polish off the bottle of wine. After we cleaned the kitchen and the girls had curled up in the living room to watch a new on-demand movie, I opened another bottle and stuck it into my knitting bag along with a wineglass.

"Everything okay here?" I asked, walking into the living room. "Do you guys want popcorn or anything?"

"Not right now, Mom," Haley said. "Maybe I'll put some in the microwave later. Do you want to watch this movie with us?"

"No, I think I'll go upstairs and knit. If I fall asleep, be sure to shut off the lights down here before you go to bed."

"Will do. Love you, Mom."

"Love you too," I told her and headed up to my room.

I removed the wine bottle and glass and felt like a teenager being sneaky. I poured a glass and curled up on the lounge in the sitting area of my bedroom.

Taking a sip, I glanced around the room. It was so beautifully decorated and furnished with the mahogany sleigh bed, carved bureaus, and vintage wallpaper, I felt like I'd stepped back in time. The room continued to be cool, but I was adjusting to the difference in temperature compared to the rest of the house. I wondered about Emmalyn Overby, the woman who had once inhabited this room. According to Chloe, she had been quite the independent female, always doing things her way, and not always for the good. When Emmalyn became pregnant with Yarrow, she refused to tell Mavis Anne or their father who the father of the child was. Both her sister and her father enabled her, and Emmalyn took full advantage of it. Learning her story had made me feel that some women flit through life with a sense of entitlement. Sometimes to the detriment of those around them—much as my mother had.

I awoke at three in the morning to find the wine bottle almost empty. I was cold and still curled up on the lounge. Heading into the bathroom, I recalled a dream I'd had. Or was it a dream? It had seemed so real. A beautiful woman in a red evening gown with long auburn hair had been sitting on the edge of the bed.

She was shaking her head and saying, "You just don't get it."

"Get what?" I asked.

She got up and began walking around the room. She touched the lamp on the bureau and then picked up the ivory hairbrush and pulled it through her hair. She walked over to the French doors that led out to the small balcony, opened them, and stood staring outside before turning around and saying, "Life is difficult, and it isn't always as it might seem."

Even in the dream I could feel myself getting agitated. "I don't know what you're talking about," I told her.

A sad expression crossed her face. "I know you don't. Not right now. But maybe in time, you will."

That was when I woke up.

I came out of the bathroom and my gaze immediately went to the French doors. They were open.

Chapter 10

I awoke the next morning with a throbbing headache. My punishment for the wine consumption. I glanced toward the French doors and saw that the rain from the day before was gone and sunlight was streaming into the room. That's when I recalled the dream.

How crazy was that? Was the woman in my dream really Emmalyn Overby? I had never even met her, but the dream woman certainly fit the description I'd heard from Chloe.

After my shower, I headed downstairs to the kitchen and found Chloe sipping coffee while reading the newspaper. She'd spent the previous night at Henry's condo.

"Good morning," I said, pouring myself a mug of coffee. "You're back. Nice evening?"

"Very nice. And yours? Did the girls have fun with their sleepover?"

The evening before was a bit foggy in my mind, but I nodded. "Yeah, I think they did. They're still sleeping."

"I'm so happy that Haley has found a new friend. Tina seems like a nice girl."

I nodded. "I like her too."

Chloe folded up the newspaper. "Anything else going on?"

"Well, let's see. My mother changed her mind about coming here at the end of March."

I saw Chloe raise her eyebrows. "Oh, she's not coming to check out the area for retirement?"

"Ah, no. She already made a decision on that. She's arriving in about three weeks and . . . she'll be staying permanently."

Now surprise covered Chloe's face. "Really? What brought this about?"

"Well, it seems her mind had really already been made up about moving here. So she figured why bother with the pretense of a hotel. She found a townhouse to purchase in The Trails and got everything arranged."

"Hmm, yeah, that's quite a shift in plans. So she's bought a place sight unseen?"

I took a sip of coffee. "Apparently so. She said the photos online were very descriptive."

"Well, that *is* how I originally found Henry's condo to rent. But I had never planned to stay there permanently." She let out a chuckle. "Gee, and look how that worked out."

"So she's arranged for the movers and will be flying down the day before, on the twenty-fifth."

"You're not happy about this, are you?"

"No. Not really. I mean, she's been out of my life for thirty years. And now, what? She thinks she can just wiggle her way back in? Hey, she can do what she wants. Haley might be happy to have her grandmother in her life, but it doesn't mean I have to be involved."

"Hmm, true," was all she said.

"Oh, I wanted to ask you about my room and Emmalyn."

Chloe's head shot up. "What do you mean?"

"I remember you said you had some weird dreams when you stayed in that room."

"Are you having dreams?"

"I did last night. Didn't you say she was quite beautiful, with long auburn hair, and she always wore a red evening gown in your dreams?"

Chloe nodded.

"Well . . . I think she's back. I mean this is just plain silly. I never even knew her. Why on earth would I be dreaming about her?"

"Remember I also told you we think Emmalyn never really left this house? She loved it here and Mavis Anne is convinced that her sprit has remained."

I waved a hand in the air and laughed. "You've got to be kidding. You sound like you believe that foolishness too."

Chloe remained quiet.

"Well, *do* you?"

She let out a deep sigh. "I can't discount it. I've had too many experiences here involving Emmalyn not to consider the possibility. What was your dream about? Was she out by the fishpond?"

I shook my head. "No, she was right there in my bedroom. At first she was sitting on the edge of the bed and I was sleeping on the lounge. Then she walked over to the French doors and opened them. She told me that I just didn't get it, whatever that's supposed to mean. But the really bizarre part was after I woke up, I went into the bathroom and when I came out . . . the French doors were wide open just the way she left them. With all the rain yesterday, I sure as hell had not opened those doors."

Chloe's lips were pursed as she fiddled with the handle of her coffee mug.

"So am I to believe that I'm sharing my room with a ghost? Is that what you're saying?"

Chloe smiled and shrugged. "I honestly don't know what to tell you, Isabelle. All I can say is that if it is Emmalyn, she's harmless."

"Oh, gee. Thanks. That's very comforting."

"Will you and Haley be here tonight for supper? Henry plans to come over and grill some steaks and he's hoping you'll both join us."

"Yup. No plans for us."

The house phone rang. I answered to hear Mavis Anne's voice.

"Isabelle, I'm glad I caught you. I wasn't sure if you'd be in the shop later and I wanted to ask if you were free this afternoon."

"Yes, as far as I know. Why?"

"Well, David and I thought perhaps you could come over and we could show you around the house and explain what will be required when he and Clive leave for Italy next week."

"Oh, sure. Would around two be okay?"

"Perfect. See you then."

I hung up and explained to Chloe that Mavis Anne wanted to instruct me on my upcoming caregiver duties.

She shook her head and laughed. "She wants to be sure she's cared for in the manner she's become accustomed to. I hope she's not too demanding. It's really nice of you to do this."

"She'll be fine. I like her a lot and I'll enjoy her company. I'm just not a great cook, though. Certainly not even close to David and Clive, so I hope she's not disappointed with my cooking skills."

"Nah, I'm sure she'll appreciate whatever you put together. I think their main concern is safety and that you'll be company for Mavis Anne." She glanced up at the clock on the wall. "Well, I need to get over to the yarn shop and open. It's going on ten. What're your plans for today?"

"Since I have no deliveries, I think I'll get caught up on laundry and straightening up a bit around here."

"Well, don't forget that Marta comes to clean on Monday, so don't go crazy. Will you be over to the shop later?"

"Yeah, I'll come by for a while. I want to keep working on that baby blanket."

"Okay, see you later."

A few minutes later Haley and Tina walked into the kitchen laughing.

"Good morning," I said. "Sleep well?"

"Very well," Tina said. "It was nice having my own bed." Then, as if realizing what she'd said, she looked down and refrained from saying any more.

"Mom, can we have pancakes? We're starved."

I laughed. "Of course you are," I said, but once again I was surprised my daughter was willing to abandon her usual yogurt and fruit. "And yes, I'll whip some up for you."

"We're going to the beach after. Is that okay?" she asked.

"Sure. The water might be a little chilly, though. It's only early February."

"That's okay. I'm not sure we'll go in. We're going to walk."

She might be deviating a bit from her stringent diet but not the exercise.

"Okay, then," I said, reaching into the cabinet for pancake mix. "I'll have these ready in a jiffy."

They each pulled up a stool at the counter and watched as I mixed and measured.

"Have you lived in Ormond Beach long?" I asked Tina.

"No. We moved here last year from Texas. My parents got a divorce and my mom was able to get a job over here."

"Oh, so you don't have any family here?"

"Nope. Just the two of us."

"What kind of work does your mother do?" I asked as I poured batter onto the grill.

"She's a nurse. She works in the emergency room at the hospital in Daytona Beach."

"That's great. So do you both like it here?" I questioned.

"Yeah, I like it a lot. I guess my mom does. She works a lot."

I was beginning to get a picture of a single mom struggling to make ends meet, and not for the first time, I felt fortunate that Roger had been so generous regarding the breakup of our marriage.

"Well, I'm very glad that you and Haley have become friends. You're welcome to come here any time you want. Although we're just living at Koi House temporarily. We'll be finding our own place within the next few months."

I saw the look of awe that crossed her face as her glance took in the designer kitchen. "Gosh, I don't know how you could leave this house. It's so beautiful. I'd want to live here forever and never leave."

I laughed as I stacked pancakes onto a platter, but Emmalyn Overby crossed my mind.

Chapter 11

The girls left for the beach and I got a few loads of laundry done in between filling the dishwasher, emptying trash, and running the vacuum through the downstairs. After I had a sandwich with iced tea for lunch, I got my knitting bag and headed to the yarn shop before meeting with Mavis Anne.

A few customers were browsing when I walked in, and Chloe was knitting. I joined her at the table and removed my blanket.

"Oh, that's working up very nice," she said, leaning over to get a better look. "Once you finish the blanket, I have to get you working on new stitches so you can broaden your knitting skills."

"That would be great. I'm surprised that I'm enjoying it as much as I am. What's going on here?"

"Not much. Quiet this morning but a group will be here at two. Louise teaches a crochet class on Saturday afternoons. Oh, I wanted to run something by you before I mentioned it to Haley. My wedding is going to be small and I really don't want a lot of fuss, but I do need somebody to stand up with me, so I thought it might be nice to have Haley. Do you think she'd be interested?"

"Oh, definitely. That's so nice of you, Chloe. I know she'd be thrilled."

"Oh, good. Well, Henry and I talked it over and he doesn't really have anybody to stand up with him, so we thought we'd be a bit unconventional and Haley could be a witness for both of us. And I'd love to include my niece, so I was thinking Solange could carry a basket of flowers and be the first to enter. I really don't want a traditional wedding party."

"I think that's a wonderful idea. I'm sure Haley will love it."

"Great. Well, we'll make plans to go shopping together for our dresses. Maybe you'd like to join us?"

"Absolutely. That would be fun."

Chloe went to ring up the purchases for her customers. I thought of my father. I wondered, if he hadn't died, whether Chloe would have ended up marrying him. I had a feeling that probably wouldn't have happened. I'd only observed the two of them together once when they came to visit me in Atlanta, but I hadn't seen the same interaction between them as I saw when she was with Henry. It made me realize that some couples just exuded a chemistry that was real and solid. I had to admit I had never shared this with anybody. Certainly not Roger. He was a nice guy, friendly and a very good provider, but passion wasn't something that he had in abundance.

Chloe returned to the table. "You know, I was thinking of designing a new scarf. Something to welcome you as you begin a new chapter in your life."

"Really? Like the Chloe's Dream shawl you did last year when you moved here?"

"Yeah, it would be a nice keepsake for you, and I'll include some new stitches for you to work on."

"I'd like that. Thanks. Well, I have to get over to Mavis Anne's. It's almost two."

I walked through the gate that separated the two houses, across the lawn and up the steps of David and Clive's home.

David opened the door and pulled me into a hug. "Isabelle, how nice to see you. Come on inside."

I followed him to the living room, where Mavis Anne sat knitting in a wingback chair. She looked up with a smile. "Ah, Isabelle. Right on time."

"How about some coffee?" David asked. "I just brewed a pot."

"That would be great," I said, sitting on the sofa. "Thanks."

"So everything's going well? Do you still like the house, and are you settling in okay?"

"It's wonderful. I can't thank you enough for allowing Haley and me to stay there. She had a sleepover last night with a new friend. I haven't seen my daughter this happy in ages."

"That's wonderful. Koi House loves people, and people fill it with happiness. So really, you're doing the house a favor."

I indulged her thoughts on the house having feelings and just smiled and nodded.

"Okay, here we go," David said, returning with a tray holding three cups of coffee, a sugar bowl, and creamer.

"Thanks," I said, adding a bit of cream to my cup.

David passed a cup to his sister and sat down.

"You and Clive must be so excited about leaving for Italy," I said.

"Oh, we are. We've been to Rome and Tuscany but we're renting a villa on Lake Como. We're looking forward to exploring that area."

"And do not forget your promise," Mavis Anne said. "You *will* look for some Italian yarn to bring back to me."

He laughed and patted her arm. "Not to worry. It's at the top of my shopping list."

"Okay, so let's discuss what I will need you to do for me in David's absence. First of all, you will not be required to do any heavy cooking. Marta will take care of that."

I was relieved to hear this.

"I may need you to prepare a sandwich and some soup a few evenings, but any larger meals will be taken care of by Marta. Now, David disagrees; however, I don't think it's that necessary for you to actually sleep here. I think—"

David interrupted her. "Mavis Anne, we had a deal. I don't like the thought of you being here in this house alone overnight. What if you fell? What if you needed something?"

"I totally agree," I said. "It's really not safe for you to be here by yourself overnight."

"I think you're both being a bit silly."

"No, we're not," I said. "Listen, I just had an idea, and I'm not certain she'd agree, although I think she will. How about if Haley stays here with you? I know you have a guest room, and to be honest, I think she'd love it. She adores you and she's extremely responsible."

Mavis Anne sat up straighter in her chair and smiled. "Oh, now that plan I would agree to. I adore Haley and love spending time with her. If she agrees, that would work out very nicely. And I wouldn't feel as if I was imposing on you. I know you're busy with a lot of other things."

"Great. I'll speak to her later when she gets home."

"Okay. I have a doctor's appointment the first week David is gone, on Friday, and I have a hair appointment every Thursday at two. Would you be able to drive me?"

"Of course," I said. "That won't be a problem."

"Good. Marta does the cleaning and laundry, so you won't be responsible for that either. During the day, I'll be at the yarn shop. Oh, and maybe once a week you could take me food shopping? Would that be okay?"

"Absolutely," I told her. "Maybe we could go out for lunch before we do the shopping."

"Oh, yes. That would be fun. Well, Isabelle, I can't think of anything else at the moment except to discuss your pay."

I put my hand in the air. "No. What I'm doing for you is minimal and I won't accept any money. I insist. You've given me an incredible break on the rent at Koi House, so consider this a small repayment."

"Well, I won't argue with you, but if Haley agrees to stay here each night, I'll get her a gift. Maybe you could take me shopping for that."

"That would be nice."

David stood up. "Okay, well, if we're finished here, I'm heading to Publix. Chloe invited us to dinner this evening. Henry is grilling steaks and I offered to make some scalloped potatoes to go with them and I need to get a few things."

After David left, Mavis Anne said, "Chloe tells me that your mother is moving here permanently. She bought a townhouse in The Trails?"

"Hmm," I mumbled.

"You don't sound too happy about this. Is there a problem?"

"I think you know she left when I was fifteen. She left my father and me and took off for Oregon."

"Yes, Chloe did explain that to me. Oh, so you've never forgiven her for leaving?"

"No, I guess I haven't. It just irritates me that she chose to have her own life thirty years ago and now . . . all of a sudden she wants back into mine."

"Yes," Mavis Anne said and let out a sigh. "I can understand that would be difficult for you. My mother left when I was fourteen."

"She did?" I was surprised to hear this.

"Well, different circumstances. She passed away. However, no matter the reason, I was fourteen and without my mother. David was twelve and Emmalyn was only eight. I think it was probably the hardest on her. My father tried, and I did the best I could, but I don't think she ever adjusted to losing her mother. So I know it's not easy."

"Exactly. And your mother had no control over what happened. My mother did. She *chose* to leave."

"Yes, that's true. But you know, Isabelle, we all make mistakes in life. It seems to me that she wants to make amends with you. She could have stayed in Oregon or chosen anyplace else to retire. But she chose here. Near *you*. Believe me, I know a thing or two about forgiving, and it's one of the hardest things to do. I don't mean to badger you, but you might want to see what happens when she gets here. Maybe things will work out better than you think."

"I seriously doubt that," I said, and recalled that Petra had told me the same thing.

When Haley and Tina returned from the beach, Haley asked if her friend could stay one more night.

"That would be fine," I said. "But doesn't your mother want you home with her?"

"She's working night shift tonight. I did call to ask if it would be okay and she said as long as you were okay with it."

"Oh. Well then, yes. That's fine. Do you like steak?"

Her face lit up. "I love it."

"That's great. Henry is grilling for supper."

"Thanks, Mom," Haley called as they ran out the back door to the patio.

I stood watching them out the window. Haley was attempting to teach Tina how to knit. Another common interest they would share. It was then it hit me that I should invite Tina and her mother over for dinner sometime. This would give me a chance to meet the woman and she'd probably appreciate an evening out. I'd be sure to get her phone number from Tina and give her a call the following week.

Chapter 12

The next Tuesday I was with the charity knitting group working on my blanket when my cell phone rang. I was surprised to see Chadwick's name on the caller ID. Yes, he had said he'd call, but I wasn't certain that would happen.

"Oh, ah . . . I'll just take this outside," I told the group as I walked out of the yarn shop.

"Chadwick, hi. How are you?"

"Very good. I'm calling to see if you're free on Saturday evening."

"Yes, I am."

"Great. Now I don't want to seem presumptuous because it's the night before Valentine's Day, but I'd like to take you to a fairly new supper club that opened in Ormond Beach. Are you familiar with it? It's called Thirty-one."

"No, not at all."

"It's pretty unique and has a 1930s décor. Based on a speakeasy from that era. I hear the food is excellent and there's music and dancing."

"It sounds wonderful. What's the dress code?"

"Business dressy. Do you feel like getting all dolled up?"

I hadn't done glam in ages, but this was sounding very appealing.

"Sure," I told him. "It sounds like fun."

"I think it will be. I'll pick you up at seven. Is that okay?"

"Yes, perfect. Thanks, Chadwick. I'll see you Saturday evening."

I disconnected the call and stood outside feeling the smile that warmed my face. When I walked back into the yarn shop, the women all looked at me and remained silent. I felt heat radiating from my neck to my face and knew they were waiting for an explanation.

Sitting down, I said, "Oh . . . that was Chadwick Price. He had said he'd call to make plans for dinner."

"Well, honey, don't keep us in suspense," Mavis Anne said. "Where is he taking you?"

"To Thirty-one, that new supper club in town."

"Oh, wow, I told Henry we really need to go there," Chloe said.

Maddie nodded. "I heard it's pure elegance. Like going to the Ritz."

"Well, aren't you the lucky girl," Fay said. "And being escorted there by Chadwick Price."

"So what are you wearing?" Chloe asked.

"I have no clue," I said. "He said it's 1930s décor."

Mavis Anne raised a palm in the air. "I have just the perfect item. I saved a few of the fancier dresses my sister, Emmalyn, used to wear. They're in the cedar closet in my old bedroom at Koi House. After we finish knitting, we'll have a look."

A few hours later Mavis Anne, Chloe, and I were gathered in the bedroom. Mavis Anne had removed six dresses from the closet and laid them across the bed. Each one was stunning.

"Take your pick," she said.

They were all beautiful, but I was especially drawn to the black one. It was a floor-length Grecian silhouette. Small pearls and jet black rhinestones were embedded in the halter top band. With a natural gathered waist, the soft jersey material was striking.

"I love this one," I said, fingering the dress. "I wonder if it'll fit."

"Try it on," Chloe said.

I slipped out of my cropped pants and T-shirt, pulled the dress over my head, and turned so Chloe could fasten the hidden zipper and hook in the back.

"Oh, Isabelle," she gasped. "It's stunning. Go look in the full-length mirror."

She was right. Even with minimal makeup and my hair due for a cut, I had been transformed. And the dress fit like a dream. Almost as if it had been created for me.

Mavis Anne clapped her hands as excitement crossed her face. "Oh, Isabelle. You are a vision." She dabbed at her eyes. "I remember when Emmalyn wore that dress. You remind me a lot of her."

I ran my hand down the side of the dress. "Are you sure you don't mind if I borrow it?"

"Don't be silly. I'd be thrilled to see the dress worn again. Such a shame that it's been hidden away in a closet for so long."

I nodded. "Well, if you're sure."

"I'm positive. Oh, and I just remembered," she said, walking to the bureau and opening a drawer. She removed a box and took out a gorgeous black rhinestone headband. Holding it up, she said, "Emmalyn wore this with the dress. It was the perfect accessory."

I took the headband and knew that Emmalyn Overby had had class and style. Shaped in a curlicue design, the gems glittered. Two velvet ties would secure it across the forehead.

"Here," Chloe said. "Let me fasten it for you."

I turned back to the mirror and this time I gasped. It was the ideal finishing touch. I looked like a starlet from a 1930s film.

"Wow," I whispered. "This really is gorgeous."

I turned around and pulled Mavis Anne into an embrace. "Thank you so much. I really appreciate your letting me borrow this."

"Just wait until Chadwick Price sees you Saturday night. But I suggest you pay a visit to Helen, my hairdresser, that morning. The dress would look even better with your hair in a French twist."

She was right. I'd hold off getting a trim until after our date. "I have to agree. With the headband, a French twist style would look really nice. I'll give Helen a call and see if she can squeeze me in Saturday morning."

Tina hadn't been over in two days, so I wasn't surprised to see her arrive after school with Haley.

"Hey," I said, looking up from my knitting. After I had tried on the dress, Chloe and Mavis Anne had returned to the yarn shop and I sat outside on the patio. "Good day at school?"

"Yeah, it was," Haley said. "What's for supper?"

I smiled. It seemed ever since she had started hanging out with Tina, her appetite for food had returned. She certainly wasn't overeating, but she ate enough to convince me I didn't have to worry about an eating disorder.

"Nothing special. I have a meatloaf in the oven and we'll have au gratin potatoes and fresh green beans with it. Is that okay?"

"Sounds really good." She paused for a second and then asked, "Would it be okay if Tina stayed for dinner?"

I didn't mind at all, but I could see this was becoming a habit. I was also coming to see that if not for Haley, Tina would have a pretty lonely life.

"Of course it's okay. As a matter of fact, I was thinking I'd love to have both you and your mother over for dinner, Tina. Could you give me her phone number so I can give her a call and see when she's free?"

Tina smiled and nodded. "Oh, yeah, that would be great. I'll write it down for you. She's working tonight, though, but you can reach her on Friday and find out when she's off again."

"We're going up to my room to do our homework," Haley said. "And then we're going jogging for a while before dinner."

"Okay." I resumed knitting and thought about Tina. She was a very pretty girl. Actually, she was striking. With coal black hair and olive skin, she might be Hispanic; I wondered if her mother was also. Tina had said they'd moved to Florida from Texas, but I wondered if any family remained in Mexico.

A few minutes later both Haley and Tina came running back out to the patio.

"Oh, Mom! What is that gorgeous dress hanging on your bedroom door?"

I had been wondering how to break the news to my daughter that I had a bona fide date. She did know about the episode I had falling and that Chadwick had come to the rescue, but I'd neglected to tell her he might call for a date.

"Oh, well . . . Remember the man who helped me out the day I slipped in the parking lot in the rain?"

Haley nodded and waited.

"Well . . . he called me earlier. He'd like to take me to dinner. This Saturday. To a supper club." I felt like I was a teenager trying to explain to my father that I had a date. I was nervous about how my daughter would take this news, but the happy expression that crossed her face told me I needn't have been concerned.

She jumped up to hug me. "Wow! Really? That's great, Mom. I'm happy for you. And you're wearing that dress?"

"I am. Mavis Anne was kind enough to let me borrow it. It had belonged to her sister."

"Wow, Mrs. Wainwright," Tina said, "you're going to look the bomb."

I burst out laughing. "Hmm, you think?"

"Oh, definitely, Mom. Can Tina stay over Saturday night? We can help you get ready and you know . . ."

I laughed again. I was pretty sure she meant she wanted to check out my date.

"Yeah, that would be fine. Don't forget, though, you promised to help Maddie at the florist shop on Saturday for Valentine's Day."

"Right. Not a problem. I'm going there on Friday too."

The girls headed back into the house and I smiled. All of a sudden things seemed to be going in a good direction for me. I knew Haley had been in touch with her father via phone calls and texting quite a lot, and that was a good thing. Though our marriage hadn't worked out, I wanted my daughter to have a good relationship with her father. Like I had. She had mentioned that during April vacation she'd like to fly to Atlanta for a few days to visit with him. I wasn't sure how Roger felt about that, with having a new person in his life, but I hoped it worked out for Haley's sake.

Yes, I thought. *Things are going very well.*

And then I remembered that in a few short weeks my mother was moving to Ormond Beach.

Chapter 13

After I returned from my deliveries on Friday morning, I filled the washing machine with a load of clothes and decided to give Petra a call. I hadn't yet had a chance to tell her about my date the following night.

"Well, you go, girl," she said after I told her. "And it sounds like quite the swanky date. Your dress sounds gorgeous. Good for you, Isabelle. It's time you begin a new chapter for yourself. Any further word on the divorce from Roger?"

"He texted me the other day and said his attorney was mailing out the documents for me to sign. Since it's uncontested and we both agree to the settlements, it's pretty cut and dried. He'll be free to re-marry soon."

"Have you explained anything to Haley yet?"

"Not yet. And she wants to fly up to visit him in April during her vacation."

"Isabelle, you have to be honest and share the entire situation with her. Kids are more resilient than you think. Especially Haley. She'll hate it more if you don't say anything."

I let out a sigh. "I know. And I will. Soon."

When we hung up I had made a promise to call Petra on Sunday with all the details of my date with Chadwick. I smiled as I recalled how many times we had each done this throughout our teen years. Life seemed so much simpler then with our biggest problem being a blemish or what to wear to an upcoming dance. Now I was faced with a divorce and a mother I hadn't had much contact with in thirty years.

I hunted for Tina's mother's phone number. I wanted to make arrangements to have them over for dinner.

"Hi," I said when Brenda answered the phone. "This is Isabelle, Haley's mother."

"Oh, hi. How are you?"

I heard just a hint of an accent in her voice. "I'm good. The reason I'm calling is that I'd like to invite you and Tina for dinner some evening next week when you're free."

"Oh, yes, Tina had mentioned that. I'd like to meet you. Well, I'm off work next Wednesday if that will work for you."

I walked to the cabinet door in the kitchen to check the hanging calendar. "Yes," I told her. "Wednesday would be great. Why don't you come over around five?"

"Okay. And Isabelle, thank you so much for the invitation."

"Great. See you then."

Shortly after three, Haley raced through the back door and headed upstairs.

"Hi, Mom," she called. "I have to change and get to the florist shop."

That's right. Haley had agreed to help Maddie for the busy Valentine's holiday.

A few minutes later she ran into the living room. "I'm not sure what time I'll be back," she said. "But Maddie said it wouldn't be any later than nine. She's going to order takeout for us for supper and she said she'll drive me home when we close."

"That's fine," I told her. "Tell Maddie I said hi, and do a good job, which I'm sure you will."

She ran over to kiss my cheek and flew out the door.

I felt a smile cross my face. I was convinced that moving from Atlanta had been a wise decision. I hadn't seen Haley so happy and content in a long time. But then I realized I had to sit my daughter down very soon and explain to her the real reason for the breakup of my marriage. I dreaded the repercussions this might have.

I had spent the rest of the afternoon knitting my baby blanket, so when I heard my stomach growling, I was surprised to look at my watch and see it was after six.

Walking into the kitchen, I debated whether to have a glass of wine. It had been a week since I'd consumed almost two bottles. I hadn't had any since. I decided to pour a glass while I prepared myself a salad.

I turned on the radio and began to sauté some shrimp while humming to a tune I recalled from my college days. I was always struck by the way music had the ability to transport one back in time.

I set the shrimp aside and began slicing tomatoes, cucumbers, broccoli, and other vegetables. I recalled how fortunate Petra and I had been to take almost a year off following college graduation to do a road trip out to the west coast, stopping here and there, following only our own schedule.

When we returned, I wanted to use my journalism major and I was able to secure a position with the local newspaper covering community events. That was how I'd met Roger Wainwright. He had a top position with our local television news station and I had been sent to cover a fund-raiser that the station was having.

Tall, personable, and good looking, he had been extremely kind to me. By the time the evening ended, he had asked me out on a date. Our dating lasted for eight years until finally I gave him an ultimatum—either we take our relationship to the next step or I was moving on. We were married within six months and Haley was born the following year. Even at the beginning, Roger and I had never shared a romantic kind of love. It had always been just a notch above friendship.

I mixed my salad together and brought it to the table before refilling my wineglass. I couldn't help but wonder how my life would have gone had I not given Roger an ultimatum but rather had just moved on. I discarded this thought immediately when I realized that had I done that, I also would not have Haley. And that was unthinkable.

After eating and cleaning up the kitchen, I topped off my wineglass and headed to the living room for some knitting. Just as I began my row, Chloe called to tell me she'd be staying at Henry's condo and she'd see me in the morning.

Thinking of Chloe and Henry made me think back to my parents. I remembered some minor disagreements between them, but certainly I never witnessed any fights that would warrant my mother taking a lover and leaving my father and me. At the time I'd often wondered if there was more to the story, but over the years I came to accept what my father had explained to me, and all that remained was resentment toward my mother.

I must have dozed off, because I heard Haley calling, "Mom?"

I sat up on the sofa and rubbed my eyes as I glanced at my watch. Just after nine.

"In here, Haley," I called.

My daughter came into the living room and plopped down in a chair. "Whew," she said. "Maddie and I really worked hard, but it was so cool. You should see some of the flower arrangements people will receive tomorrow. There are going to be some happy sweethearts in Ormond Beach."

I laughed and saw the look of accomplishment on my daughter's face. "That's great. I'm sure Maddie was very happy to have your help."

"Yeah, I think she was. She taught me how to do the bows and even taught me how to do a few of the simple arrangements. I'm tired, but I really enjoyed the work. I felt like I got to use some of my creativity."

"What time do you have to go back in the morning?"

"Eight. And she's going to leave me alone in the shop while she goes out to do the deliveries. So she must trust me."

"I have no doubt she does. You're a real asset, Haley. Oh, don't forget that you'll be spending the night at Mavis Anne's tomorrow night. David and Clive leave for Italy tomorrow. Henry is driving them to the airport."

She yawned and nodded. "Yup, I know. Mavis Anne said Tina could stay too. The three of us are going to play cards and I told Mavis Anne we'd be over after you leave on your date. Tina and I want to see you."

I laughed as I got up to bring my empty wineglass into the kitchen. "Well, you'd better get to sleep, working girl."

She came to give me a hug and kiss and headed upstairs.

I placed my glass in the sink and began shutting off lights. That was when I recalled the dream. Another one. With Emmalyn.

In this dream we were in the yarn shop. Once again, Emmalyn was wearing the red evening gown. She was piling up skeins of yarn on a table and then turned to me and said, "Choose."

I felt bewildered. "Choose what?" I had asked her.

"Choose what you have to do."

"I don't understand," I told her, feeling annoyed.

She had nodded and begun to rearrange the skeins of yarn on the table.

"Can you choose now?" she'd asked.

"I don't know *what* to choose," I yelled at her.

She nodded again. "That's right. You don't."

And that was the end of the dream.

Chapter 14

I awoke Saturday morning and my first thought was my dream of the previous evening. *Total nonsense,* I thought. I had no idea why I was having these silly dreams but I had more important things to think about today. I glanced at the clock to see it was just before seven and remembered Haley had to be at the florist shop by eight.

I heard her in the shower, so I headed downstairs to prepare coffee and my daughter's breakfast.

"What would you like to eat?" I asked as she walked into the kitchen.

"Oh, just some yogurt and fruit this morning," she said, heading to the fridge. "Are you excited about your date tonight?"

"Yeah, I think I am."

"Good." Haley opened a yogurt container and perched on the stool at the counter. "I think it would be nice for you to have a male companion."

I laughed. "Why is that?"

"Well, Dad has somebody new in his life and I think you should too."

It was at times like this that my daughter seemed much older than her fourteen years.

"It's just a dinner date, Haley. We may never see each other again."

"Oh, Nana texted me and asked if I could help her the day the movers arrive. She said she'll have a lot of boxes to get unpacked. Would it be okay if I go over to her new place?"

"Sure," I mumbled, but it annoyed me that my mother seemed to be luring Haley into her web. What if my mom ended up not liking it here and took off again? I didn't want to see my daughter hurt in the way I had been.

＊　＊　＊

I arrived at Glam just before ten and was ready for Helen to work her magic. By the time she finished, I had to admit that this woman had a talent for doing hair.

I reached up to touch the gorgeous French twist at the back of my head. Taking the mirror she passed me, I spun around in the chair to see her creation.

"Oh, Helen, it looks beautiful. So sophisticated."

"I heard about the dress you're wearing tonight and I think this style is the finishing touch."

I had to agree.

I spent a quiet afternoon knitting and then decided to pamper myself with a bubble bath. By the time I emerged from the tub, it was after five, and I could hear Haley and Tina downstairs. I walked into the kitchen, where Haley was making grilled cheese sandwiches. Both girls looked up and gasped.

"Oh, Mom," Haley exclaimed. "Your hair looks gorgeous."

"It really does, Mrs. Wainwright," Tina agreed.

I smiled and secretly hoped that Chadwick Price would also think so. "Thanks. Are you girls all set for supper?"

"Yeah. I'm making grilled cheese and soup for us."

Tina jumped up from the stool. "I'll open the can of soup."

"And after I leave, you'll lock up here and go over to Mavis Anne's?"

Haley nodded as she flipped a sandwich on the grill. "I told Mavis Anne we'd be there shortly after seven."

"Okay. I'm going upstairs to put my makeup on and get dressed."

I walked over to the vanity where I kept my makeup bag only to discover it wasn't in the usual spot. I twirled around the room wondering where on earth it could be. My gaze flew to the top of the bureau, the bedside table, the desk. And no makeup bag.

I went to the top of the stairs and hollered down to Haley. "Do you know where my makeup is?"

She appeared at the foot of the stairs. "No. It's always on your vanity."

"I know. It's not there. You didn't take it to borrow something?"

Haley shook her head. "No. It has to be in your room. Do you want me to help you look?"

"No, that's okay. You go eat your supper."

I walked back into the bedroom and stood on the threshold feeling confused and upset. Maybe I'd left it in the bathroom? I walked in, and after a thorough search, still no makeup bag.

Walking back into the bedroom, I said, "Where the hell *are* you?"

The only place I hadn't looked was the bureau drawers. I just knew it couldn't be in there, but I pulled the top drawer open. An aroma of Chanel No. 5 drifted up to me—at the same time I spied my makeup bag nestled on top of my underwear. Reaching for the bag, I felt a chill go through me. How on earth had it gotten in my drawer? I never would have put it there. It was then I recalled Chloe's story about also smelling this particular French perfume when she sometimes opened one of the bureau drawers. The very same signature perfume that Emmalyn Overby was noted for.

I took the bag and went to sit at the vanity table to begin applying my makeup. By the time I finished, I had decided that I must have inadvertently tossed the bag into the bureau drawer.

I was ready to slip the gorgeous dress on and called down to Haley again.

"Any chance you could zip and hook the dress for me?"

"Come on, Tina," she called into the kitchen. "My mom needs help."

We slipped the dress over my head and Haley fastened the back. I put on a pair of strappy black heels and then sat at the vanity. Holding the rhinestone headband on my forehead, Haley tied the back to hold it in place.

I stood up and walked to the cheval mirror in the corner of the room. I had to admit that a transformation had taken place. While I was always confident about how I looked in public, what I now saw in the mirror made me take in a breath. If I hadn't known better, I would have thought the image that stared back at me was a very beautiful and chic woman of the 1930s.

"What do you think?" I asked as I turned toward Haley and Tina.

I could see their approval in the expressions on their faces.

"Oh, Mom," Haley said. "You are drop-dead gorgeous."

"Mrs. Wainwright . . . you're smokin' hot."

I laughed as I turned back to the mirror for another look and nodded. "You know, I think I have to agree with both of you."

The ringing of the doorbell interrupted any further indulgence.

"Oh, let me go let him in, Mom. I'll introduce myself. You have to make an entrance down the staircase."

"Are you sure?" I asked.

Haley was already racing from the room. "Absolutely," she called over her shoulder with Tina close behind. "And wait a few minutes before you come down."

I let out a deep breath and allowed myself another glance in the mirror. I walked to the bed and picked up the black lacy shawl that Chloe had let me borrow and a small black evening bag.

I blew out a puff of air, looked around the room, and said, "Okay. Time to get this show on the road."

I heard chatter as I descended the staircase. A moment later conversation stopped and three sets of eyes were staring up at me as I took the final steps.

"Hi, Chadwick. I see you've met my daughter and her friend."

He nodded, and for a second I thought perhaps he'd lost his voice as his gaze went from my face down the length of my body and back up to my face. He cleared his throat and nodded again. "Yes, I have. You look amazing."

I grinned as I realized Chadwick, the confident professional, seemed to have reverted to an awkward teenage boy on his first date.

"So do you," I said. And he did.

Wearing a black suit, crisp white shirt, and gray tie, he was the kind of man that definitely turned female heads. Curly dark hair with just enough gray to be distinguished, a bronze tan and fit body, Chadwick Price caused my heart to skip a beat—and he was my date for the evening.

"Okay," I said, regaining my own composure before giving last-minute instructions to Haley. "I think we're ready."

Before we walked out the door, I turned around and glanced toward my daughter. She smiled, nodded and gave me a thumbs-up. I was pretty sure she approved of Chadwick Price.

Chapter 15

On the short drive to Thirty-one, Chadwick and I made small talk about weather, my daughter, and a recent sale he had completed. He handed the keys to the valet to park the car and we walked into the supper club.

A Sinatra song filled the air and the décor made me feel I'd stepped back in time. Tables covered with white cloths and chairs upholstered in black-and-white zebra print filled the center of the room. Dark walls held large prints of Florida natives, giving one the feel of the tropics. A small stage with red velvet curtains was located to the side of the dining room with a highly polished bar opposite. We were escorted to a table for two where the waiter pulled out my chair for me to be seated and passed a wine list to Chadwick. After perusing it for a few moments, Chadwick made a choice, ordered a bottle, and then turned his full attention to me.

"So," he said, leaning forward with a smile. "Amazing doesn't seem to be an adequate enough word to describe how you look tonight."

I couldn't recall the last time a man had been so complimentary. "Thank you. I have to thank Mavis Anne for letting me borrow this dress and headband."

"I wondered where you found a vintage gown like that."

"Actually, it belonged to her sister, Emmalyn. She was Yarrow's mother."

He nodded. "Yes, that's right. I remember hearing about her. She was tragically killed pretty young, wasn't she?"

"Yes, a car accident when she was only twenty-eight."

The waiter returned, and I was surprised to see that Chadwick had ordered champagne and not just regular wine. The waiter popped the cork, poured a small amount into a flute, and passed it to Chadwick to sample.

He took a sip and nodded. "Very nice."

The waiter then proceeded to fill my glass before topping off Chadwick's.

When the waiter retreated, Chadwick lifted his flute to touch mine. "Here's to us," he said. "A new friendship and wherever it might lead us."

I smiled and nodded. "To friendship. Oh, this is wonderful."

"I'm glad you like it. Piper-Heidsieck, from the Champagne region of France."

I took another sip. In addition to his good looks, this man projected a cosmopolitan demeanor.

The waiter brought the menus, and Chadwick told him he'd signal when we were ready to order.

"Tell me about yourself," he said, leaning back in his chair as if he had all the time in the world to listen. Just to me.

"There really isn't much to tell. I grew up in Pennsylvania. My mom left when I was fifteen, so it was just my dad and me."

"That had to be rough on you."

"It was. Especially because she left us to be with her lover. She took off for Oregon and taught art classes at the university there."

He nodded and waited for me to continue.

"I went to Penn State and married Roger after eight years of dating. We had a decent life—until we didn't. But Haley was the bonus from our marriage."

"She seems like a really nice young lady."

"She is. Sometimes I feel she's more mature than I am. We've had our ups and downs, but I think we're on a good track now. I just always wanted the two of us to have the relationship that my mother and I never had."

"That's understandable. And your mother? You never hear from her?"

"Not much over these thirty years. But she's retired now, apparently the lover is no longer in the picture . . . and she wants to worm her way back into my life."

Chadwick took a sip of champagne before saying, "And I take it that you're not interested?"

"Not really, no. But she's not going to make it easy. She's decided to relocate here, to Ormond Beach."

"Hmm. And how do you feel about that?"

"I certainly can't stop her. She's bought a place at The Trails and will be here in two weeks."

"Yeah, you could have some difficult times ahead."

I was surprised that Chadwick didn't try to placate me, by telling me it might all work out and things would be fine.

"Shall we look over the menu?" he asked, passing the large leather booklet to me.

We decided on identical choices: an appetizer of baked herb goat cheese and roasted peppers followed by a spinach salad. For our entrée we both chose chicken cordon bleu roulade.

Chadwick gave our order to the waiter, who then refilled our flutes.

When he left the table, I said, "Your turn. Tell me about you."

"Well, I grew up in the Atlanta area. My father still owns a real estate company there. I had an older brother, Aaron, who passed away from cancer about twenty-five years ago. Maybe Chloe mentioned this to you?"

When I shook my head no, he paused a second before continuing.

"After Aaron passed away, I decided to move down here. I had just turned thirty and it was time for me to establish my own business and life."

"And you've never been married?"

He laughed. "No, never. Had a few serious relationships that eventually led nowhere, but that was it." He took a sip of champagne and locked his eyes with mine. "I never found the right woman."

As silly as it sounds, I had the strangest feeling that he wanted to add, *not until now.*

We moved on to less personal topics such as sports, movies, music, and food. I was surprised to discover that we had a lot in common.

Our appetizers arrived and we continued talking. A singer had now taken the stage and was crooning old Dean Martin songs into the microphone.

I nodded toward the stage. "He's very good," I said.

"He is," Chadwick agreed. "Do you enjoy dancing?"

"I do, but it's been a million years. I'd probably step all over your toes."

He laughed. "I doubt that. We'll give it a whirl after dinner."

Our conversation continued through the main course and I was beginning to marvel that talking with Chadwick was so easy. As if I'd known him forever, and no matter what I told him, he wouldn't be shocked or disappointed or judgmental.

We both passed on dessert. After the waiter cleared away our dishes, he topped off our flutes with the remaining champagne.

The music was just beginning again. Chadwick stood, held out his hand to me, and said, "Dance with me."

The moment I went into his arms and we began dancing, I had a feeling that we'd danced together before, which of course we hadn't. But he was so easy to follow and his arm around me felt right. He squeezed my hand, looked down at me, and smiled.

It was then I focused on the song and realized it was another old Dean Martin song, "Memories Are Made of This." And I wondered. Were we beginning a journey of memories together?

After a few more dances Chadwick suggested we have a nightcap in the Havana Bar on the patio. We walked outside and found a padded loveseat in front of the fire pit. I was surprised that nobody else had claimed this spot. I held out my hands near the flame.

"Nice," I said.

"Are you cold?"

"Not at all. This throws great heat." I put the lace shawl over my shoulders and sat down.

We both remained quiet staring into the flames. A few minutes later a waiter placed two snifters of cognac on the table beside us.

When he left, Chadwick passed one to me and held up his glass. "Thank you for an incredibly great evening, Isabelle. I can't tell you how much I enjoyed it. You look so beautiful."

He made me *feel* beautiful. "I did too. It's been a wonderful evening."

We touched glasses and each took a sip.

He sat back and I felt his arm go around my shoulders, causing me to shiver.

"Are you sure you're not cold?" he asked, pulling me a little closer.

I smiled and shook my head. "No. Not at all."

"So are you divorced now or are you still going through the process?"

"Actually, the documents will arrive this coming week. It's an amicable divorce . . . well, at least now it is. It was pretty shocking to me when Roger first left. But it's for the best. I know that now."

Chadwick was quiet for a moment before saying, "So you don't love him anymore?"

I let out a sigh. "I'm not sure I ever did. After Roger left, I began to be honest with myself. We met shortly after I graduated college. I had majored in journalism and was working for a small newspaper as a reporter covering various events in the area. Roger worked for a local television station. They were having a fund-raiser and I was assigned to cover it."

I took a sip of cognac and thought back to those years.

"I found myself flirting with him, he seemed to be flirting back, and before I left the event, he had asked me out on a date."

"And I take it that date led to marriage?"

I laughed. "I guess you could say that. Eight years later."

"You dated for eight years? That's a long time."

"Exactly. By then I was pushing thirty. I was ready to settle down, start a family, and be a wife."

"But Roger wasn't?"

"Looking back now, no, I don't think he was. And in all honesty, what followed was probably my own fault. I gave him an ultimatum. I told him either we took the next step or we were finished."

Chadwick took a sip of cognac and nodded. "And so . . . you got married."

"Yup, and Haley was born within a year. The first few years were okay. He worked a lot at the TV station; I was the stereotypical wife and mother. And actually, I loved it. But the older Haley got, the more I found I wanted more of my husband's company and attention. He was never a romantic sort of guy, but . . . I was hoping that might change over time."

"And it didn't?"

"No. Not for him anyway." I paused for a moment. "Roger left me for somebody else."

I felt his arm pull me a bit closer. "I'm sorry," he said quietly. "It makes no sense that he would leave *you* for another woman."

"He didn't," I blurted out. "Roger left me for a man. He's gay." I squeezed my eyes tight to prevent the tears from sliding down my face. I couldn't believe I'd just said that. Nobody except Petra knew this. I'd allowed everybody to think he'd left me for another woman. And I'd taken the pain, the rejection, the betrayal, and the hurt deep inside me and let it fester there for almost two years.

"Come on," Chadwick said, standing up and taking my hand. "Let's go for a drive."

Chapter 16

Chadwick headed south on A1A and pulled into the parking lot of Andy Romano Park overlooking the Atlantic Ocean. We had both remained quiet on the drive.

He reached for my hand and gave it a squeeze. "Feel like talking?"

"Are you shocked or disgusted by what I told you?" I asked.

"Not at all. Discovering that your husband is gay has nothing to do with you."

I was surprised to hear him say this. "That's not what I've felt these past two years. I thought maybe if I had been different. Sexier. More beautiful. More . . . something."

I heard him let out a sigh and squeeze my hand again. "Isabelle, this isn't about you. It's about marrying a person you simply didn't know. Even after eight years. But that's not uncommon. People have a way of projecting only what they want us to see. We all have secrets. Some are minor and not that important. But others have life-shattering consequences. I'm afraid that's the kind of secret Roger had."

I nodded. He was right. Then why did I still feel so inadequate as a wife and a woman?

"I just can't help but feel that maybe if I had done something different, maybe—"

Chadwick interrupted me and shifted in his seat to face me. "Look at me," he said.

I turned and saw the concerned expression on his face.

"Isabelle, there isn't a thing *you* could have done differently. Nothing. Unfortunately, Roger was never honest with you. For that, he was wrong. However, you also have to know how difficult it's been for homosexuals. It still is in many places. Some of society has become more accepting and of course laws have helped that to happen. But it's still not always easy. People discriminate and many are consumed with hate. Maybe he felt the time had finally come to be honest, and federal laws probably helped his decision. Do you know the fellow he's with?"

I nodded. "I don't really know Gordon, but yes, I've met him. He works at the television station with Roger. I just assumed they were good friends. You know, *guy* buddies. I sure as hell never thought they were *gay* buddies."

"Does your daughter know about this?"

I shook my head. "God! No! And she wants to go visit him in April. Roger and Gordon are now living together. I have no idea how I'm going to tell Haley. And apparently, now that the laws have changed, they're planning to make it legal and get married." I let out a groan. "I can't even imagine explaining this to my daughter."

"You know, kids today aren't like we were. Everything is out in the open now. Being gay or a lesbian is something today's generation is exposed to and I think that's gone a long way to make kids more broadminded. They might not all accept homosexuality, but it's not hidden like it was in my parents' generation."

I knew Chadwick was right about the sweeping changes in society but I dreaded having to tell my daughter why her father had really left.

"When the time is right, you'll tell her, and her reaction might surprise you."

I nodded and recalled that Petra had said the same thing.

He leaned toward me and took my face in his hands. "You'll do just fine."

I felt his lips brush mine and all thoughts of Roger were gone. The pressure of Chadwick's lips increased as I slid my arms around his neck and returned his kiss. A few moments later we broke apart, both of us breathing heavily. Without a doubt this man made up for all of the passion that Roger had lacked.

He pulled back and stared into my eyes. "That . . . was incredibly nice."

"It was," I whispered.

He bent his head to kiss me again and there was no denying the desire that he created in my body.

But what really surprised me was when we broke apart and I looked into his eyes, I saw my own desire reflected there—a desire I had never witnessed with my husband.

He buried his face in my neck and whispered, "Thank you for a wonderful evening."

I released a sigh of contentment and nodded.

Chadwick pulled away, and I saw the dashboard clock read almost midnight. The entire evening had slipped away much too quickly.

"Gosh, I can't believe the time," I said.

"I know. I'll drive you home."

He backed the car out of the parking spot, reached for my hand, and gave me a smile. "I'm hoping this was the first of many dates to come."

I returned his smile. "I hope so too."

When he pulled into the driveway of Koi House, he was still holding my hand. He leaned over to kiss my cheek before getting out, opening my door, and walking me to the porch.

Putting his hands on my shoulders, he leaned toward me for another kiss, which was quickly becoming more heated than the previous ones.

He abruptly pulled away, held me at arm's length, and said, "Okay. If I don't leave now, you're going to end up having a guest overnight." He kissed my cheek and smiled. "I'll call you tomorrow."

I watched him jog to his car, get in, and wave good night as I wondered why having him as an overnight guest would be a bad thing.

I walked into the house, shut off the porch light, and locked the door before heading to the kitchen for a glass of ice water to bring upstairs.

Walking into the bedroom, I noticed the aroma of Chanel No. 5 was much stronger than earlier and I smiled. The entire night had been magical. Wearing Emmalyn's gorgeous dress, the supper club, the champagne, the dancing—but most of all, Chadwick Price had been enchanting and made me feel like I'd just lived a page from a fairy tale.

Sunlight streaming through the windows woke me the next morning. The bedside clock read just after eight. I stretched and smiled as I recalled the previous evening. Had it all been a dream? No, this time it was real. I really had shared a very special evening with Chadwick. I was pretty sure he liked me. A lot. I certainly had not been looking to get involved with somebody. But maybe it's accurate that we truly have no control over matters of the heart. Love is involuntary—it happens with no control from us.

And what was with those passionate kisses, I wondered. I recalled Chloe saying she detected chemistry between Chadwick and me the first time we'd met at LuLu's. Was there also some truth about love at first sight? Many people seemed to think so. I was more of the belief that people didn't *fall* in love but rather *grew* in love. But after spending the previous evening with Chadwick, I was beginning to have my doubts about this.

I got up, headed to the bathroom, and then went downstairs. The house was so quiet with Chloe at Henry's condo and Haley at Mavis Anne's house. I started the coffee and opened the front door to get the newspaper. I smiled when I saw the newspaper had a bouquet of flowers attached to it with ribbon. Bending down, I picked it up and noticed there was also a small envelope there.

My smile increased as I took the newspaper and flowers into the kitchen. After pouring myself a mug of coffee, I settled on the stool to read the card written in bold, masculine script.

Just a small thank you for an evening that I wish didn't have to end. It was signed, *Fondly, Chadwick.*

I glanced at the bouquet and wondered when he had stopped by to leave them. And then I looked more closely at the flowers. They weren't from a florist shop. Had he handpicked these roses and daisies? I had visions of him sneaking into a neighbor's yard and burst out laughing.

I was filling a vase with water when Haley walked in the back door with Tina.

"Good morning," I said. "How'd it go staying with Mavis Anne?"

"She's so cool," Haley said.

"Yeah," Tina agreed. "We had the best time. Oh, pretty flowers, Mrs. W."

I grinned at the new moniker that Tina had recently begun using. "Thank you."

"From Chadwick?" Haley questioned.

I nodded. "Yeah. I found them on the porch this morning with the newspaper."

"Oh, wow," Tina gushed. "Straight out of a Jane Austen novel."

I laughed. "Have you girls had breakfast?"

"Yes," Haley said. "Marta came over and made French toast for all of us. She brought her daughter Krystina and the three of us are going to the beach. Is that okay?"

"Sure. So Mavis slept okay and everything went well?"

"Yup," Haley assured me. "Oh, and David called this morning. He and Clive had just landed at the airport in Milan and were getting their rental car to drive to Lake Como."

"Oh, good. I'm sure that made Mavis Anne feel good to know they arrived safely."

The mention of David made me think of something else.

"What time will you be home, Haley?"

"Probably by two. Tina's mom gets done with work at three today, so she's going home to be with her."

"Okay."

"Why? What's going on?"

I waved a hand in the air. "Oh, nothing really. I just wanted to talk to you about something."

Chapter 17

After I showered and dressed, I walked next door to check on Mavis Anne. She was sitting on the patio knitting.

"There you are," she said. "Details. I want details of that date last night."

I laughed as I sat down to join her. "Well . . . *magical* would pretty well cover it. It was simply . . . magical. All of it. The supper club, the food, the champagne, and, of course, Chadwick."

Mavis Anne grinned. "Ah, yes. Chadwick. He's a special guy. I've known him for quite a few years and he's never failed to impress me. So I can assume that the two of you hit it off quite well?"

"Hmm, you could say that. He left me some flowers this morning on the porch with the newspaper and he said he'd call me today."

Mavis Anne put her knitting down and leaned forward to pat my hand. "I'm happy for you, Isabelle. I had no doubt that you'd make a good couple. I excel in the romance department. Unfortunately, I lost my Jackson way too soon, but the time we had together has always stayed with me."

I recalled Chloe telling me about the love of Mavis Anne's life. But she was right. She'd lost him much too soon to the war in Vietnam. But it seemed that over the years her love for Jackson had only deepened.

"The entire evening just felt so *right*," I told her. "I surprised myself by sharing things with him that I never discuss. And he's so understanding. Yeah, he's a pretty special guy."

"Sounds to me that your fall in that parking lot was meant to be."

"You really believe that sort of stuff?"

A look of surprise crossed Mavis Anne's face. "Oh, yes, of course. Nothing happens by chance. We might think it does, but no. I've always felt the universe knows precisely what it's doing. Especially when it comes to the heart and love."

"Hmm, maybe you're right. So what are your plans for today? Can I prepare your lunch?"

"Oh, thank you, but no. Louise is coming to get me. We made plans to drive down to Cocoa Beach and do some browsing in the shops and then we're going to have lunch at that great French restaurant, Café Margaux. Would you like to join us?"

"Thanks but no. I have some chores to get done around the house and Haley will be back from the beach by two."

I kept Mavis Anne company for another hour and then went home.

I had just walked in when my cell phone rang and I saw Chadwick's name on the caller ID.

"Hello," he said. "And how are you this morning?"

"I'm great. Thank you so much for the flowers."

His laughter came across the line. "Oh, good. You found them."

"I did. With the newspaper. Did you steal those from a neighbor's yard?"

I heard him laugh again. "No. I picked them from my own garden. Unfortunately, Maddie's florist shop was closed today."

"Well, you did a great job. I have them in a vase and I love them."

"That was my intention. So what are your plans for today?"

"Actually . . . I've decided to have that talk with Haley later this afternoon. About Roger."

"Good for you. I think it's the right thing to do. I hope it goes well."

"Yeah. Me too."

"The beginning of the week is busy for me, but I was wondering if you might be free on Thursday evening."

I walked to the cabinet to check the calendar. "Yeah. I have to take Mavis Anne for a hair appointment in the afternoon, but I'm free that evening."

"Great. How about if I pick you up about six? I'd like to bring you to my house for dinner."

"That would be nice. So, yes."

"Okay. Well, if I don't talk to you before, I'll see you Thursday at six."

I hung up and recalled what Mavis Anne had said about love at first sight. I wasn't sure about love, but I did know I had been strongly attracted to Chadwick Price from the moment I'd met him the year before. And that attraction seemed to be getting stronger.

Haley returned home shortly after two and headed to the fridge to make herself a salad.

"So, what's up?" she asked as I finished loading the dishwasher. "You wanted to talk to me about something?"

"Yeah," I said, dreading the impending conversation. "Fix your salad and we'll talk." I poured myself a glass of iced tea and watched my daughter place lettuce, tomatoes, cucumber, and onions into a salad bowl. She added some tuna fish and dressing and joined me at the counter with an expectant look on her face.

I took a sip of iced tea. "Well, I wanted to talk to you about visiting your father in April."

"Oh, okay. You said I could go, right?"

"Yes, of course you can, and we'll get your flight tickets soon. But . . . ah . . . well, there's something I wanted to tell you about why your father left me."

Haley nodded. "I know. You said he had somebody else in his life. I hope you know I'd never take sides, Mom. I love you both but I'm sorry he did that to you."

I let out a deep sigh. "Well, Haley, sometimes things just aren't meant to be. Sometimes things happen in life that are good and wonderful, but . . . they're just not supposed to last a lifetime. Things change. People change. And sometimes things were always a certain way but people just weren't honest with themselves or others."

I saw the blank expression on my daughter's face and realized I was beginning to ramble.

I cleared my throat. "What I'm trying to say is . . . this person that your father left me for . . . well, it wasn't another woman."

Haley's head shot up as she stared at me. "Oh," was all she said.

"No. It was a man." Her expression told me she was trying to digest this information.

After a few moments, she said, "Are you saying that Dad is gay?"

I nodded as a pain shot through my heart. This was probably one of the hardest things I'd ever had to do. "Yes. He is." I waited to see which way she'd take the conversation.

She put down her fork and stopped eating. "Was he always gay?"

"Yes, he was. Although he never told me until a couple of years ago. I'm not sure he could admit it to himself until then."

Haley blew out a loud puff of air. "Wow." She shook her head. "Wow," she said again. "Is the man Gordon?"

Now it was my turn to be surprised. "Yes, it is. But how did you know that?"

"Well, I never knew for sure. But a few years ago I'd stopped by the television studio to see Dad after school. I went to his office but didn't knock before going in. Dad and Gordon were hugging. I didn't think too much of that because a lot of men hug in a friendly way. But this was different. First of all, they both looked embarrassed and then they got all awkward. Dad tried to explain they'd just been notified they'd both won some kind of award for broadcasting. But something just didn't feel right. I never said anything because I thought it was my imagination."

"I'll be damned," I said.

"But I guess it wasn't my imagination."

I shook my head. "No, it wasn't. It is Gordon and they've been together for about three years now."

"So that's who Dad wants to marry? Gordon?"

I nodded. "Yes. How do you feel about all of this?"

Haley jumped up to give me a hug. "Oh, Mom. This isn't about *me*. How do *you* feel about all of it? Why didn't you tell me any of this before? It had to have been so hard on you."

I felt moisture stinging my eyes. This was one of those moments when the maturity of my daughter blew me away.

I wiped at my eyes. "I'm okay, Haley. Really. Well . . . I am now. It took a while to soak it all in but . . . yes, I'm okay with it now."

She pulled me into another embrace. "Well," she said in a matter of fact tone, "if you're okay with it, then I'm okay with it."

"Really? Do you still want to go visit your father?"

"Of course I do. He'll always be my dad. And I only met Gordon that one time, but he seemed really nice. They're living together, aren't they?"

"Yeah. Do you think that'll be a problem with visiting?"

"No. Dad's moving, you know."

"Really? No, I didn't know. We've really only texted since I left Atlanta. Where is he moving?"

"To a beautiful house just outside of Atlanta. He sent me photos on the computer. Three bedrooms and a pool. He said he'll have my room decorated any way I want. They'll have a guest room, too, but nobody will use my room. That's just for me."

I knew this made Haley happy and made her feel special, which was great. "That's wonderful. So they'll certainly have the room for you to visit anytime you want. Will they be in the house when you go in April?"

"Yes. They're moving next month."

"That's wonderful," I said again. And it was. It was apparent that Roger was making the proper provisions to keep his daughter in his life. Even though things had changed with me, he was doing the right thing for Haley.

"Do you have any questions?" I asked.

"Yeah. Can I go to their wedding?"

I was surprised about her request. "You'd really like to go?"

"Sure. Why not? A girl at school went to her mom's lesbian wedding a couple weeks ago. It was held at some fancy place in Orlando."

Yup. This new generation was definitely more openminded and accepting than previous ones. And I could see that this was a very good thing.

"Of course you can go," I told her. "I'll take you shopping for a nice outfit to wear."

Haley finished her salad and we continued to discuss Roger, Gordon, and their situation. By the time my daughter left the kitchen to go do some homework, I knew she was a well-adjusted, compassionate, and loving young lady. And I was mighty proud of her.

I brewed a pot of coffee and decided the time had come to speak to Roger on the phone. He had a right to know about the conversation that had transpired with Haley.

"Roger, this is Isabelle," I said when he answered.

"Isabelle, how nice to hear your voice." I could tell he meant it by his tone.

"How have you been?" I asked.

"Fine. And you? How have *you* been?" I could detect a sincere concern.

I let out a sigh. "I wasn't good for quite a while. I won't lie. But now . . . I'm fine. I really am. I feel like I've turned a corner."

"You have no idea how happy it makes me to hear this. Isabelle . . .

I never wanted to hurt you. Not ever. I'm not sure you can ever forgive me for what happened, but . . . I've always hoped at least you would have a chance to go on and be happy."

It suddenly struck me that I *was* happy. "I am. I love living here and Haley's happy too. It was the right thing to do, moving away from Atlanta. Listen, the main reason I'm calling is about Haley. I know she's planning to come visit you in April and, well . . . I thought the time had come to be honest with her about you and why our marriage really broke up."

There was a moment of silence before he said, "Are you saying you told Haley that I'm gay?"

"I did. And I told her your upcoming marriage isn't to a woman, but you'll be marrying Gordon."

"Oh, Isabelle, I never wanted you to have to be the one to tell her. I was planning to do that when she came here in April. I'm so sorry."

"No, it was okay. I thought it might actually be better if the news came from me."

"How did she take it?"

"Surprisingly, she took it way better than I would have expected. We really have a daughter to be proud of. That's one thing that you and I got perfectly right."

I heard a whoosh of air come across the line. "Haley has always been extra special. So I shouldn't be surprised. But are you sure she's okay with all of this?"

"Very sure, Roger. She can't wait to visit you and she wants to attend the wedding."

"That's way more than I could have hoped for. Isabelle, thank you. Thank you for telling her in a way that she understood. This could have all gone very differently."

"Hey, you're her father. And you always will be. I'll be getting her flight tickets as soon as you both decide on dates."

"Absolutely not. I'm paying for her flight and I'll get it booked after I speak to Haley. By the way, are you okay financially? Can I send you more money?"

I felt a smile cross my face. "No, but thank you. I'm doing just fine. Oh, and Roger . . . I've met somebody. It's a brand new relationship and I'm not sure where it will go, but right now . . . I'm very happy."

"And I couldn't be happier for you. You deserve all the love and good things there are in life."

"Okay, well, you take care and keep in touch. I'll sign the divorce documents when they arrive this week."

"Thanks again, Isabelle. You're the best. You really are. We'll talk soon."

I hung up as I felt a warm spot touch my heart. Roger and I would always have the connection of our daughter. And I had no doubt that, in his own way, Roger loved me. It just had never been in the way I had wanted to be loved as a woman.

Chapter 18

Marta had come Wednesday morning to clean while I was out doing my deliveries. I could have paid her to prepare something for dinner, but I chose to make a batch of lasagna to have with Brenda and Tina. Salad and garlic bread would top it off.

I thought the dining room would be too formal and decided we'd eat at the breakfast nook table. I'd just finished completing the place settings when Haley walked into the kitchen.

She placed a kiss on my cheek. "It looks so nice, Mom. Thanks for having them over for dinner."

"I like Tina and I'm looking forward to meeting her mom. Do me a favor and fill that vase on the counter with water and then arrange the flowers."

"Oh, pretty. Did you get these at Maddie's?"

"Yeah. I thought they'd brighten up the table."

I began preparing the salad while Haley tended to the flowers.

I was lost in my thoughts concerning Chadwick and looking forward to dinner at his house the following night. I certainly had not planned to dive into another relationship but I was beginning to see that relationships were another thing that we have no control with. I had always been a planner and organizer and decided that maybe it was time for me to let go and see where life took me.

"Mom, did you hear me?" I heard Haley ask.

"What's that?" I said.

"Do you want me to put the garlic bread into the oven?"

"Not yet. I thought I'd offer Brenda a glass of wine and we'd sit on the patio for a little while before dinner. The lasagna comes out of the oven at six thirty and we can stick the garlic bread in then."

"Okay," she said, just as the front bell rang. "Oh, there they are. I'll get it."

I placed the salad in the fridge to stay crisp and followed Haley to the front of the house.

"Hey," she said, opening the door wide. "Come on in."

"Hi, Brenda," I said, extending my hand. "I'm Isabelle. I'm so glad you could come."

A smile covered her face. "Thank you so much for inviting us. What a beautiful house you have," she said, stepping into the living room.

She was medium height, slim build, and had thick, dark hair like her daughter's. But unlike Tina, Brenda had a stunning, exotic quality about her. Dark eyes and olive skin added to her looks.

"Oh, it's not really our house," I explained. "We're just renting it, but yes, it's a very nice home. Come on, let's go sit on the patio till dinner is ready. Would you like a glass of wine?"

"Yes, that would be nice," she said, following me to the kitchen.

"We're going up to my room," Haley said. "Call us when dinner is ready."

"Oh, my goodness," Brenda exclaimed. "This kitchen is nicer than some restaurants."

I smiled as I uncorked a bottle of red wine. "Yeah, it *is* pretty wonderful."

"Do you do a lot of cooking? I think I'd be in here all day and night cooking," she said.

I passed her a wineglass and shook my head. "Not nearly as much as I probably should. Do you enjoy cooking?"

"Oh, yes, very much. My mother owned a restaurant in Mexico before we came to America. Then my father died and we went to Texas. My mother opened a small restaurant there and I used to help out as a kid."

We walked out to the patio and sat down. "Oh, that's great. Does your mother still have the restaurant?"

Her expression looked sad. "No, I'm afraid not. My mother passed away three years ago and I wasn't able to keep it going on my own."

"That's too bad. I love Mexican food. I know you're an RN, but have you thought about opening a restaurant here?"

"I'd love to, but financially I couldn't do that right now."

I nodded. "Well, maybe in time." I saw the doubtful look she gave me. "Haley told me you moved here last year for your job."

Brenda paused a moment before saying, "That was one of the reasons, yes. But I had just gotten divorced . . . and . . . I just thought it best if we left the area and started over."

"Right. I did the same thing when we left Atlanta. Actually, my divorce documents just arrived today."

"Are you still in touch with Haley's father?"

"I wasn't very much at first, but I think we've arrived at a good place for all three of us. Haley has plans to fly to Atlanta in April to spend some time with her dad. Tina said she's not in touch with her dad at all?"

"No. She's not," was all she said.

That seemed to be a subject she'd rather not discuss.

"So you like it around here?" I asked.

Brenda took a sip of wine and nodded. "Yes, very much. I really like my job and my coworkers have been kind and friendly. When we arrived here last year, we didn't have much with us and people were so giving."

I had a feeling there was a lot more to Brenda's story than she wanted to discuss on our first time meeting each other.

"I've also found this to be a wonderful community."

"Do you have family here? Is that why you chose Ormond Beach?" she asked.

"Actually, no. Chloe wasn't really family but close enough." I went on to explain about my father and Chloe and how Haley and I came to be here.

"Chloe sounds like a wonderful person. You were fortunate she took you under her wing and introduced you to Mavis Anne."

I was beginning to feel more grateful each day. "Oh, you have to meet Mavis Anne. You'll just love her. Well, let's take our wine inside. That lasagna should be about ready."

The girls and Brenda helped me clean up after dinner. We had just finished loading the dishwasher and I looked around the kitchen.

"I think that's it," I said. "Thanks for your help."

"That was delicious," Brenda said. "I can't thank you enough for having Tina and me to dinner. I'm not sure if she told you, but we just have an efficiency apartment on the beach. So my ability to cook is very limited."

For somebody who loved to cook that must be difficult. I recalled some of the run-down motels along the beach and assumed that was where they lived.

"Do you want me to go check on Mavis Anne?" Haley asked.

I glanced at the clock and saw it was just past seven thirty. "No, that's okay. There are cupcakes for dessert if you girls would like some. I'm going to make coffee for Brenda and me and then I thought I'd take her over to meet Mavis Anne."

"Oh, okay. Tell her I'll be over by nine thirty to spend the night with her. We're going to go watch a video."

I saw a smile cross Brenda's face. "I'm very happy that Tina met such a nice girl as Haley. It's so scary today with kids."

"I feel the same way. Haley had a bad experience with bullying at school before we moved here, so I was hoping she'd meet some nice kids. She's made a good circle of friends, but it's obvious that Tina is her favorite."

Brenda nodded. "Yeah, Tina feels the same way. Having a close female friend is good. I've never had one."

I was surprised to hear this. "Really?" I said, thinking of Petra and was not able to picture my life without her in it.

She shook her head. "Oh, as a kid in Mexico I did, but when we came to America, I lost touch with them. I had a few friends at school in Texas but I didn't have a lot of free time, helping my mother at the restaurant after school and on weekends. So it made it difficult to be part of a group. And then I went to college for nursing and I guess I was more focused on my studies than socializing."

I found this to be sad. Every girl or woman should have that one special person she could depend on, no matter what. But Brenda had never experienced that kind of friendship.

She accepted the mug of coffee that I passed her and waved her other hand in the air. "Oh, I'm not complaining. Not at all. I'm very grateful to be here, to have my job and to see my daughter so happy."

I liked Brenda Sanchez. I'd only known her a few hours but I could tell she was a special person and we were developing a connection.

"Come on," I said. "Take your coffee and let's go check on Mavis Anne."

We walked out the French doors and Brenda said, "Oh, is that the yarn shop over there?"

"Yes. Do you knit or crochet?"

"I love to knit. My mother taught me when I was a child. She was an expert knitter. But I haven't knitted in quite a while. I had to fill the car only with essentials when we came here, so I didn't bring any of my yarn stash."

Leaving a yarn stash behind? Yes, Brenda was special and made me realize she was the type of person who not only wasn't selfish but also didn't seem resentful of the hand life had dealt her.

"Well, you should stop by the shop sometime. We have loads of yarn and needles and all kinds of fun stuff."

"Yeah, maybe," was all she said, and I could have kicked myself. It was pretty obvious that money for yarn wasn't an option right now.

"It's so nice to meet you," Mavis Anne said after I made the introductions. "And I simply adore your daughter. She and Haley are my two favorite girls."

Brenda smiled as she sat down. "Thank you. She's a good girl. I'm not sure what I would have done without her these past few years."

"And Isabelle told me you're a nurse at the hospital. So you like our community?"

"Oh, I do. Very much. Koi House is your childhood home?"

"Yes, I grew up there with my sister and brother. But I won't lie, I love living here with David and Clive. Not that they spoil me or anything, but I'm happy Koi House has the energy of Isabelle and Haley living there."

If Brenda thought it odd that a house could have energy she didn't say anything. I saw her glance at the sweater that Mavis Anne was working on.

"That's a beautiful sweater. I love doing cables."

"Oh, you're a knitter? How nice. You'll have to join us for a knit-along or one of the knitting groups."

"Thank you, but we'll see. I work a lot of hours . . . and right now my time is limited."

"Well, you drop by whenever you want. You'll be very welcome."

After about thirty minutes, Brenda looked at her watch and said she needed to get Tina and head home.

"I'm working day shift tomorrow for some overtime, in addition to my normal night shift," she explained.

I walked back to the house with her and we hugged before Brenda thanked me again for dinner and a wonderful evening.

I watched her pull out of the driveway in an older model car and knew she was one of so many single parents trying to get along in life. For the first time, I felt a twinge of guilt. I had thought I'd had hard times, but I had a feeling they were probably nothing in comparison to what Brenda had endured since she was a child.

Chapter 19

We had just returned from Mavis Anne's hair appointment. "Can you stay and have coffee with me?" she asked.

It wasn't quite four and I had two hours before Chadwick was picking me up. "Yes, that would be nice. Have you heard from David?"

"I have," she said as she prepared the coffeemaker. "They're having a wonderful time. He said the weather is perfect. They're shopping, enjoying the Italian food and wine, and also relaxing. So it sounds like the perfect getaway."

"That's wonderful. Any mention of your yarn yet?"

Mavis Anne laughed. "Not yet, but he assured me they're going to focus on that tomorrow."

A few minutes later we were settled with our coffee, and Mavis Anne asked about my mother.

"Isn't she arriving next week?"

I nodded. "Yeah, I haven't heard from her, but Haley told me she flies down here a week from today."

"Are you feeling any better about her coming?"

"I can't do anything about it, so it really doesn't matter," I said, and heard that sulky tone in my voice again.

"Well, I hope you won't think I'm disloyal . . . but I'd really like to meet her."

I wasn't surprised to hear this. Mavis Anne Overby was a people person. She welcomed meeting new people; my mother would be no exception.

"Oh, I'm sure you'll meet her. My mother is a knitter. Or at least she used to be when I was a kid. I don't know that much about her now. But I'm sure Haley will convince her to stop by the yarn shop after she gets settled in."

"That would be nice," was all Mavis Anne said on the subject. "So Chadwick is having you to dinner this evening. I'm sure you'll enjoy that. In case you haven't gathered, he's one of my favorite people."

I laughed. "Yeah, I sort of thought so."

"Chadwick is such a wonderful addition to the community. He's quite the philanthropist and hosts fund-raisers for various causes. We really appreciate all that he does."

I recalled that Chloe had mentioned this to me.

"He does seem to be a very giving person and that's a good trait to have."

"Oh, he is. Wait until you see the Fourth of July gala that he'll be hosting. He has it at his home every year and the proceeds go to the local hospital."

That was still five months away; I didn't know if Chadwick would continue to be in my life then. After the breakup of my marriage and the reason behind it, I still wasn't feeling all that confident when it came to romance.

"Well," I said after finishing my coffee, "I need to get home. Chadwick is picking me up at six."

"You be sure to tell that handsome man I said hello, and you have a wonderful evening," Mavis told me.

Chadwick arrived just before six. I opened the door to see a huge smile on his face.

"Hey," he said. "Ready to dine at Chez Chadwick?"

I laughed. "I am. Just let me grab a sweater."

"Your daughter isn't home?" he asked when I walked back to the living room.

"No, she's having dinner with Mavis Anne tonight. Which reminds me, Mavis Anne said to be sure to say hello to you." I left out the part about him being handsome.

"She's a character," he said and laughed. "All set?"

"I am."

We drove the short distance down Beach Avenue and pulled into a circular driveway on the right. Not ostentatious but certainly a lovely brick home that sat back from the sidewalk and was surrounded by a black wrought iron fence.

As I walked in the front door, my gaze went straight back to the open living room and patio area, which overlooked the Halifax River.

"This is just beautiful," I said.

"Come on in the kitchen. We'll have a glass of wine before I start grilling the steaks."

"Sounds good," I told him as I followed behind.

Chadwick uncorked a bottle of red, filled two glasses and passed one to me.

"Cheers," he said.

I nodded and took a sip. "Oh, this is very good."

"I hoped you'd enjoy it. I brought it back from Italy last year."

I noticed a stainless steel built-in wine cooler and realized this man certainly knew his wines.

"Do you travel a lot?" I asked.

He reached into the fridge and removed a platter of various cheeses before filling a bowl with crackers.

"Let's sit on the patio," he said, and I followed him out to the screened area. "I don't really travel a lot," he explained. "But I do enjoy visiting Europe. The food, the wine . . . I love all of it. Have you been to Italy?"

I was almost ashamed to admit that I'd never been to Europe. I didn't even own a passport. My college dream of traveling the world never materialized after I met Roger.

I shook my head. "No, I'm afraid not. I always wanted to travel, especially to Europe. Of course, Paris, and I wanted to visit Prague and Vienna. But, well . . . life kind of intervened and that never happened."

"Oh, that's a shame," he said, and he looked sincerely sorry. "Everybody should visit those places at least once."

Call me silly, but I had the strangest feeling that Chadwick Price was determined to make that happen for me.

"Well, if this wine is any example of the great wines in Italy, I'd say it was well worth the trip." I couldn't help but wonder if he'd visited there solo or had a female companion with him.

"So how did your dinner with Tina and her mother go?" he asked.

I was surprised that he showed interest in the little things going on in my life.

"Very well. I like Brenda a lot. She's another single mom, but she's really struggling. Working full-time and finding it difficult, I'm sure. But she's not a complainer. She seemed really happy to just be living here. I'm not sure what kind of situation she left back in Texas, but it's obvious she's happy to be away from it. It makes me feel extra grateful that Roger has been generous financially to Haley and me."

He nodded. "Yeah, some women go through very difficult times. I sponsor various fund-raisers for the domestic abuse center in town and I'm always amazed at the strength and resilience of some of those women." He took a sip of wine. "Have you heard from your mother? Doesn't she arrive soon?"

"Yeah, a week from today. I haven't heard from her, but she's been in touch with Haley. She'll be staying at a hotel for one night and the movers arrive the next day."

"I imagine Haley is happy her grandmother will be living so close."

I nodded. "I think she is. With so much distance between them, they never had a chance to develop a proper relationship. So I imagine they will now."

"How do you feel about that?"

I shrugged. "Hey, it's between them. I certainly would never stop Haley from seeing her. I just plan to keep my own distance."

He took the last sip of his wine and stood up. "Well, let me get the grill fired up."

"Can I do anything to help?"

"Sure. You can get the table set out here. I thought we'd eat on the patio."

I followed Chadwick into the house, where he pointed to where the dishes and silverware were located.

I arranged the place mats and table settings and then stood gazing out at the river. Such a pretty spot—a beautiful terraced area with brick steps leading down to a brick patio, all of it surrounded by a black wrought iron fence. That was when I noticed a pontoon boat moored to the dock.

"Is that your boat?" I asked as Chadwick placed steaks on the grill.

"Yeah, it is. We'll have to take it out sometime. Maybe Haley and Tina would also like to go for a ride."

That was considerate of him. "Oh, I'm sure they'd love that."

Following a delicious dinner of steak, salad, and rice pilaf we settled down on the patio sofa to finish off the wine.

"Are you sure you don't want coffee?" he asked.

"No, the wine is fine. Thanks."

"How are the wedding plans coming for Chloe?"

"Very well. We're going shopping in a couple of weeks for our dresses. She's asked Haley to stand up for her and, needless to say, Haley is thrilled."

He laughed. "Yes, all young girls love a wedding. I'm really happy for Chloe—Henry seems like a great guy."

"He is. Haley and I like him a lot. After losing my dad, Chloe deserved another chance at love. I'm just glad that my father met her and she came into my life. We've become very close these past few years."

"That's really nice. Yeah, I think everybody deserves another chance. Especially when it comes to love."

He took my wineglass and placed it on the table before he leaned over to kiss me. My arms automatically went around his neck. This man definitely had kissing down to a science. Like the last time, when we pulled away we were both breathing heavily.

He nuzzled his face in my neck. "You're a great kisser. Did you know that?" he said, and I detected huskiness in his tone.

"Hmm . . . no . . ." I began to say before he kissed me again.

"You are," he whispered when he moved away and let out a deep breath. "Very much so."

There was no doubt about it. His kissing turned me on. But it also confused me. I wasn't at all sure where we were going from here. I wasn't even sure exactly where I wanted to go.

I let out a deep sigh.

"Everything okay?" he asked.

I nodded. "Yeah."

He passed my wineglass back to me and took a sip of his own.

Reaching for my hand, he said, "Isabelle, I like you. A lot. I know you're just coming out of a bad relationship. But I need you to know . . . I want you to know . . . you mean a lot to me. I enjoy being with you and I'd like us to continue seeing each other. I have no idea where we'll end up . . . but for right now, I want to be with you. If that's what you want."

I knew that I did. "Yes," I said, and smiled. "Yes. I'd like that very much."

His smile matched mine. "Good."

He leaned over and placed another kiss on my lips.

"So does that mean I can be your plus-one at Chloe's wedding?" he asked.

I laughed. "Oh, so all of this was only to wangle a wedding invite?"

He pulled me into an embrace. "Not at all," he said. "Not at all."

And I knew I was about to embark on a new chapter in my life.

Chapter 20

I was in the yarn shop the following Thursday afternoon knitting with the group and only half listening to the conversations going on around me. My mind kept wandering to Chadwick. I had seen him twice more since dinner at his house. We had gone to the movies one evening and out for Italian food and drinks the night before. Things were definitely heating up with us—and this had me both excited and apprehensive.

I looked up to see Haley walk in the door.

"Did you come to knit with us?" Yarrow asked.

Haley plopped down on the sofa and shook her head. "Not really," she said. "Mom, do you think you could drive me over to the hotel so I could see Nana?"

I felt a table of women's eyes staring at me. My mother had flown into Orlando that morning but I hadn't thought Haley would want to see her immediately.

"You have homework, don't you?" I said.

"Yeah, but I can do it after supper. Nana said I could have dinner with her at the hotel restaurant."

For somebody who hadn't been around for thirty years, my mother was wasting no time making arrangements with my daughter.

"Oh, that's nice," I heard Mavis Anne say.

"So can I, Mom?" Haley asked again.

I didn't see any way I could refuse. "Yeah, okay. I'll drive you over." I got up and placed my knitting on the table. "I'll be back," was all I said to the group before walking out the door.

I had remained silent driving up Granada Boulevard with Haley. "So do I have to come back and get you?" I now asked.

"No. Nana said she'll drive me back. She just doesn't know the area yet but she said I can show her where we live and she'll drive me back."

How nice, I thought, but only said, "Okay. But I want you home by seven. You'll still have to get your homework done."

When I pulled up to the front door of the hotel to drop Haley off, she looked at me and said, "Oh. Don't you want to come in to see her?"

"No. I really don't. You go and visit with her and I'll see you at home by seven."

She leaned across the seat to place a kiss on my cheek. "Okay. Love you," she said before getting out.

I drove back to the yarn shop with thoughts swirling in my head. I didn't even know what my mother looked like now. I hadn't seen her in fourteen years, since Haley was a baby. My mother was now sixty-eight. While certainly far from old, she was no longer the young mother of my youth. I had to admit I was a tiny bit inquisitive. After all, I had her genes. So would I age in the way that she was aging? I pulled into the driveway at Koi House and pushed all thoughts of Iris Brunell out of my head.

Mavis Anne looked up and smiled as I walked into the yarn shop. "So how is your mother?" she asked.

I sat down and picked up my knitting. "I have no idea," I told her.

"Oh, didn't you go inside to see her?" Chloe asked.

I began working on a new scarf I was making. "No. I did not."

There was a moment of silence before Yarrow said, "Chloe, how is Treva doing? That little grandchild of yours will be here in four months."

"She's having a very good pregnancy. Henry and I drove up to visit them in Jacksonville last weekend. She's really beginning to show now and she looks so cute."

"Have they found out yet if it's a girl or boy?" Louise asked.

"They're being old-fashioned about it. They don't want to know until the baby is born."

"Nothing wrong with that," Mavis Anne said. "Not knowing makes the actual birth a bit more exciting."

"True," Chloe said. "But it keeps the knitting limited to white, yellow, or mint green."

"Oh, I don't know about that," Fay said. "I recently saw on some

TV show that today some baby boys are wearing pink. Even Target or someplace is trying to get rid of gender-specific toys for kids. In my day, it used to be that dolls were for girls and trucks were for boys."

Mavis Anne shook her head. "Well, I have no problem with children playing with different toys, but there's no reason to make everything unisex today. My goodness, I was in a restaurant recently and got thoroughly confused. The bathroom had a sign with both a male and a female. It finally dawned on me that it was to be used by either one."

Everybody laughed, and Louise said, "Things certainly have changed over the years. I'm just not sure that all of it is good. Why does everything have to be taken to the extreme? So a girl wants to play with trucks and a boy wants to cuddle dolls. Nothing wrong with that at all, but to have a major store getting involved . . . that's where I have a problem."

"Oh, please," Yarrow said. "Today everybody gets involved in everything. The media races to be the first with breaking news, whether it's true or not. Things are put on social media with the speed of lightning. Everybody has an opinion about something, and this can be a good thing, except when it's done in a nasty and condescending way."

"Very true," Louise agreed. "Politeness is a thing of the past. Worrying about offending somebody? Gone! And I feel the major cause is because on social media people can remain anonymous. If you have something to say, say it. But it should be required that you also have to identify yourself."

"Anything new with your wedding plans?" Maddie asked, moving on to another subject. "Your sister and her family are coming from France, right?"

Chloe nodded. "Yes, Grace will be here with Lucas and Solange. Everything is pretty much on hold until we go shopping in a couple of weeks for our dresses. Henry is checking on the trellis for the fishpond area and he's also looking for a person to marry us."

"Oh, it won't be a priest or clergyman?" Louise asked.

"No. Both Henry and I are nondenominational in our beliefs and so we agree we'd prefer to have a wedding officiant with the same beliefs."

"Hmm," was all Louise said.

"Well, I think couples should be free to choose whichever way they want to be married. Or not. Love is love and that piece of paper doesn't make it more so," Mavis Anne said, making me love her liberal streak even more. "Years ago society demanded that a couple in love be married and I think couples today have proved it doesn't always have to be that way. Especially for older couples. Being in love and wanting to be together should be the primary concern."

Mavis Anne Overby was a forward-thinking woman and I admired that trait in her.

"Well, I guess I'm from the old school," Louise retorted.

"Yes, I guess you are," Mavis Anne said with finality, causing the rest of us at the table to smile.

By five o'clock the regulars had left the yarn shop, and I gathered up my knitting.

"Guess I should get moving too," I said. "Do you have any errands for tomorrow?" I asked Mavis Anne.

She shook her head. "No, I'm all set. Thank you. And thank you so much for looking out for me, Isabelle. David and Clive return home on Saturday, and it has been so nice having you and Haley around."

I smiled. "It's been our pleasure. Okay, well, if you decide you need anything, just let me know. Yarrow, I'll see you in the morning for the deliveries."

I walked back to Koi House and cut up some cooked chicken for a sandwich. Without Haley home for dinner, I decided to have something easy. After I prepared my sandwich, I opened a bottle of white wine and poured myself a glass. I took a sip and realized that I couldn't recall the last time that I'd had a glass of wine alone. Not since I had been seeing Chadwick. I had a nagging feeling that prior to meeting him my drinking had been getting more and more frequent. But since meeting Chadwick I had no desire to drink on my own just for the sake of drinking. Sharing a glass of wine with him allowed me to fully enjoy the social experience, making it a special event.

After finishing my sandwich, I poured a second glass, which I took into the living room with me, where I turned on the television to catch the local news and weather. Nothing new there. Murders, shootings, car-jackings, robberies, domestic abuse. I recalled the conversation at the yarn shop about things changing. We probably always had these crimes but somehow with increased technology we seemed to be hearing about them 24/7.

"Isabelle," I heard Chloe call from the back of the house.

"In here," I hollered, and a moment later she walked into the living room.

"Have you got a second?" she asked.

"Sure. What's up?"

She reached into her knitting bag and brought out a partially finished scarf. "I wanted to show you what I have so far. The scarf I designed for you."

I looked at the very pretty pattern and fingered the yarn. "Oh, Chloe. I love it. It's a great pattern. And I like the yarn a lot."

"Good. The yarn is Bamboo Pop. The same one you're using for your top, so I was hoping you'd like it."

"I do. Very much. Have you named the pattern yet?"

"Not quite. I have a name in mind and I'll let you know as soon as I decide. Haley's not back yet?"

I glanced at the clock, which read six thirty-five. "Not yet. She's due home shortly."

"Okay. Well, I'll be at Henry's tonight, so you have a good evening and I'll see you tomorrow."

About ten minutes later I heard a car pull up in the driveway. I wanted to go to the window to get a glimpse of my mother, but I'd forgotten to close the blinds; with the lights on she would see me peeking out, so I stayed put.

A few moments later I looked up to see Haley walk in the front door—followed by my mother. I honestly didn't think she'd come in the house. I jumped up to face both of them. In a split second I took in the sight of my mother and was surprised at what I saw. The last time I had seen her she bordered on pudgy, had a drab and unbecoming hairstyle, and wore clothes that looked like they had come straight out of the hippie sixties.

The woman walking in my door appeared taller, was slim, had an air of confidence, and wore black yoga-style pants with a leopard print tunic top. But it was her hair that drew my attention the most. Very short and in a pixie style, it had a wide strip of blue coming across her side bangs. My daughter's pink hair was finally beginning to fade and my mother showed up with blue hair? Oh. My. God. Was that a tattoo on her ankle?

"Isabelle," I heard her say and found myself being caught up in an unexpected embrace. "You look as beautiful as ever."

She held me at arm's length and nodded while I remained speech-less.

"It's so nice to see you," she said, obviously waiting for me to say something.

"Hi, Mom," was all I seemed able to manage.

Apparently catching my frostiness, my mother backed away and nodded again. "So Haley and I had a nice dinner together and it gave us a chance to catch up."

"That's nice," I mumbled.

"Mom, can I go to Nana's new house tomorrow after school? The movers arrive in the morning and I can help her unpack."

"Ah . . . yeah . . . I guess that would be okay."

"She'd be a huge help to me, so thank you, Isabelle. I appreciate it."

I noticed her glancing around the living room, but I remained silent.

"You have a gorgeous place here," she said.

I wasn't sure if that was a hint to see the rest of the house, but all I said was, "It's not *my* house. We're just renting."

"Right. Okay. Well, I'll say good night then. It was good to see you, Isabelle." She looked as if she was trying to decide whether to hug me again and thought better of it. "And Haley, sweetie, you just call me when you get home from school and I'll come by and get you."

My mother and my daughter exchanged a hug and a kiss, and Iris Brunell walked out the door. Just like she had thirty years before.

Chapter 21

"So does it bother you that Haley wanted to spend the night at your mother's house?" Chadwick asked.

I curled up closer to him on the sofa and shook my head.

"No. Not really. I understand that Haley would like a relationship with her grandmother. That's fine." I took a sip of wine.

"But?" he asked.

I felt a smile cross my face. This man was getting to know me pretty well.

"But . . . well, Haley is about the same age I was when my mother left. She sure didn't have maternal instincts back then."

But I knew this wasn't quite true.

"So you were never close?"

I shrugged. "I guess we were when I was younger." I took the final sip of wine and placed the glass on the table. "My father taught a lot of evening classes, so my mom and I were alone a lot. Yeah, I remember we used to color together and play board games. But those last couple years before she left . . . we were drifting apart."

"Isn't that natural, though, when a girl hits the teen years?"

I thought of Haley and the little ways she was attempting to show her independence. "Hmm, maybe. Anyway"—I flung a hand in the air—"she's here now and it is what it is. I just don't have to be happy about it."

Chadwick nodded and reached for my hand. "I wanted to ask you something. I need to go back to Atlanta next month for a day or so on business. I was wondering if you'd like to go with me?"

"Oh," I said, sitting up straighter to turn and face him. All of a sudden, whatever we had seemed to be moving along faster.

"My parents have a large house and we could stay there. You

would have your own room," he explained as if this might be the deciding factor.

"Oh," I said again. "Yeah, that might be fun." But meeting his parents? I wasn't sure I was ready for that.

"Okay. Well, give it some thought. We'd only be gone overnight. That would be enough time for me to take care of things. Another glass of wine?" he asked.

I'd had three. Or was it four? "Sure, what the heck," I said, passing him my glass.

He returned, placed the glasses on the table, and leaned over to kiss me. This guy certainly did know how to kiss.

"Hmm, nice," he said, slowly moving his hand down my back.

We were interrupted by his cell phone ringing.

"Sorry," he said. "I have to get this. We had a problem with a rental this afternoon."

I listened as he discussed something about an elevator being out of service.

Fifteen minutes later he joined me on the sofa.

"I'm sorry about that. Sometimes the job never ends."

"Everything okay?"

"Well, we had a couple check into one of the vacation condos and apparently the elevator was being repaired. Needless to say, they weren't happy. But my excellent assistant, Betty, managed to get them placed into another building. I don't know what I'd do without her."

"Has she been with you for a while?"

"Yeah, almost twenty-five years, since I opened my business down here. Unfortunately, she's been hinting about retiring at the end of the year. She'll be tough to replace." He took a sip of wine. "You wouldn't be interested in being my assistant, would you?"

I laughed, pretty sure he was joking. I had no experience at all in whatever it was Betty's job entailed.

"I know nothing about the real estate or rental business."

"You can always learn," he said, making me realize he hadn't been joking. "Something else for you to think about."

His phone rang again.

"I'm so sorry. This seldom happens, but we had a lot of people checking in for the weekend. Excuse me again," he said, and reached for his cell.

I stifled a yawn. "That's fine," I assured him. Getting up so early to do the coffee shop deliveries was catching up with me. Maybe having a nine-to-five office job wasn't such a bad idea after all.

The aroma of coffee woke me. I snuggled more into my pillow and realized I wasn't at home. When I opened my eyes, it took me a moment to orient myself and remember I was at Chadwick's house, with sunlight streaming through the windows. Oh, my God! Had I fallen asleep on him the night before?

I rubbed my eyes, got up, and followed the coffee fragrance to the kitchen. Chadwick was filling a mug. He looked up and smiled.

"Good morning, sunshine. Sleep well?"

"I can't believe I fell asleep. I'm so sorry."

He passed me the mug and pulled another one from the cabinet. "It's fine. I was on the phone for a while, and when I hung up I didn't have the heart to wake you. You were snoring away."

"Snoring? Oh, God, I'm so embarrassed. Did I have drool on my chin too?"

He pulled me into an embrace and laughed. "It was a nice light snoring and no drool. Have some coffee," he said and kissed my forehead.

"Bathroom first," I told him.

"Okay. There's a new toothbrush and toothpaste in the vanity drawer on the right."

What? Did he keep a stash for female overnight guests?

I returned from the bathroom to find him beating eggs in a bowl.

"And breakfast too?" I said. "Do you treat all your female guests so well?"

I saw a smile cross his face. "I'd have to say that you're the first female who has spent the night here."

Surely he was joking. A handsome, eligible bachelor like him?

"Do you like French toast?" he asked.

"Love it," I said, taking a sip of coffee. "Oh, this is good. Yarrow better be careful."

"Thanks. Glad you enjoy it."

"Did everything work out okay with the rental properties last night?"

He dipped some sourdough bread into the batter and nodded. "Yeah. Finally. That doesn't happen too often. But this time of year is our busiest season, so there are bound to be problems now and then."

"You don't just sell property but have rentals also?"

"Right. Just vacation rentals. We do property management. I have a staff who does the cleaning, but Betty handles all the rental agreements and problems. She knows I like to be kept abreast of what's going on, so that was the reason for the phone calls."

"She sounds pretty conscientious."

He placed the egg-soaked bread onto a grill. "She is. I'm going to be lost without her when she does retire."

"Can I do anything to help? I feel useless sitting here."

"You're not useless, but sure. In the cabinet over there, you can grab some plates. In the drawer below are placemats and silverware. I'll fill the juice glasses. It's such a pretty morning; we can eat on the patio."

"You're spoiling me," I said after we finished eating. "That was delicious."

Chadwick laughed. "Glad you enjoyed it. More coffee?"

"Yes, please."

He reached for the French press on the table and refilled my mug.

"So what are your plans for the rest of the day?" he asked.

"Well, David and Clive return from Italy today, so Mavis Anne asked if I could take her place at the yarn shop helping Chloe." I glanced at my watch and saw it was just after eight.

"What time do you open?"

"Ten, but I'll have to go home and shower and change first."

I spent another thirty minutes lingering over coffee and then stood up.

"I really have to get going," I said. "Thank you so much for a wonderful evening and breakfast this morning."

He walked me to the door and pulled me into an embrace. "It was all my pleasure," he said, before kissing me.

It only took a second for desire to return and I could feel his desire matching mine.

"Okay," he said, pulling away and kissing my forehead before letting out a deep breath. "Okay. Maybe next time you spend the night, you won't be all alone on my sofa."

No doubt about it, I thought as I drove the short distance home. *Chadwick Price is definitely as attracted to me as I am to him.*

Chapter 22

I had just finished dressing when Haley called on my cell.

"Hey, what's up?" I said.

"Nana and I went out for breakfast. Is it okay if I stay till this afternoon to help her with more unpacking?"

"Yeah, that would be fine. I'm helping out at the yarn shop today, so I'll be there till around four. You'll be home for supper?"

I heard a hesitation on the other end of the line before Haley said, "Well . . . ah . . . I was wondering if I could stay one more night. Nana said it's been so long since we got to spend time together like this."

And whose fault was that? But I said, "Yeah, okay. But I want you home tomorrow morning, Haley. The entire weekend will be gone and you'll be back to school on Monday. I thought maybe you and I could spend the day together tomorrow."

"Oh, cool. Definitely, Mom. I promise to be home by ten. Love you."

"Love you too," I said, before hanging up.

I walked into the yarn shop to find Chloe attaching price tags to skeins of Cascade yarn.

She looked up and smiled. "Good morning. Thanks so much for pitching in today."

"Not a problem. Glad I could help."

"Hey," Yarrow called from the back. "A cup of tea or coffee?"

"I'm fine right now, but thanks. What time do David and Clive arrive?"

"Just about noon. Henry left for the airport to get them. I'm sure Mavis Anne will be happy to have her guys back home."

"Yeah, but it was good they could have such a nice trip. So. What can I do here for you?"

"Well, there's a box of needles and accessories over there that need to be unpacked."

After Chloe and I finished our tasks, she said, "Oh, I want to show you the scarf I finished for you. I've decided to call it Isabelle's Challenge."

She removed a beautiful scarf from her knitting bag. It was white with a lace edging and little bumps at the center. "Oh, it's gorgeous," I said. "I love it. But why that name?"

"I feel you've had a few challenges over the past couple years. Losing your dad, the breakup of your marriage, and now your mother. So maybe every time you wear it, you'll remember the obstacles that you overcame and realize there will most likely be more ahead, but you can handle them."

I wrapped the scarf around my neck. "Thank you so much, Chloe. I just love it."

We both turned around to see Maddie walk in the door.

"I had a quiet morning at the shop so I closed early," she said, setting her knitting bag on the table. "Oh, very pretty." Maddie came to finger my scarf. "Is this the one you designed, Chloe?"

"Yeah. And I'm calling it Isabelle's Challenge."

"Very appropriate. When does the knit-along begin? I can't wait to make one."

"I thought we'd start next week. I'll send out an email telling everyone and give them a chance to choose their yarn. Since you're here, you can get yours today. It's the Bamboo Pop cotton over there." She pointed to the center table, where an arrangement of various colors reminded me of ice cream and cotton candy.

We had a busy morning with sales. I handled the purchases while Chloe tended to the questions or knitting problems from customers.

By two things slowed down and we took time for lunch. Yarrow had made chicken salad sandwiches for us, and the three of us sat at the table in the yarn shop area.

"So how's it going with Chadwick?" she asked.

I took a bite of my sandwich and nodded. "Good. Very good, actually. He's a really nice guy."

"I just knew you two would hit it off," Chloe said. "Will he be your escort at the wedding?"

"Yes. I asked him and he accepted. Actually, he hinted first about coming."

Chloe laughed. "I'm not surprised."

"Wasn't he ever seriously involved with anybody else? He told me this morning I was the first one to spend the night at his house," I said, and then realized exactly what I'd said.

Both of them stared at me and waited.

"Oh . . . well . . . no. It's not what you think."

Yarrow laughed. "No? What is it then?"

"No, I mean, yes . . . I did happen to spend the night at his house last night. But not with him. I mean . . . I slept on the sofa where I fell asleep. I hadn't intended to . . . I just nodded off . . . and next thing I knew I was waking up on his sofa this morning." I realized how lame this sounded and stopped talking.

"Oh, okay." A smile crossed Chloe's face.

"So what you're saying," Yarrow asked and I didn't fail to miss her smirk, "is that you didn't sleep in his bed?"

"Right," I said, becoming annoyed. "We didn't have sex. If that's what you were thinking."

Chloe and Yarrow looked at each other, shook their heads and laughed.

"It wasn't what *I* was thinking. Were you?" Chloe asked Yarrow.

"Not me," she said emphatically. "You sure sex isn't on *your* mind, Isabelle?"

"Okay, enough," I said, putting my hand in the air. "Enough with the kidding. No, we haven't taken our relationship to that level."

"Yet," I heard Yarrow say under her breath.

Chloe laughed again. "Sorry for teasing you. I'm just happy for you, Isabelle. Wherever this goes with Chadwick, I'm glad you two found each other."

"I'm happy for you too. Now on to the mother subject. How's she doing?" Yarrow asked. "Getting settled in okay?"

"I guess so. Haley spent the night with her last night and will be staying there again tonight helping her unpack."

"Oh, that's good." Chloe took a sip of iced tea. "Isn't it?"

I shrugged. "Yeah, I guess so."

"Do you feel left out?" Yarrow asked.

"No. Not at all." And I didn't. "At least not now. But I guess it ticks me off that when I was Haley's age, that's when my mother decided to leave. She didn't choose to spend these teen years with me . . . but now she wants to be with Haley."

Chloe nodded sympathetically. "I can understand your feelings. So you'd rather have your mother be punished and not get to spend time with her granddaughter?"

"Well . . . no. Not exactly. I don't know how I feel." Maybe Chloe was right. I was glad for the distraction of Mavis Anne walking in the door.

"They're back," she said, settling herself at the table. "My boys are back home."

"Did they have a good flight?" I asked.

"Yes, and they landed a little early. They'll be over shortly. Oh, Henry said to tell you he'll see you at home later, Chloe. He wanted to get back to let the dogs out."

A few minutes later David and Clive walked into the yarn shop carrying assorted tote bags.

"Welcome home," we said in unison.

"These are for each of you," David said, passing us each a bag.

"When the owner of the yarn shop in Lake Como found out that David's sister owned a yarn shop in the States, she gave him a nice discount on this yarn," Mavis Anne said. "And she said if we liked the yarn, she'd be more than happy to ship it to us to sell here."

I peeked inside my bag and removed a skein of soft, squishy beige yarn. "Oh, this is really nice."

Mavis Anne nodded. "Yes, and we each have enough to make a cowl and a pair of socks. She even gave David a nice pattern for each."

"I really like this," Chloe said, fingering her skein of what appeared to be an alpaca in a gorgeous shade of lavender.

"Me too," Yarrow said. "Well done, David."

He laughed. "Well, I knew I couldn't come back without yarn. I spent over an hour with Maria, the owner of the shop, talking. Poor Clive was such a trooper waiting for me."

I saw a smile cross Clive's face as he waved a hand in the air. "Not a problem. She had a very comfortable shop. Much like this one. So I found a comfy chair and relaxed. David had me going from morning till night doing this and that."

I laughed. "So you had to return home to get a vacation, huh?"

"Oh, please," David said. "You loved every minute of it."

Clive laughed. "Hmm, I can't lie. You're right. Okay. Well, I need to go get started on dinner. I want you all to come. Chloe, call Henry and tell him he's invited too. I'm going to try out one of the Italian recipes I learned in my cooking class."

David rolled his eyes. "I swear half of his luggage is filled with assorted spices and pasta that he brought back."

"And don't forget the wine," Clive said. "Wait until you try some of the Italian wine I got over there."

"Are you sure you're up to cooking tonight?" I asked. "Aren't you exhausted from your trip?"

"Not at all," Clive said. "We had a good night's sleep at the airport hotel in Newark last night. So I'll see you for dinner at six."

David shook his head and laughed. "I'm not sure where Clive gets all his energy. Oh, and Isabelle, feel free to invite your mother and Haley to dinner also."

That wasn't going to happen. "Oh, thanks, but they have plans for tonight. I'll be there at six, though."

I wondered if this was how it was going to be now. That my mother would automatically be included in various events right along with Haley and me. Well, it wasn't going to happen as long as I had something to say about it.

Chapter 23

Two weeks later I began to breathe a sigh of relief concerning my mother. Haley had spent time with her, but my mother had only called me twice, and each time we had a short and superficial phone conversation. Maybe she really was going to back off about having a relationship with me.

I finished dressing and headed downstairs to see if Haley was ready to meet Chloe to go dress shopping for the wedding.

I found her in the kitchen on her iPad.

"All set? We're picking Chloe up at the condo."

"Yeah. Hey, Mom. Remember you said I could get a dog? I know we're not in our own place yet, but who knows when that will happen. I found this website where they need people to adopt dogs in the area."

Not the dog thing again. "Hmm, gosh, I don't know, Haley. I'm not sure Mavis Anne would want us having a dog here."

"Why not? She had no problem with Chloe living here with Basil."

Leave it to my daughter to be right.

I grabbed my keys and handbag. "Okay. Right. Well, we'll talk about it later. We have to pick up Chloe in ten minutes."

Chloe was outside her condo building when we arrived.

"Hey," I said when she got in the car. "All ready to find that perfect dress?"

She laughed. "I only hope I find something."

Haley leaned over the backseat. "Are we going to a bridal shop?"

"Ah, no," Chloe told her. "I'm well beyond the proper wedding gown phase. We'll hit the shops at the mall. I'm thinking more along the lines of a cocktail dress."

"Perfect," I said.

By the end of the afternoon the three of us were happy with our purchases and enjoying a stop at Starbucks before heading home.

"I think that dress was made for you," I told Chloe. And it was. I knew the moment Chloe came out of the dressing room it was the one for her. It fell to the knee, the beige color complemented her tan, and the fit showed off her slim figure. With the tiny seed pearls sprinkled across the dress, it was ideal for a late-afternoon wedding.

"I have to agree," she said. "I just love it. And your dress and Haley's are also perfect."

She was right. I'd chosen a simple sheath style, sleeveless, in a dressy black-and-white design. Haley finally decided on a mint green dress with spaghetti straps that fell just above her knees. All three dresses were simple but elegant.

"I can't wait," Haley said. "I've never been in a wedding before. What will I have to do?"

Chloe laughed. "Your duties are minimal. You just have to look pretty and walk to the trellis where we'll be married. Solange will have a little basket of flower petals and she'll walk in front of you."

"Sounds pretty easy," Haley said. "I think I can manage that."

"Has Henry arranged for the caterer and the tents?" I asked.

Chloe took a sip of her iced coffee and nodded. "Yeah. He's right on top of things and working with David and Clive. He also arranged for a little three-piece combo to play music before the ceremony and when we walk to the pond area."

"Will we have dancing after the ceremony?" Haley asked.

"Absolutely. Henry even hired a DJ to play when the reception begins and then after for dancing."

"You must be getting excited about going to Hawaii," I said.

"I am. But we still have so much to get done in the next seven weeks. We have to meet with the DJ to choose our music and also with Maddie to finalize the floral selections. Oh, and we have to interview the pet–house sitter that Henry found."

"I told you that we'd keep Basil and Delilah for you," I said.

"I know you did and I appreciate that. But you have enough going on in your life. We were fortunate to hear about Carol through our vet. She's single, in her forties, and is able to stay at the condo while we're gone. So I think this will work out well."

"Oh, Mom, I forgot to ask you. Is it okay if I spend the night at Nana's? I haven't stayed over for a couple weeks."

I saw the look of expectation on my daughter's face. I had to admit that my mother had managed to keep her distance from me and also wasn't smothering Haley.

"Sure," I said. "I guess that'll be okay."

"Oh, cool. She told me to come for supper around five. Will you be with Chadwick tonight?"

I shook my head. "No, he had to go down to St. Pete on business and won't be back till pretty late. But I'll be fine on my own." I gave my daughter a smile and ruffled the top of her hair to assure her.

When my mother came by to get Haley, I noticed she didn't bother to come into the house. She gave a short toot of her horn, Haley kissed me good-bye, and they pulled out of the driveway.

"Well, isn't that what you wanted?" I said out loud as I watched the car drive away.

Yeah, it was. I had made it perfectly clear to my mother that she could have a relationship with Haley but I wasn't the least bit interested. Then why did I have a nagging sensation in the pit of my stomach?

"Ah, well," I said, and headed to the kitchen.

I poured a glass of wine and debated what to make myself for supper. Opening the fridge I saw leftover chicken, a few slices of quiche, salad in a plastic container, and plenty of turkey breast and cheese for a sandwich. But nothing appealed to me.

Taking my wineglass, I went to sit on the patio. It was a beautiful March evening with the scent of lantana in the air. I glanced toward the fishpond and realized I hadn't had a dream with Emmalyn in quite a while, which convinced me that all of it was merely coincidence and meant nothing. My mind wandered to Chadwick. I did love being with him. He was easy to talk to and had a good sense of humor. Not to mention he was also a pretty good kisser, which led me to wonder if we would progress beyond kisses. He certainly didn't take advantage of me the night I fell asleep at his house. Instead he got me a pillow and covered me with a blanket. A definite gentleman. But what did *I* want? Did I want to take it a step further and develop a bona fide relationship? I honestly wasn't sure.

I let out a deep sigh and headed back into the house. Instead of another glass of wine I opted for some ice water with lemon. Opening the fridge again and glancing inside, I reached for the covered bowl of onion dip and a block of Muenster cheese. Reaching into the cabinet, I pulled out a bag of chips and box of crackers. After placing everything on a tray, I carried it into the family room, where I settled myself on the sofa and reached for the television remote. I skimmed the channels and found one showing a marathon of *Bones* reruns. Dead bodies and bones seemed to match my mood.

By nine o'clock I had binged on both the TV episodes and the junk food. As I brought the empty tray into the kitchen, a feeling of loneliness crashed over me. How pathetic was I? Here I was in my mid-forties, home alone on a Saturday night, confused about a relationship with a really great guy and a mother who showed no interest in me.

But that wasn't really true. I knew I was feeling sorry for myself. I might have no idea where Chadwick and I were headed, but I was pretty sure that if I gave my mother half a chance, our relationship would improve.

I walked back into the family room and plunked down on the sofa to turn off the TV. I'd had enough of Bones and Booth, and clicked the remote just as my cell phone rang.

"Hey, girlfriend," I heard Petra say. "I wasn't sure I'd catch you home on a Saturday night."

"Oh, yeah. Here I am. All by my lonesome."

"Well, don't you sound cheery. What's up?"

I blew a breath of air into the phone. "Nothing. Really. It's just me. Chadwick is out of town and Haley is spending the night at my mother's house."

"Ah. Feeling sorry for yourself, huh?"

Petra was famous for not coddling me. I smiled.

"Hmm," was all I said.

"Well, cheer up. I'll be down there in a little over two weeks. I plan to whip you back into shape. I take it things haven't improved with your mother?"

"You could say that. But in her defense, I made it crystal clear to her that she could visit with Haley but I wanted nothing to do with her."

"Be careful what you wish for. So how is everything else going? Are things moving along with Chadwick? I can't wait to meet him.

You do know you're not allowed to get serious until I give my approval, right?"

I laughed. "Yes. I wouldn't dare to let things progress till that happens."

"Good. Well, I just wanted to touch base with you. Stop feeling sorry for yourself and go have a big bowl of ice cream."

I laughed again. That had always been another solution to life's problems for Petra and me since we were kids.

"Will do," I told her. "Love you, and we'll talk again soon."

I had just piled a bowl with Rocky Road when my phone rang again. I was pleasantly surprised to see it was Chadwick.

"Hey," I said. "I thought you were in St. Pete."

"Just got back a few minutes ago. I wanted to see how you are. Did you have a good evening?"

I could definitely add thoughtful to this man's attributes. "It was okay. Quiet. Haley is spending the night at my mother's."

"Oh, gee, if I had known, I'd have asked you to go with me today."

"Thanks, but I couldn't have gone anyway. We spent most of the day shopping for dresses for Chloe's wedding."

"That makes me feel better. But I'm sorry you had to spend the evening alone. I know it's short notice, but is there any chance you and Haley would like to go out on my boat tomorrow afternoon?"

"That sounds like fun. I definitely would love to go, and I'll check with Haley."

"Great. I'll call you in the morning."

I hung up with a smile on my face. I was feeling decidedly less lonely than I had earlier in the evening.

Chapter 24

The following week I was at the yarn shop enjoying the afternoon knitting group. Most of us were working on the Isabelle's Challenge scarf and they were all working up very nicely.

"When I finish mine," Fay said, "I'm going to make one for my daughter for Christmas. I think she'd love this, and it'll keep her warm this winter up in Maine."

Chloe nodded. "I'm glad all of you like the pattern. They're all turning out so pretty in the various colors."

"Oh, Isabelle," Mavis Anne said. "How did you enjoy the boat ride on Sunday? Haley told me you both went out in Chadwick's boat."

"It was fun. He took us on the Halifax River and then docked at the River Grille. The three of us went in for dinner."

"That *does* sound like fun," Maddie said. "I heard he had a really nice pontoon boat. Aren't you the lucky girl." She gave me a playful jab in the ribs.

"Speaking of boats," Mavis Anne said, "Louise and I are thinking about booking a cruise."

"Oh, how exciting," I said. "Where to?"

"It's the Alaska cruise. We've both always wanted to do this. But . . . it's in May."

"Why is that a problem?" I asked.

"Well, it's the first week of May. The same week that Chloe will be going to Hawaii. So we wouldn't have anybody to run the yarn shop."

"Oh, no," I said. "What a shame. I'd love to help out. Maybe between now and then you could train me. I probably wouldn't be much help with customers coming in with problems, but at least I could do the sales and keep the business going."

"Hmm," Mavis Anne said. "That might work, and we could look around for one other person to be here with you and help out."

"There," Louise said. "It's settled! We have to send our deposit by the end of the week—let's do it. The yarn shop will be fine. You worry too much, Mavis Anne."

Before she could reply, the door opened and my mother walked in.

"Mom. What are you doing here?" I blurted out.

All eyes at the table shifted from me to my mother and back to me again.

"Well, I *am* a knitter, Isabelle," I heard my mother say with an edge to her tone.

"Isabelle Wainwright," Mavis Anne said. "Where are your manners? Introduce us to your mother."

I made the introductions and felt like a scolded schoolchild.

"It's so nice to meet all of you," my mother said. "You have a lovely shop. Haley has been telling me I had to stop by."

"Well, that's wonderful," Mavis Anne said. "Come and join us. We're just all sitting around knitting."

I saw my mother shoot me a glance as if waiting for me to concur. When I remained silent, my mother said, "Oh, thank you, but maybe some other time. I came by to get some yarn for me and Haley. We're going to be doing a sampler afghan together."

"How nice," Chloe said, getting up. "What do you have in mind?"

Great. Just great. Now my mother had invaded my place of business and solitude. Today she was wearing capri pants and a cotton knit top. The blue streak in her hair seemed to be fading. And she still looked pretty damn good for her age.

"Gosh, that's wonderful," I heard Chloe say. "I've always wanted to take salsa lessons. I bet that's so much fun."

What? My mother was taking salsa lessons?

"Oh, it is. It's also very good exercise and a nice way to meet people."

"Well, you seem to be settling in quite well."

Conversation at the table resumed, but I had no doubt everyone had one ear on what my mother was saying.

"Isabelle," Mavis Anne said, "didn't you tell me that your mother was an expert knitter?"

"Ah . . . yeah . . . maybe I did."

"Well, there's our solution."

I knew exactly what she was going to say, and before I could stop her, she asked, "Iris, would you by any chance be interested in helping out here at the shop for about a week?"

With no input from me, it had all been decided. Of course my mother agreed to help out. After all, she was retired and had no commitments. She seemed to totally ignore the fact that her coworker during that time would be *me*. Petra's words came back to me: be careful what you wish for.

Haley returned home from school and already knew about her grandmother helping out at the yarn shop. Apparently, they had texted each other.

"Are you okay with that, Mom?"

"I really had no say about it."

"Don't forget that Tina and her mom are coming at five," my daughter said, clearly thinking it best to change the subject.

"I haven't forgotten. That was really nice of Brenda. She didn't have to offer to cook supper for us."

Brenda Sanchez had called me the week before. She thanked me again for having her and Tina to dinner and said she wanted to reciprocate. But because of her limited cooking facilities, it wasn't possible to have us to her place. She asked if it would be okay if they came to our house; she would bring all the ingredients and cook us a traditional Mexican dinner. Of course I accepted.

They arrived just before five, loaded down with plastic bags filled with various items.

"This is so nice of you," I told her. "Come on in the kitchen."

I helped them carry some bags and then waved my hand in the air. "Well, it's all yours. I'm just going to sit here and be lazy."

Brenda laughed. "That's what you're supposed to do. Is it okay if I rummage in your cabinets and drawers for cooking items?"

"Be my guest. I'll pour us each a glass of wine."

I opened a bottle of red, filled two glasses, and passed one to Brenda. "Here's to an authentic Mexican meal."

Brenda took a sip and nodded. "And I'll get to work." She reached into one of the bags and took out a bright orange apron, which she put over her head and tied in the back. Women still wore aprons?

I watched her remove tomatoes, chicken, rice, beans, and various spices from the bags as I perched on a stool. She began cooking the chicken with sliced onion in the frying pan with oil. While that was cooking, she removed a package of tortillas from a bag and placed them on the counter.

"I thought I'd make chicken enchiladas," she said. "With some black beans and rice."

"Sounds delicious."

When the chicken was cooked, she divided it on the tortillas, added some cheese, rolled each one and placed them into a baking dish. She then proceeded to melt butter and flour in a saucepan and stir chicken broth into the mixture before adding sour cream and green chilies and pouring all of it over the enchiladas.

"There," she said, after placing the baking dish into the oven. "That needs to cook for twenty minutes. I'll get the rice and beans going."

"You must miss having a proper kitchen for cooking," I said.

She nodded. "Yeah, I do," she admitted. "But I hope someday I'll have a kitchen like this again."

This bit of news caught me by surprise. "Oh, you had a designer kitchen?"

"I did. The entire house was pretty ostentatious. Six thousand square feet."

What? How did a woman go from that to living in an efficiency on the beach?

Reading my thoughts, she said, "I know. You must be wondering how I went from such a palatial home to where I am now."

I remained silent and waited for her to continue.

"I'm ashamed to say . . . my husband was a drug dealer. A big one."

"Oh. So the house was bought with drug money?"

"It was, but even more shameful is the fact that I had no idea until it was too late."

Another story of a woman being in the dark. I recalled Chloe telling me about her friend Sydney and the way she ended up in

Cedar Key. Unbeknownst to her, her husband was a major gambler, and when he died suddenly, Sydney lost her home and bank account.

"I'm so sorry, but your story isn't as uncommon as you might think."

Brenda took a sip of wine and nodded. "Actually, my husband was an attorney in a prominent law firm. We lived in a modest sized home and had a modest lifestyle when Tina was born. He certainly made decent money, and this enabled me to be a stay-at-home mom. When Tina started school, I offered to go back to work as a nurse, but Carlos insisted I stay home."

She began stirring the rice she was now cooking in a saucepan.

"Carlos was always the boss. When we were first married, I didn't mind him making most of the decisions, but I guess as I got older I began to resent the fact that I had very little say in major issues. That was when our marriage began to get rocky. He became emotionally abusive and I even thought about leaving him."

"But that didn't happen?" I asked.

Brenda shook her head. "No. Tina was about ten and he announced that he'd gotten a huge promotion at the office and that we were moving. That was when I should have left. So what happened next was my own fault. I didn't."

Why did women always think the end result was their fault? I wondered if we were genetically engineered to feel we were the cause of relationship problems when in fact it was a loss of self-esteem making us feel that way. I pushed away a thought about myself that flitted into my mind.

"So you moved?" I said.

"Oh, yeah. To that house that was never a home. It was a showplace. Carlos insisted we entertain his associates on a lavish level. He even hired staff to make it happen. So most weekends were spent with his friends and business partners coming for dinners and pool parties. What I didn't know was that most of them were also involved with dealing drugs. It was a major operation and it all came crashing down two years ago when federal agents descended on our house to arrest Carlos."

My God. It was beginning to feel like Brenda was describing a television show or a film.

"That's terrible," I said. "They certainly didn't think you were involved, did they?"

She let out a sarcastic chuckle. "I wasn't arrested, if that's what you mean. The only good thing was that Tina and I weren't at home the day the feds showed up. She was at school and I was having lunch with friends. But I was interrogated for weeks. At the end of it all . . . Carlos was found guilty and is now serving a lengthy prison term."

I shook my head. "God, I'm so sorry. That's quite a story and a horrible thing for you to go through. I guess you lost the house?"

She nodded. "Not that I wanted it, but yes, the government confiscated the house, the cars, the boat, just about everything. Tina and I were allowed to keep our clothes and only jewelry that I could prove had belonged to my mother and therefore couldn't possibly have been bought with drug money."

I shook my head again. "Poor Tina—what a thing to go through."

"She was devastated. She was the main reason I had to leave that area. The trial was all over the news and in the papers, and even at ten years old, she knew what was going on. I legally changed our last name. Sanchez is my maiden name."

Once again it made me realize the lengths to which a mother will go to protect her child. Something I felt my mother had never done.

I reached over and patted her hand. "You made the best decision possible."

She nodded. "It hasn't been easy, but yes, I know I did. I only hope that eventually Tina and I will have a decent home to live in again. But it's all okay. I have a good job, Tina is happy at school, and we have each other. That's what it's all about, isn't it? A mother and her child being together and being happy. The material things? That's all they are: things."

I thought of my own mother again. Yes, that was how it was *supposed* to be. But I knew that Iris Brunell had failed the test of motherhood.

Chapter 25

I awoke a few weeks later and my first thought was that Petra was arriving later that afternoon. But then I recalled my dream from the night before. And once again, Emmalyn had had the central role.

I tugged on my memory to piece the dream together and recalled that Emmalyn was sitting on a bench in the pond area and I was watching her knit. I wasn't sure what the item was, but I told her it was beautiful. She gave me a smile, nodded and then began to unravel the piece. I became upset and asked her why she was doing that. She replied, "Sometimes you have to take something apart, go back to the beginning and start over."

"This is getting downright crazy," I said as I headed to the bathroom.

By the time I went downstairs to start the coffee, I still hadn't figured out the meaning of the dream. Start over with what? My thinking was interrupted when Haley walked into the kitchen.

"Good morning," she said, heading to the fridge and removing a container of yogurt. "What time will Petra be here?"

"She said between two and three."

"Are we going out for dinner?"

"Not tonight. I thought after the drive Petra might prefer to have dinner here, so I'm going to make roast chicken. That okay?"

"Sure," she said, and resumed spooning yogurt into her mouth. "I can't wait to see her. Will she meet Chadwick while she's here?"

I smiled. "I don't think she'll return to Jacksonville without that happening."

"How about Nana? Will Nana be able to see her?"

A twinge of annoyance swept through me. "I don't know. Petra isn't coming to visit her." When Haley didn't respond, I said, "We'll see."

After Haley left for school, I walked over to the tea shop, loaded up my car, and made my deliveries.

When I returned, the yarn shop was filled with women knitting and chatting away.

Mavis Anne called, "Come and join us, Isabelle."

I pulled a chair up to the table and noticed that the Isabelle scarves were in various stages of completion.

"Where's yours?" Maddie asked. "Aren't you going to knit?"

"I can only stay for a little while. My friend Petra is arriving this afternoon and I have to prepare a roast chicken for dinner."

"That's so nice that your friend is coming to visit," Fay said. "Will she be staying long?"

"Through the weekend. Yes, it'll be nice to see her."

"I've been meaning to ask you," Yarrow said, looking at Fay, "how are those 'mean girls' treating you at the facility?"

I had heard the story about Fay, who lived at a retirement facility in Daytona Beach, where a group of knitters had excluded her from the group. Yarrow had met her the previous year at her original tea shop and had asked her to join our group.

Fay laughed and continued knitting. "Oh, they never change. But that's okay. I wouldn't want to be part of a group like that. Besides, a few of us have formed our own group and we're having a great time. We call ourselves the Feisty Fivesome."

All of us laughed and I said, "That's great. What exactly do you do?"

"Oh, all kinds of things. We take road trips together for a few days, we did a paint and wine class, and we pretty much just have fun. But the most important thing is we don't exclude anybody. If other women want to join us, we welcome them."

Mavis Anne shook her head. "Females are definitely complex creatures. That's why having groups like we have here is a good thing. The only requirement is a love for knitting and socializing."

"Well, I'd better get moving," I said. "Have fun knitting and I'll see you soon."

"You'd better bring Petra over to meet me," Mavis Anne said. "Are you gals free for dinner tomorrow evening? David and I would love to have you."

"I think we are free, but I'll let you know. If Petra gets here and settled in before five, I'll bring her over later this afternoon."

* * *

Petra pulled into the driveway just before three. I walked out onto the porch and watched as she opened the back door of her SUV, reached in, and removed Lotte. She placed her on the grass near the fence where she promptly squatted and peed.

"Hey, you," I called and felt a huge smile cross my face.

Petra looked up and raked a hand through her hair. "Hey. Let me just get my luggage."

I walked out to the driveway to help. "You take Lotte and I'll get your bag," I said, before she pulled me into a tight embrace.

"This new life must agree with you. You look fantastic, Isabelle."

"Thanks. You always do. I'm so glad you're here. I've missed you."

She looked up at the house and nodded. "So . . . this is Koi House. Very pretty. No wonder you like it here."

Petra followed me through the front door.

"Yeah, but I really have to find my own place soon. Come on, I'll show you your room."

I pointed out my room off the upstairs hallway and then Haley's. "And this one is yours," I said. "I hope you'll be comfortable."

"It's just gorgeous." Without asking, she placed Lotte on the bed. "I think we'll like it here just fine, won't we, sweetie?" She placed a kiss on top of the dog's head. "But why push to find your own place? It seems from what you've said that Mavis Anne would be happy if you stayed here forever."

I laughed. "Yeah, you're probably right. I don't know. I just felt when I came here it would be temporary."

"Well, living here seems to be working out quite well for you." She walked to the window overlooking the back garden. "Oh, is that the yarn shop?"

"Yeah. Mavis Anne invited us for dinner tomorrow evening. I told her I'd check with you and let her know. We can go over there later before they close at five."

"That's sure convenient for you with your tea shop deliveries. Well, I'm going to get unpacked."

"Okay. I'll be in the kitchen. Wine?"

"Absolutely."

"Just come down the stairs and straight through the house to the back where the kitchen is."

I had poured two glasses of white wine, sliced some Muenster cheese, and was arranging crackers on a platter when Petra walked in carrying Lotte.

"Isabelle, this house is a treasure. I honestly don't know how you could leave it. It has such charm and character. Thanks," she said when I passed her a wineglass.

"Here's to us and friendship." I touched the rim of her glass and took a sip. "Yeah, I know. I've grown quite comfortable here."

"Do you feel out of place? Like it's not really yours? Is that why you want to leave?"

I shook my head. "No. Quite the opposite, actually. It's just that the original plan was to come here, stay a short time, and move on to . . . well, I'm not really sure to what."

Her gaze took in the kitchen. "I think you'd be nuts to leave. Besides, original plans are always subject to change."

"Well, I'm not planning to do that next week," I said, and laughed. "Come on. Let's sit on the patio. Haley will be home from school shortly. She was so excited about you coming."

We sat down on the patio chairs with Petra letting Lotte sit in her lap.

"Beautiful garden area. Is that the fishpond?" she asked.

"Yes. I'll show you later when we go over to the yarn shop. So you had a good drive down here?"

"I did. Wednesday midday traffic is pretty light, so I made it in ninety minutes. Okay. Now when do I get to meet Chadwick Price?"

I laughed and shook my head. "You're incorrigible. Maybe I don't want you to meet him," I teased.

"Right. Like that's going to happen. You know I have to give my approval," she teased back.

"I did speak to Chadwick, and you'll meet him Friday evening. He insisted on taking the three of us to dinner."

Petra nodded. "Nice. I take it Haley likes him."

"Yeah. She seems to. He also seems to like her."

"And what about you?"

"Me?"

"How much do you like him? Is he a good lover?"

I could feel heat radiating up my neck and gulped a sip of wine. "Of course I like him. Yes."

"And?"

"And I have no idea if he's a good lover or not."

"God, Isabelle. You're not in high school. You haven't slept with him yet?"

"No."

"Why not?"

I looked up to see Haley walk through the French doors.

"Petra. You're here. Oh, and Lotte," she said, coming to give Petra a hug and scoop the dog into her arms.

"I swear you've grown a couple more inches in the two months since I've seen you," Petra said, holding my daughter at arm's length. "And even more beautiful."

"Thanks," Haley said. "I'm so glad you came." She snuggled her face into the dog's head. "Do you think I could take Lotte for a walk?"

"That would be great. She was cooped up in the car for almost two hours. I left her leash at the bottom of the staircase on the bannister."

"Okay. I won't be gone longer than an hour. I'm going to take her into the yarn shop first so Mavis Anne and Yarrow can meet her."

I saw Petra smile as Haley went into the house cuddling the dog. "She has an extended family living here, doesn't she? With Mavis Anne and Yarrow. That's good for her."

"I know. Yeah, it really is good for her, and they adore Haley."

"So what ever happened to your promise to get Haley her own dog when you moved here?"

"Hmm, yeah. We just recently had that discussion again. I had told her when we got our own place, but with no plans to make that happen . . ."

"Oh, Isabelle, don't be such a twit. Get your daughter a damn dog. You know she'd love that. And by the way . . . why on earth haven't you slept with Chadwick yet? Sometimes you really annoy the hell outta me."

I wasn't sure whether to laugh or be annoyed myself. But that was Petra—telling it like it is.

"Well, gee, maybe because he hasn't asked to sleep with me. And well . . . I don't know."

"What's wrong?"

Petra had always been famous for breaking through the fluff and getting to the core of a problem.

I let out a deep sigh and then took a sip of wine. "Well," I said, fingering the wineglass, "there hasn't been anybody since Roger." I took another sip of wine. "And even with him . . . it was never something out of an X-rated movie. I guess I feel . . ."

"Inadequate? You've lost your self-esteem. Does Chadwick turn you on?"

I recalled his kisses and the passion just under the surface. "He does."

"And no doubt you turn him on in the same way. You just have to be reminded how to be flirty. Seductive. You need to regain that confidence you once had. To feel like a woman desired. And I have just the right fix for that."

"You do?"

"Yup. You must have a Victoria's Secret around here. Girlfriend, tomorrow we're going shopping. And Isabelle is going to get her mojo back."

Chapter 26

I sipped my coffee the next morning waiting for Petra to get out of the shower and join me. Maybe she was right. Maybe I did need to ramp up my sex appeal.

"Okay," she said, breezing into the kitchen. "I need my coffee and we'll be ready to roll. That was so nice of Mavis Anne to offer to keep Lotte while we go shopping."

"She loves dogs. And she'll spoil her rotten."

"I wouldn't have it any other way," she said while filling her mug. "So if she loves dogs so much, then she certainly wouldn't mind Haley having a dog living here."

"No, probably not." I didn't feel like having the dog discussion again. Not when my mind was on matters between the sheets. "Are you sure you don't want any breakfast?"

"Nah. Coffee is fine and we'll have an early lunch after our shopping."

We brought Lotte to the yarn shop to stay with Mavis Anne and headed down A1A so I could show Petra various sights along the ocean. When we got to Daytona Beach, I turned onto International Speedway Boulevard and headed to the Volusia Mall.

Walking into Victoria's Secret with Petra, I began having doubts about this shopping spree. Scantily glad manikins displayed items I thought more suited for a pole dancer than a forty-five-year-old female attempting to look sexy.

"Are you sure about this?" I whispered as she headed to a display of panties.

"Absolutely," she assured me.

A perky young blonde approached us. "Something I can help you with?" she asked.

Petra waved her away. "Nope. We're fine. Thanks."

After a few minutes of browsing, Petra held a tiny bit of silk in the air. "These," she said. "You have to get a couple pairs of these."

Was she serious? I doubted that the v-shaped material held together with strings on the sides would even cover my crotch.

"Oh, Petra! Really?" I wasn't sure if I was more embarrassed about the blush I felt heating my face or the fact she was waving the item in the air.

"Isabelle Wainwright. Don't be such a prude. Half the women in America wear these. The days of bloomers are long gone."

I wasn't a prude, and as I fingered the material, I had to admit that they even had a sexy *feel* to them.

"If you're sure," I said doubtfully.

"Here's your size. We'll get a pair in black, red, and beige. Okay. On to bras."

By the time we left the shop with me clutching the tote bag, and my credit card feeling some serious damage, I wondered if I'd really be brave enough to wear the stuff I'd purchased. And if I did, I couldn't help but wonder what Chadwick might think of it. Should he get the chance to see it.

After shopping, I headed south on A1A to Ponce Inlet and decided to take Petra to lunch at the North Turn. With a NASCAR-themed bar and grill and beachfront deck, the location was well known for its Daytona Beach racing history.

Petra looked at the framed photos and information lining the walls when we walked in.

"This is really cool," she said.

I nodded. "Yeah. The races ran right outside there on the beach until 1958 when they opened the speedway on International Speedway Boulevard. Come on, let's get a table outside."

She followed me out to the covered deck area and we found a table overlooking the ocean.

After we gave our wine and food order to the waitress, we both sat there in silence soaking in the sight of the sun on the ocean and the waves crashing on the shore.

"Beautiful," she said. "I'm not that far from the ocean in Jacksonville, but I never seem to get to the beach often enough. Working from home can have its downfalls."

I nodded. "Yeah, I would think it could tend to become a bit isolated. But the good thing is you can live anywhere. Move down here," I said before I realized what I was saying. Petra had always made it clear she loved her house, her area, her life.

"Hmm," was all she said as the waitress approached and placed our wine in front of us.

"Hmm?" I repeated. "Are you saying you'd actually consider that?"

She touched her glass to mine. "Here's to the unknown future," she said. "We never know where life will lead us."

My cell phone rang; the caller ID listed my mother's name. "Shit," I said. "My mother. Guess I should take the call."

Petra gave me a thumbs-up as I said hello.

"Isabelle. How are you?"

"Good. And you?"

"Fine. Really doing well. Has Petra arrived?"

"Yes. Yesterday. Actually, we're out having lunch together." No way was I going to tell my mother about my shopping spree.

"That's great. Be sure to tell her I said hi. But the reason I'm calling . . . well . . . I wondered if you, Petra, and Haley would like to come to dinner tomorrow evening." When I remained silent, she said, "That is, if you're not busy."

It was obvious that she was using Petra to lure me back into her good graces. Tomorrow evening was definitely out. Plans with Chadwick trumped my mother.

"No. I'm afraid not. I've already made previous plans for tonight and tomorrow night."

There was a slight pause before she said, "Yes, of course. I probably should have called sooner. How about Saturday evening? Would that work for you?"

Was she groveling? "Ah . . . I'm not quite sure. Let me get back to you. I'll give you a call tomorrow."

"That would be great, Isabelle. Enjoy your lunch."

The call had been disconnected and I looked at Petra.

"Your mother?" she asked.

"Yup. Wants us to come to dinner Saturday evening."

"I'd love to see her new house. What's it like?"

"I have no idea."

"Isabelle! You haven't been over there yet?"

Despite animosity toward my mother, a twinge of shame came over me. "No. I haven't. Haley has been helping her and keeping her company. There's been no reason for me to go there. Besides, she never invited me."

Petra took a sip of wine. "She has now."

"Yeah. All right. Okay. But she's only extending the invite because you're here. It's more about you than me."

Petra blew out a puff of air and shook her head. "This is one of those times that you can be such a bitch. For once, cut her some slack. She's reaching out to you, Isabelle. I have no doubt she probably thought you'd be more inclined to go with me here visiting."

"Okay. Enough. We'll go to her damn house Saturday evening," I muttered through clenched teeth, and was grateful to see the waitress coming with our food.

The dinner at Mavis Anne's had been a good time. Petra adored both David and Clive and the conversation had been nonstop with a lot of laughter and storytelling.

When we came back to Koi House, we both got in our jammies. I brewed a pot of herbal tea and we curled up on the sofa.

"You know you're quite fortunate, don't you?" Petra asked. "First that Chloe invited you to visit here and then that Mavis Anne insisted you stay. You're surrounded by a lot of love, Isabelle. I hope you know that."

Then why did I always feel a void?

I let out a sigh. "Yeah. I have been fortunate. Most of the time."

She took a sip from her mug. "You know, when we were younger I used to feel bad for you. Your mother just took off and you hardly ever heard from her. But your father more than made up for it. And you and I always balanced each other, because I never even knew my father."

I recalled how Petra's mom had raised her daughter alone, refusing to give enough information for Petra to find him. But unlike me, she had adjusted to growing up with only one parent.

"But your mother is back in your life now. Yes, thirty years later. But it's never too late, Isabelle. At least for you it isn't. It's doubtful that I'll ever find my father."

"What? You've been looking for him?"

She took another sip of tea. "I haven't wanted to say anything be-cause ... well ... there really isn't much to say. But when my mother died three years ago, I had to go through all of her things." She paused while shifting her position on the sofa. "And I found some papers. And an old black-and-white photograph. It was my mother with a fellow her age. Taken on a beach and she was holding a baby. I assume it was me. Of course I don't know for certain, but I have a feeling that the fellow could be my father. He has his arm around her and they look romantically involved."

I reached over to grab her arm. "My God, Petra. I had no idea. So was this man your father? Where was the photo taken? Do you think he's still alive?"

"I have no idea. My mother always told me that my father had died and she didn't want to talk about it. I certainly couldn't force her."

"Yeah, I remember how stubborn and set in her ways she could be. So are you searching for him now?"

"With so little info, there isn't a whole lot to search. But yeah, I've been doing lots of Google searches and I even joined Ancestry.com. Because I finally do have a name for my father. My mother wouldn't even give me that, but it was written on the back of the photo."

"What is it? What's his name?"

"Peter. Peter Maxwell."

"Wow," I said, completely surprised by all of this. "Oh, my God! She named you the feminine version of his name! Why didn't you tell me before? We share everything."

"Yeah, I know, and I did think about it. But I don't know ... seems silly, I guess, but I thought if I actually verbalized any of this it would fall apart and I'd never get anywhere. Not that I've had one bit of success trying to find him."

I clasped her hand and gave it a squeeze. "I know how determined you can be, Petra. You've always been my rock. You're strong and I know you won't give up."

She nodded and squeezed my hand back. "I probably won't. But Isabelle ... your mother? She's right *here*. Just waiting for you to love her."

Chapter 27

After lunch Petra and I went to spend some time at the yarn shop. She hadn't touched knitting needles in years, but I could tell she was enjoying browsing and touching all the various yarns.

"I can't believe how much the yarn industry has changed since I was a teenager," she said, fingering a skein of soft cotton.

Fay looked up from the socks she was working on. "Well, find yourself a pattern and choose some yarn. It's never too late to get back to it."

"I think I will," Petra said. "How about that Isabelle scarf all of you are making? Do you have the pattern? That might be good to start with."

"Great idea," Chloe said, jumping up and walking to the counter. "Here's the pattern and any of that Bamboo Pop cotton can be used."

"Now the big decision," Petra said. "Which color to choose?"

Fay laughed and looked across the table at me. "I'm glad your mother decided to help out here when Mavis Anne and Chloe are gone. We met with her the other day and worked out a schedule. She'll be coming in on Wednesday and Saturday. Those are the two days I can't make it."

So it was final. I'd have to be with my mother in the yarn shop for two whole days. Alone.

"Oh, that's nice," I mumbled and kept my head down, knitting away.

"I have it," I heard Petra say. She returned to the table with two skeins of white. "This will go with anything. Now I just need needles. I got rid of all my knitting supplies years ago so I'm starting over."

"I'm happy to see you'll be returning to the wonderful world of knitting," Mavis Anne said. "Do you know they even have patterns now to make outfits for dogs?"

"No! Really?" I saw the look of excitement that crossed Petra's face. "As soon as I finish the scarf I'll get started on something for Lotte."

"Leave it to you," I said. "Knitting for a dog."

Everybody chuckled.

"So you're going to meet Chadwick tonight?" Mavis Anne asked.

Petra nodded. "I am. Anything I should know ahead of time?"

"That he's pretty hot," Maddie said.

"He is that," Mavis Anne confirmed. "But he's also a very nice man. I have no doubt you'll like him. Where are you going for dinner?"

"To the Golden Lion in Flagler Beach," I said. "Chadwick is picking us up at six."

"Oh, good choice." Mavis Anne nodded. "Such a pretty spot with the deck overlooking the ocean."

The phone rang, and Chloe jumped up again to answer it while we continued talking.

A few minutes later she returned to the table. A huge smile lit her face. "That was Treva. She had her OB checkup this morning and everything is fine. Right on schedule for a June delivery."

"Do you plan to go up to Jacksonville when she's in labor?" Maddie asked.

"Gee, I hadn't really thought about that. But I guess I could. I'd love to be right there when my grandchild is born. I'll see what Eli and Treva think."

"Oh, I'm sure they'd love to have you there. Treva doesn't bother with her stepmother or her father, does she?" Mavis Anne asked.

Chloe shook her head. "No. I'm really it for family. Well, me and Eli and Henry."

"Right," Mavis Anne said and nodded. "A girl always needs a mother figure in her life. No matter her age."

The glance she shot in my direction didn't escape me.

Chadwick rang the doorbell at precisely six. Haley reached the door first. I got up from the sofa and found I was nervous to be introducing my best friend to a man who might be in my life forever or possibly drift away.

Chadwick stepped inside as butterflies fluttered in my stomach.

"Chadwick," I said, and grabbed Petra's hand as she came to stand beside me. "I'd like you to meet Petra Garfield."

"Hi," she said, not the least bit nervous, reaching out to shake his hand. "She just neglected to say that I'm her *best* friend like for a million years."

Chadwick laughed and returned her handshake. "Very important information," he confirmed, kidding with her.

And there—right in front of my best friend and my daughter—he leaned over to place a brief kiss on my lips. "You're looking as beautiful as always," he said without one ounce of shyness.

"Thanks," I said and smiled. All of a sudden my nervousness evaporated, and the scene felt natural and right. "Okay. I think we're ready."

"I thought you had a little dog," Chadwick said. "I'd like to meet him."

That was *it*. No matter what, I knew Petra would always be Chadwick's staunchest supporter and defend anything he said or did.

"Oh, I do," she gushed. "But it's a *she*. Lotte. And she's staying with Mavis Anne this evening until we get back. You can meet her when we pick her up later."

"That would be great," he said. And once again I was surprised by his sincerity.

We were seated at a table near the railing with an unobstructed view of the ocean, and the conversation hadn't lagged once in the hour we'd been at the restaurant.

I only made comments when necessary, allowing Chadwick and Petra time to get to know each other. He asked Petra about her line of work, growing up in Pennsylvania, and of course lots of questions about Lotte. He then moved on to Haley, asking about school, Tina, and various teen subjects. A couple of times I caught him sending me a wink across the table and my heart melted.

It struck me that Chadwick Price was what guys referred to as a man's man. He was sociable and knew how to work a group. But the thing was, it wasn't fake or being done for some ulterior purpose. He was genuinely interested in other people and what they had to say. A rare quality in today's world.

"Yeah, so we went shopping yesterday," I heard Petra say.

"Ah, a woman's love," Chadwick said. "Did you find something specific or just browsing?"

"Oh, no, we found—"

I kicked Petra under the table to prevent her from saying any more. "Yes," I interrupted. "We found a few nice things. But mostly, we just browsed and then I took Petra to lunch at the North Turn."

Chadwick looked from me to Petra and back again as a smile crossed his face. Maybe this man was a bit too astute for his own good.

"Nice choice," he said and moved on to another subject, but I didn't miss his smirk.

By the time we headed back to Koi House, I had no doubt it had been a very good evening and Chadwick and Petra liked each other. For some reason, that meant a lot to me.

Haley went into the house but Chadwick came with us to get Lotte. After much patting and telling Petra how sweet Lotte was, he said, "It's been a very enjoyable evening. It was really great meeting you, Petra, and I hope we'll see each other again."

"Same here," she said. "Oh, you will. I'll always be in Isabelle's life."

Somehow the way she said that made it sound like Chadwick would also be in my life forever.

"Thanks so much for dinner," she said, before heading toward Koi House with Lotte in her arms.

"I like her," he said, as we stood near the gate. "You were right. She's a no-nonsense person and tells it like it is. That's a good trait to have."

"Hmm, sometimes," I said, and laughed.

I felt his arms go around my waist and I looked up into his handsome face. As his lips touched mine, my arms circled around his neck. His kisses only continued to get better, and at that moment I recalled the sexy lingerie wrapped in tissue paper stashed away in my bedroom drawer. Would I ever be wearing that for Chadwick?

After a few more kisses, I pulled away. "I guess I should go inside," I said.

"Hmm," he mumbled, but kept his arms around me.

"Okay," he said after a few seconds. "I guess I have to let you go. Does Petra leave on Sunday?"

I nodded.

"Can we get together on Monday evening? I have to leave Tuesday for Miami and some business meetings until Friday."

I had no idea what I had going on Monday evening but whatever it might be, it didn't take priority over Chadwick.

"Absolutely," I told him.

He brushed his lips with mine again. "I'll call you," he said before walking to his car.

I walked into the house to find Petra curled up on the sofa, two wineglasses on the table. She picked one up and held it in the air.

"Here's to Chadwick Price," she said. "He's definitely a keeper."

I laughed and sat down beside her as I reached for the other glass. "Thanks. Then I guess you approve?"

She rolled her eyes. "Seriously? What's not to like?"

"Yeah. I agree. I mean, nobody's perfect, but I've yet to find his flaws."

"Oh, you will, but I have a feeling they'll be pretty minor ones. I do like him a lot, Isabelle, and it's plain to see, he's crazy about you. Haley adores him too and they seem to have a nice rapport between them."

I nodded. "Yeah. I never gave that much thought because I never dated anybody after Roger and I broke up. But having them like each other is a nice bonus."

"Oh, trust me. If the kid doesn't like the boyfriend or vice versa, it can be a game changer. So yes, you lucked out in that department."

"I'm glad you like him, Petra. That means a lot to me."

"Hmm," she said, a grin covering her face. "If it means that much— this might be headed in a pretty serious direction."

Chapter 28

O^{ne} thing I had to admit: my mother had taught me the basic manners in childhood. In retrospect, I knew she hadn't been a bad mother. She had just been an absent mother. For thirty years.

So early Saturday morning I headed to Maddie's florist shop and purchased a houseplant to take to dinner that evening.

I came in the back door of Koi House to find Petra sitting at the counter sipping coffee.

"Nice touch," she said. "For your mother?"

Leave it to Petra to know me.

"Yup," I said, nonchalantly going to pour myself a mug of coffee. "I'd do the same for a stranger. Haley still sleeping?"

"I think so. Haven't seen her yet. What's up for today? Are we due at your mother's at six?"

"Yeah," I said, and thought about my call to her the day before. It was difficult not to hear the happiness in her voice when I said we accepted her dinner invitation. "Well, you can't go back to Jacksonville without our visiting Angell and Phelps chocolate shop. So we can go down there and then have lunch out."

"Sounds like a plan." She took a sip of her coffee and placed the empty mug in the dishwasher. "Well, I'm headed to the shower. See you in a bit."

I sat there lost in my thoughts when she left the kitchen. Over the past few days I had been getting flashbacks of various incidents from my childhood, when my mother was still in my life. How she was always there for school events, even when my father was working and couldn't make it. Her worry and concern the time I had chicken pox at age nine. My eighth grade graduation when I insisted I wanted a perm for the ceremony—and proceeded to do it myself at home, resulting in me looking like a French poodle. I then insisted I wasn't going but my mother took me to her hair stylist and had my hair straightened, cut, and styled. Little things—but things that a loving mother does for her daughter. And yet—she was able to just walk away as if she never cared at all. All these years later, I still found it difficult to understand.

I looked up as Haley walked into the kitchen and came to place a kiss on my cheek.

"Good morning," she said, and I knew that although I might have lost my mother, the gods had shined down on me when I had Haley.

"Good morning," I told her. "Sleep well?"

"Yeah. And Mom, I'm really glad you agreed to go to Nana's tonight. She's excited about us coming for dinner."

No doubt, I thought, and once again the old resentment returned.

A little before six I was driving down Granada to The Trails and wondering whether I should have left well enough alone and refused the dinner invitation. Too late now.

I pulled into the cul-de-sac and my mother's driveway. Before we even got out of the car, my mother had the front door open to welcome us.

Hugs were exchanged and she waved a hand toward the family room.

"Come on in," she said. "I'm so glad you came."

I passed her the plant. "For you," I said.

"Thank you so much, Isabelle. It's lovely."

She placed it on the counter and shot us a huge smile.

"Okay. Dinner will be ready shortly. How about a drink? Wine for you gals and a soda for you, Haley?"

"Thanks, Nana."

"Sounds good, doesn't it, Izzy?" Petra said, when I mumbled sure.

She only called me Izzy when she was irritated with me. I had a feeling she thought I wasn't being friendly enough.

I walked into the family room and glanced around. Beautifully furnished, just like our home had been when I was growing up. My gaze caught framed photos on a credenza and I walked over. I was surprised to see one of me with Buster, my childhood dog. I had begged and begged for a dog, and on my fifth birthday my parents took me out to the country to choose a pup from a litter of cocker spaniels. Buster lived to be ten years old, but we lost him to cancer a few months after my mother left, making his loss doubly hard.

I picked up another frame that was a collage of photos of me. On family vacations, dance recitals, and my eighth grade graduation. The other frames were the few photos of Haley that I'd sent to my mother over the years.

"Here you go," she said, passing me a glass of wine.

"Something smells delicious," Petra said.

"I made roast pork with cheese potatoes and fresh green beans."

"Sounds yummy, Nana. And my favorite ice cream for dessert?"

My mother laughed and nodded. "Yes, I got Rocky Road."

"You have a beautiful place, Iris," Petra said.

"I love it here. Come on, I'll show you around."

I followed them as she pointed out the two bedrooms, a room she called her knitting room filled with shelves of yarn and a day bed, and then the kitchen/dining area.

I noticed that the French doors in the family room led to an enclosed patio outside.

"This is really ideal for you," Petra said. "And you like the area? You're keeping busy?"

My mother laughed. It was then I noticed that she was sipping ice water and not wine.

"Probably too busy," she said. "I joined a salsa class and I'm starting a yoga class next week. And the first week in May I'll be helping out at the yarn shop while Mavis Anne and Chloe are gone. In addition to my meetings, yes, I seem to have plenty to do. And I do love the area. I've made a few new friends and I love that the beach is so close."

"Sounds like it was a good choice moving here," Petra said, and I caught the glare she sent in my direction.

I knew she felt I'd been too quiet and was making no attempt to join the conversation.

I took a sip of wine. "Well, it certainly sounds like you're the social butterfly."

I had to acknowledge that I'd been secretly hoping my mother would feel her relocation here was a mistake. But apparently, that wasn't happening.

Dinner was cooked to perfection. We were enjoying coffee while Haley savored her bowl of ice cream.

"Haley tells me you have a special man in your life," my mother said. "I'd love to meet him some time."

"Why?" I blurted out before I realized how hurtful the question was.

But she had never met any of the fellows I had dated in high school or college. And she hadn't even met Roger until long after we had gotten married.

I saw the wounded expression that crossed her face and said, "Well, I mean . . . we've only been seeing each other a short time. Who knows where it will lead or if it will even continue?"

I knew this was probably a fib, but it was the best I could come up with.

My mother nodded. "Yes, true. Well, I just want you to know that I'd be happy to meet him. If you thought that I should."

"You know, Iris," Petra said, "it's only a ninety-minute drive from here to where I am in Jacksonville. If you ever feel the need for a little getaway, just give me a call and come visit."

A smile crossed my mother's face. "Thanks, Petra. You've always been such a sweet girl."

Unlike me, I thought.

"Nana," Haley said, "show Mom what you're knitting. Wait till you see this, Mom."

My mother reached into a tote bag beside the sofa and brought out a gorgeous lace shawl. It was very intricate, done in a shade of ecru, which made it look vintage.

I had to admit it was stunning. I reached over to touch it. "It really is gorgeous," I said. "Those stitches must be challenging."

My mother nodded and I could tell she was pleased with my compliment. "Yes, they are. But anything worthwhile is always a challenge," she said, and I wondered if that had a double meaning.

We made more small talk, and when I glanced at my watch I saw it was almost nine.

"Well," I said, "we should get going. Thank you for the dinner, Mom. It really was excellent."

"It was, Nana. Thanks. Mom, maybe Nana could come to our house next time for dinner."

Leave it to my daughter to make me squirm.

"Yeah, maybe. We'll see," was all I said.

My mother hugged me good-bye and whispered in my ear, "Thank you for coming, Isabelle. I know it wasn't easy, but it meant a lot to me."

I nodded and followed Petra and Haley to the car. I resented the lump that had formed in my throat.

Chapter 29

Two weeks later I drove Haley to the Jacksonville airport for her flight to Atlanta to stay the week with Roger. Petra insisted I spend the night at her house after I dropped Haley off.

I pulled into her driveway and smiled. Even though we'd recently been together, I always looked forward to spending time with my best friend.

"Hey," she said, opening the door with Lotte in her arms. "I'm so glad you agreed to stay the night. I have lunch all ready."

I followed her into the kitchen and perched on the stool while she uncorked a bottle of white.

"So what are your plans for the week with Haley gone?" she asked.

"Well," I said, taking a deep breath, "I've been summoned to my mother's house tomorrow evening for dinner."

She passed me a wineglass. "And I'm thinking you're not happy with this?"

"I just wonder what it's all about. Why would she invite me alone without Haley?"

"Maybe because she'd like some private time to talk to you?"

I shook my head. "I doubt it. What could she possibly have to say that I don't already know?"

"I guess you'll find out tomorrow night. You *are* going, aren't you?"

"I'll probably be sorry, but yeah, I agreed to go. And Wednesday morning I'm going with Chadwick to spend the night in Atlanta at his parents' home."

Her head shot up as her eyebrows arched. "Oh, really? And what's that all about?"

I waved a hand in the air. "Don't get too excited. He has to go up there for business and asked me to go along. He'd like me to meet his parents, so we'll be staying there for one night. That's all."

A smile crossed Petra's face. "Hmm, that's all? Sounds rather important to me. When a guy would like you to meet his parents, you've moved beyond the friendship stage. Trust me. I know these things."

"Oh, right," I said. "And that's because you have somebody special in your life?"

"Hey, do as I say, not as I do. Are you nervous? About meeting them?"

"I haven't given it much thought. Should I be?"

"Nah. Except for a woman's wedding day, it's only that other really major day in her life. Meeting people who could potentially turn out to be family by marriage."

I held my palm in the air. "Hold on. First of all, I never realized what a hopeless romantic you are, and secondly, we're simply spending the night there rather than doing the drive back the same day." I took a sip of wine. "That's all it is." And I wondered which of us I was trying to convince more. Petra? Or myself?

I arrived back in Ormond Beach the next morning around ten, dreading dinner with my mother later that evening. Once or twice I thought about calling her to cancel, fibbing that I was sick, but I couldn't bring myself to do that.

And so here I was ringing her doorbell just before six.

As on my previous visit, she opened the door wide with a huge smile on her face. But this time I was alone and didn't have Petra and Haley to pick up the slack if conversation flagged.

"Isabelle, I'm so glad you agreed to come. Would you like a glass of wine?"

"Great," I said, and followed her to the family room, where I sat on the sofa as she uncorked a bottle of red, poured one glass and brought it to me.

She sat across from me in a wingback chair. "So is Haley having a nice time visiting her father?"

I ignored her question and blurted out, "Why don't you drink wine? This is the second time I've come here and you haven't had any."

She took a sip of ice water and nodded. "Right. It's part of the reason I wanted to talk to you. I'm a recovering alcoholic. There's a lot you don't know about me, Isabelle."

What? My mother was an alcoholic? I pictured a falling-down, word-slurring, unkempt person when I heard the word *alcoholic*. Surely she meant that sometimes she just had a few too many. Like I did. Besides, I couldn't remember seeing my mother drunk when I was a child.

"I don't understand," I said.

"I know you don't and that's what I hope to fix." She let out a deep sigh.

"Were you a drinker when you left me and Dad?" I asked.

"I was. I just kept it pretty well hidden. From you, at least. But your father knew."

"Oh, so that's why you left? You preferred booze over me?" I knew my words had taken on a nasty tone, but I didn't care. I was angry to learn this about my mother, but also pissed that I hadn't been told before now.

"Let's get something straight right now," she said, and I heard an edge to her tone. "I never left because of *you* and I never preferred anything above *you*. If you don't believe anything else that I have to tell you, I need you to believe this. Do you understand?"

Instantly, I felt as if I was ten again and was being chastised by my mother for something I had said or done wrong. I nodded and said, "Yes."

"Okay," she said and stood up. "I have a lot to tell you and I know you'll have a lot of questions, but I'd like us to have dinner first and enjoy the pasta and meatballs that I made. No discussion about the past until we're finished. Deal?"

My head was spinning, but I nodded. "Okay," I said. "Can I help?"

"No, I'm all set. Let me just put it on the table."

I followed her to the dining area and saw she had already set the table.

Somehow we managed to make general conversation about Haley, Petra, the yarn shop, and various other topics as we ate salad, pasta, and garlic bread.

I helped my mother clear the table and clean up and then she brewed a pot of coffee.

"I think it might be a long evening," she said, shooting me a smile.

After we settled ourselves in the family room, each with a mug of coffee, she said, "Let's see, where do I begin?"

"At the beginning would be nice," I retorted. All through dinner I failed to understand how anything she could tell me would take away the hurt and resentment I'd harbored for thirty years.

She nodded. "Right. Well, that would be back to college where I met your father. Your grandparents were gone by the time you were born, so not only did you never meet them, but you never saw the area where I grew up. Shamokin was a coal mining town in the middle of Pennsylvania. It was less than three hours from Philly, where I went to college, but believe me, it was a whole other world."

When I'd asked my mother about her childhood, as I think all kids do, she'd never said anything bad about it. Only that she grew up in the country, she was an only child as I was. Because her childhood seemed so boring, I never questioned her any further.

"My father worked in the coal mines," she now told me. "And in February of my senior year of high school, he was killed in a mine explosion."

"Why did you never tell me this?" I asked.

She shrugged. "You never asked. Besides, it didn't affect me being your mother. But who knows . . . maybe it affected me more than I realized. I had worked hard all through high school and managed to get a full scholarship to college. I remember the day I left home. I think I'd felt smothered by coal dust all my life and I felt like I was getting a chance to gulp fresh air when I arrived at college. Meeting your father was another gulp of fresh air. He came from the city and a middle-class family. I knew he was going places and I wanted to join him."

"Did you love him?" I asked.

She paused a moment before saying, "I did. But probably not in the way I should have. Over the years I came to see that his love for me was no greater than mine for him."

I recalled that I'd never really witnessed any great affection between my parents, but as a kid I think I assumed everybody's parents were like that.

"So why did you stay together?" I asked.

She let out another deep sigh before taking a sip of coffee. "Why does any couple? You're in a rut. You're not sure where to go or what to do. You just keep putting one foot in front of the other—thinking maybe tomorrow will be different. I don't know, Isabelle. I can't answer that."

"But you had no problem leaving when I was fifteen. Was it because you had a lover to make the leaving easier?"

"What? Is *that* what your father told you? That I had a lover?"

I saw the genuine look of astonishment on her face.

"Yes," I said, and for the first time in thirty years I began to question what I had been told. "Yes. After you were gone about a month, he sat me down and explained that you wouldn't be coming back. That you had been in touch with him and told him you were in Oregon. He told me he wasn't surprised because you had been seeing somebody—another man."

My mother slowly shook her head from side to side. "Oh, Isabelle, there's so much you don't know, but no . . . when I left it had nothing to do with another man. It had everything to do with protecting myself and ultimately protecting you—but maybe I was wrong about that."

"I don't get it," I said. "I have never understood why . . . not why you left him . . . but why you left *me*. Why didn't you take *me* with you?" I was fighting to prevent the tears trying to form in my eyes.

"Because I was not in a good place and I didn't want to damage you. We had always been close, but when you turned thirteen we began to drift apart and that's not unusual. Most teen girls go through this with their mothers. But you had grown even closer to your father during this time and I knew the best thing to do was let you stay with him." She paused for a moment as if formulating her thoughts. "What I'm going to say is in no way an attack on your father. I want you to know that, but it's time you know the truth. He was a wonderful and caring father to you, but he was a difficult husband. Your father was demanding and a perfectionist and that in itself is fine . . . except when it destroys another person's confidence and identity."

"What are you saying?" I asked, but I remembered that my father always expected only the best from me. Instead of rebelling, I acquiesced and became a model daughter and student.

"I'm saying that emotional and verbal abuse can be every bit as bad as physical abuse. If a woman hears long enough that she's a disappointment and a failure as a wife and mother, over time she just might come to believe it. And I did. By the time you were ten, I was convinced that while I might have been an average mother, I really sucked as a wife and a woman. And so . . . that was when I began to find solace in alcohol."

"I don't remember you drinking very much. Yeah, you'd have a glass or two in the late afternoon and with dinner, but so do I and so do many other women. That doesn't make you an alcoholic."

She nodded. "That's true. But remember all those migraine headaches I had? When I locked myself in the bedroom most evenings? That's when there is truly a problem. When you hide away with a bottle or two and claim you're resting because of a headache."

My mind immediately flashed back to Atlanta shortly after Roger left and how I had done the very same thing—hidden out in my bedroom with a bottle of wine. And I did the same thing last summer when I came to visit Chloe at Koi House. Was I headed down the exact same path my mother had taken?

"And so, what happened? Dad said you were staying with some guy out in Oregon. But you weren't?"

"No, I was not. Do you remember Sylvia? My very good friend from college?"

"Sure," I said. "She came to visit us a few times in Philly. Wasn't she a social worker in Portland? Is that where you were?"

"Yes, but even if your father didn't tell you this, I told you in those first letters I sent."

Letters?

"What letters?" I felt a twinge of anger course through me and I wasn't sure whom it was directed toward.

"I wrote you quite a few letters, Isabelle, when I first got to Oregon. It was such a difficult time for me, but I wanted you to know my leaving had nothing to do with you. Your father kept those letters from you, I guess. But I'm not surprised."

Oh, sure, I thought. *Blame it on my father.*

"No, I can see now that you're right. It had nothing to do with me. And everything to do with your selfishness. You were unhappy in your marriage, so you chucked it all, including your daughter, and headed out west." I stood up and reached for my handbag. I'd waited thirty years to find out why she'd left and it all boiled down to my mother being selfish.

"Isabelle, sit *down*. You are not leaving until you hear all of my story."

As if on cue, I heard the ringtone on my cell phone telling me I had a call from Chadwick.

"I have a call," I said, stating the obvious. "It's Chadwick."

"You can take it on the patio, where you'll have some privacy," she said, in a determined voice.

I walked outside and for the first time in months I craved a cigarette.

"Hi," I said.

"Hey, beautiful. How was the dinner at your mother's?"

"I'm still here."

"Oh. Okay. I hope it's going well. Give me a call when you get home."

"I have no idea when that will be."

I glanced at my watch and was surprised to see it was already eight.

"If you feel it's too late, then I'll talk to you in the morning."

"Okay."

"And Isabelle . . . you're doing the right thing. Giving her a chance to explain."

I wasn't sure I agreed. Sometimes ignorance truly is bliss.

"Bye," I said, then disconnected the call and walked back inside.

Since my mother clearly seemed to be in control of the conversation, I remained silent and sat down.

Chapter 30

"Okay," she said, placing a fresh mug of coffee on the end table beside me. "So yes, it was Sylvia that I ran to. And I *was* running. But I want you to know, I was never running from you, Isabelle. I was running from myself."

I took a sip of coffee and waited for her to continue.

"I should have been stronger, I should have stayed and sought help, I should have done a lot of things differently. But I didn't."

"And Sylvia gave you the help you needed?" I asked.

"No. Nobody can give you that help. You have to want it and then it's a long, tough road back, but you have to do it yourself. Sylvia was the means to set me in the right direction. Within a few days of my arrival, she knew I had a major problem with alcohol. I didn't have to hide it anymore at her place and I guess that's when I hit my bottom. I felt like I'd lost everything. There was nothing more for me to lose. I won't go into the sordid details, but before the week was over she gave me an ultimatum—either I began attending AA meetings, got a sponsor and stayed sober, or I couldn't live with her."

"As simple as that?" I said.

My mother laughed. "Right. Just that simple. Like the program says, easy does it. Except it's never easy. I did find a meeting, hated every minute I spent there, insisted to myself I didn't have a problem, could stop any time I wanted. All the usual excuses."

"What happened?"

"After thirty days of sobriety, I began slowing down on the meetings. Thought I had it licked. I didn't need meetings and then I didn't need a sponsor. And within thirty more days, I was right back to square one."

"Did Sylvia kick you out?"

She shook her head. "No. She stuck with me. Gave me another chance but said it was the final one. She said everybody deserves a second chance . . . but she refused to enable me. And beyond a second chance, she felt that's what she'd be doing."

I remained silent, but I had a feeling my mother wanted that second chance with me and our relationship.

"And so?" I asked.

"I knew she meant it. Was it easy? Never. But I knew I only had two choices. To continue drinking or to go forward and build a new life for myself."

"A life that didn't include me."

She ignored my comment. "I checked myself into a rehab facility. I was there for ninety days and still pretty fragile when I was discharged. I wrote to you, and when you didn't answer, I assumed you just didn't want to bother with me. The few times that I called and your father put you on the phone, I could tell how angry you were. I felt maybe I should go easy and let you come to me if you wanted to. You have no idea how thrilled I was when you called to tell me I was a grandmother. I thought maybe things would improve between us then, but . . . that really didn't happen." She took a sip of her coffee.

"If you had it to do over, would you do things differently?"

She paused a few moments before answering. "I'm honestly not sure, Isabelle. I know you consider it selfish, but I had to do what was best for me. Because if I wasn't right and in a good place, you wouldn't have been either. Had I stayed, I think my drinking would have continued and only gotten worse. I think that over time, I would have ended up damaging you. I'm not trying to justify what I did . . . but I know now, in my soul, that I left to protect myself and in doing so, I also protected you. Maybe I did do the right thing. You've turned out to be a daughter to be proud of. You're an excellent mother. And although I probably had nothing to do with any of that . . . I love you and couldn't be any prouder."

The tears that had threatened earlier now stung my eyes and I swiped at them. I had nothing to say. My head felt like a computer on overload, exploding with too much information. I knew it was going to take a while for me to digest all that I'd been told this evening.

"Any more questions?" she asked.

I shook my head. "Not right now. No."

She slapped the palm of her hand on her thigh and got up. "Okay, then. We're going out."

"Out?" I looked at my watch and saw it was going on nine. "Where?"

"Get your jacket," she said. "You'll see."

On our way out the door she grabbed two scarves from the coatrack. "Here, you might need this when we get where we're going."

My mother drove toward A1A. It reminded me of childhood excursions with her. She'd suddenly announce, "Get a sweater, Isabelle. We're going out." And she'd surprise me with a trip for ice cream or to the park, where I could play on the swings and slides. I remembered one rainy day when we ended up at the library. I was only about seven; that was the day I got my first library card. It was strange how over the years I hadn't recalled any of these fun events. Maybe that's what anger does: it blots out everything that was good and only allows you to focus on the negative.

My mother pulled into the parking lot at Andy Romano Park. We were going to the beach at night?

"Are you familiar with the sea turtles?" she asked.

I'd read in the newspaper and seen on television something about sea turtles nesting and dropping their eggs on the east coast beaches of Florida.

"Not really," I said.

"Well, my sponsor in AA is a woman named Charlotte, and she's very involved in this program to protect the sea turtles. I've been to a few of their meetings and it's something I want to be a part of."

My mother continued to surprise me. She'd been living in Ormond Beach less than two months and during that time she had managed to join a salsa dancing class, yoga, and now a program for sea turtles.

"I'd like you to meet Charlotte. She's here tonight doing her watch and if we're lucky, we'll see a mother turtle coming out of the ocean to make her nest. Come on."

I got out of the car, wrapped the scarf around my neck, and felt the Atlantic wind on my face as I followed my mother to the sand. I saw a handful of people walking around; most of them seemed to be carrying a red light.

"There's Charlotte," she said. I saw a woman raise her hand in greeting and walk toward us.

She gave my mother a hug and in a hushed tone said, "I'm so glad you could make it; this must be Isabelle."

Silly, I know, but it made me feel good that my mother had told her about me and she knew who I was.

"Yes," I said as I extended my hand. "Nice to meet you."

"Same here," she said. "And I think you're in luck. You just might get to see a mama turtle make her nest here tonight."

"What's with the red lights?" I asked.

"Sea turtles gravitate toward light, and light pollution from the beach area is a death sentence for them when the baby turtles hatch from their shells. They will automatically go toward the water because of the reflection of the night sky and moon, but if there are bright lights along the beach from houses and businesses, they get confused and wander onto A1A."

"Oh, my gosh," I said. "That's terrible."

Charlotte nodded. "It is. A lot has been done the past few years to prevent this, but we have to keep our light to a minimum on the beach, so we carry special flashlights with a red light. This enables us to see the mother turtles and babies when they hatch, but it doesn't disorient them. Are you planning to stay awhile and patrol with us?"

I looked at my mother.

"It's up to Isabelle," she said softly.

"Yes. Definitely." I felt like I was about to embark on a unique experience.

And it was.

We joined the others walking the beach, staying quiet and keeping an eye on the ocean. Any conversation I heard was soft and limited. I had lost track of time as I walked beside my mother and allowed myself to absorb the night sky, the water, and the energy that surrounded me. My mind wandered to the information she had shared with me, and I felt like I was in a state of suspended animation—unsure whether to let go and move forward or to grip the hurt tighter and hold on.

I wasn't sure how long we had been walking the beach when my mother touched my arm and pointed as she increased her pace.

"I think we have a female coming to nest," she whispered, and we both followed Charlotte, who was in the lead.

We joined the small semicircle of volunteers, our eyes glued to the huge sea turtle emerging from the water a short distance away. She made her way up the sand, leaving large tracks behind her that resembled those of a small truck. When she finally found what she thought was a good spot, she got to work. Using her front flippers, she began to dig out what my mother whispered was a body pit. I was intrigued with the amount of work that the preparation took. After some time she began using her hind flippers to dig.

My mother leaned toward my ear and whispered, "She's digging the egg cavity now to deposit her eggs," and I nodded, totally captivated with what I was witnessing.

We then watched as she deposited her eggs and proceeded to work just as hard using her hind flippers to cover the nest with sand. The entire process lasted a few hours, but it was as if time stood still as I stood there entranced by all of it.

The female sea turtle then headed back to the shore and into the ocean while the other volunteers got to work putting poles into the ground, attaching survey tape and sectioning off the nest area for protection.

The three of us walked away from the area and I shook my head.

"That was utterly amazing," I said. "When will the mother be back to take care of the eggs?"

"Oh, she won't," Charlotte said. "Her job is finished. She drops the eggs and the hatchlings have to fend for themselves."

I felt an ache in my heart. "Oh. She'll never come back to check on them?" I wasn't liking the end to this amazing process.

Charlotte shook her head. "No, but she will eventually come back to this exact beach to nest again. Studies show that it has to do with the magnetic field of the earth—that's how they always return to the same beach to nest."

I nodded and mumbled, "Hmm," as I realized there seemed to be a connection between the mother sea turtle and my own mother. No, she hadn't dumped me before I was born. And yes, she had been with me for fifteen years of my life. But like the mother sea turtle, when she left, she left me with the feeling she had never looked back—until now.

And like the sea turtle mother, my mother was now working at building a nest.

Chapter 31

By the time I had arrived home it was after three, and I had fallen into bed fully dressed.

My alarm went off at six and I groaned as I reached over to silence it. The emotional impact of the night before washed over me. My first thought was to call Yarrow and fake a sickness, but then I remembered she was doing me a favor the following day by doing the deliveries herself so I could drive to Atlanta with Chadwick.

Forcing myself out of bed, I stripped out of my clothes and headed to the shower. I didn't bother to take the time to blow-dry or style my hair, and applying makeup was out of the question. I just wanted to fulfill my duty with the delivery of coffee and muffins and return to my cozy bed.

Yarrow looked up when I walked into the tea shop.

"Tough night?" she said.

"You could say that," I told her, then grabbed the basket and headed out.

When I returned to the tea shop a few hours later to drop off the empty basket, Yarrow was busy with customers. I gave her a nod and walked across the garden to Koi House.

I must have gotten a second wind because I made myself a cup of tea and dialed Petra's number.

"Holy shit," she said, after I related the events of the night before. "That was some night you had."

"Yup, it was. In more ways than one. Did you know that my mother was an alcoholic? Had your mother ever said anything to you?"

"No. I had no idea, but you know . . . I do seem to remember there was a time shortly before your mother left that my mother was worried about her. She was backing out of lunches and plans they had made. But I don't think my mother considered she was drinking. She was concerned that maybe your mom was ill."

I let out a sarcastic chuckle. "Hmm, well, I guess she was. Some people feel that alcoholism is a disease."

"Wow, so she hasn't had liquor for all these years? You really have to give her credit."

When I remained silent, Petra said, "How did the two of you leave everything? Any change in your relationship?"

"I honestly don't know. I just don't know what to think. I mean, sure, it's easy now for her to tell me her side of the story, but my father isn't here to debate it or tell a different version."

There was a pause on the line before Petra said, "Isabelle, listen. I don't want to get you mad . . . and I know you adored your father . . . but did you ever think that maybe he told you what *he* wanted you to think?"

"Are you saying he lied to me?"

"No, that isn't what I'm saying. But many times we're told something because the person telling us truly thinks it's the truth and that's the way it happened. But don't forget . . . all of us have defense mechanisms. I think drinking was your mother's way of coping, but she told you she left to protect you. Maybe your father did the same thing. He wanted to shield you from your mother. Maybe he thought you'd be better off without her in your life."

"But it wasn't up to *him* to make that decision."

"Exactly," Petra said, and I heard the sadness in her voice.

My mind had been racing all afternoon with thoughts of my parents, myself, and where I was headed. I'd spoken to Chadwick briefly, explained it had been a late night, and promised to give him all the details when he picked me up the next morning. Another thing I loved about him: he gave me room to breathe and didn't press me for answers.

I curled up on the sofa with a cup of tea and realized that my father had been the opposite of that. Especially with my mother. A kid doesn't pay much attention to those things, but as an adult they suddenly become clear. Looking back, I recalled that my mother could never seem to measure up to my father's standards. Whether it was her cooking, the way she looked, what she wore, what she said. And

I now remembered snippets of unkind comments he would make to her. I couldn't help but wonder if that was why I tried extra hard—to avoid those barbs being directed at me. I also wondered if that was why I was drawn to Roger. He never intimidated me or demanded more than I was able to give.

I let out a deep sigh and suddenly came to understand that living in that type of environment—where no matter what you did or said, it was never good enough—must be a living hell. And while it was no excuse to leave your child behind, I was coming to understand the reasons behind my mother's behavior.

Thinking about this made me recall one of my psychology courses in college. I had read that all behavior has a reason. It doesn't always make sense or justify certain actions, but it does make one stop and at least try to figure out why a person acts or behaves the way they do.

I had skipped both breakfast and lunch and by five I was starved. I didn't feel like preparing a full dinner so I opted for canned soup and a grilled cheese sandwich. I had just finished eating when Haley called.

"Hey, sweetie, how's it going?" As soon as I said the words, a deep sense of loneliness came over me. My daughter had only been gone two days and already I missed her terribly.

"Really good," she said, and I could hear the happiness in her voice. "Dad and I are having a great time and I adore Gordon. He's so funny and has a super sense of humor. We've been busy getting everything ready for the wedding Friday evening."

I smiled. When Roger found out that Haley could come in April and stay a week during spring break, he and Gordon set about to plan their wedding while she was there.

"Oh, good. I bet you're enjoying that."

"I am. I went with them to the park where the ceremony will take place, and it will be so nice. They've hired a company to have it all decorated and you should see the swanky hotel where the reception will be. The room overlooks a lake and it's going to be really cool."

I smiled again at my daughter's happiness.

"Oh, and guess what? They said I could sit with them at the head table and I get to say something and toast them."

"I'm impressed," I said. "I know you'll do a good job. Is it a large group attending?"

"About a hundred people. I can't get over how many friends they have, and they've invited colleagues at the television studio. Somebody is going to film the ceremony and reception for them too."

"All of it sounds wonderful. And you like their house?"

"I love it. Oh, and I almost forgot . . . they have a new kitten. Her name is Irma and I just adore her. She's so sweet and she's been sleeping with me since I got here."

It was obvious that my daughter was in her glory.

I laughed again. "I'm so happy for all of you, Haley."

"Oh, how'd it go last night with Nana? Is everything okay there?"

"Yeah. Yeah, it went okay. We had a long talk . . . and well . . . we'll see what happens."

"Oh, good. Okay, I need to go. Dad and Gordon are taking me out for dinner. I'll give you a call in a couple days. Love you, Mom."

"Love you too, and give my best to your dad and Gordon," I said, before hanging up.

I cleaned up the kitchen, did a little bit of knitting, and by seven I could barely keep my eyes open. I definitely did not function well on only three hours of sleep. So I put on my jammies, grabbed the book I was reading, and headed to bed.

I was having a hard time focusing on the book because my mind kept wandering and I recalled my last dream about Emmalyn. She had said something about unraveling and going back. That sometimes we just had to take something apart and then start all over.

I couldn't help but apply this idea to my mother and me. I was smart enough to know that I couldn't go back. That I could never recapture those lost years with my mother. They were gone. Forever. But if I decided to start over with her—what would I have? Could we possibly build a decent mother-daughter relationship? Would she tire of living here and take off again? Would I be exposing myself to a possible repeat of hurt? All of it was a huge risk. I knew that. And I was pretty sure that was why I had no answers. Because I wasn't entirely sure it was worth taking that risk.

Chapter 32

I had dozed off the night before by eight o'clock and slept straight through till six. Yes, I had been exhausted, but I think stress factored into my fatigue too. And the entire situation with my mother was notching up my stress level. All the more reason I was looking forward to getting away with Chadwick overnight.

By the time he pulled up in my driveway promptly at ten, I was on the porch, my overnight bag beside me, ready to bask in the company of Chadwick Price.

"Hey, beautiful," he called, getting out of the car and walking toward me to take my bag.

"Good morning," I said, as he leaned in for a kiss.

"Feel more rested today?"

I nodded as he placed my bag in the trunk.

"Yes, much better." I slid into the passenger seat and smiled as he backed the car out of the driveway.

He patted my knee and returned my smile. "Good. Well, we'll be at my parents' house before six."

He headed toward I-95 and all of a sudden I felt nervous about meeting Virginia and Austin Price.

"What are they like?" I asked.

"My parents? Oh, I think they're pretty likable people. And they can't help but like you."

I wasn't sure why he was so certain about that.

"So," he said, "you had quite a long night with your mother."

"I did." I proceeded to bring him up to speed and when I finished, he remained silent.

"No comment?" I asked.

"I'm not sure I have a right to comment. This is between you and your mother. How do *you* feel about it? Do you think there's a chance to have a relationship?"

I shrugged. "I don't know. I think I'm still trying to absorb everything she told me. One thing I don't understand is why my father wouldn't tell me the truth about her drinking. Or why he kept her letters from me."

"Well, you said your mother felt she was protecting you by leaving. Maybe your father did the same thing. He might have thought it was better to keep you to himself."

Petra had said pretty much the same thing. "So you think he was the one being selfish?"

"I didn't say that. I'm just saying that generally people do the best they can. They don't mean to intentionally hurt somebody, but that's what often happens when information is withheld."

I nodded. "Yeah, I'm annoyed that he didn't tell me everything and then let me decide."

"He may have also felt somewhat responsible for your mother leaving. He knew how angry you were with her and maybe he didn't want to ruin what you shared with him."

I hadn't thought of that. "Could be," I said.

"What did you think of the sea turtles? You were fortunate you got to see one of the females making her nest."

"It was amazing. I'm glad my mother took me with her."

"It's a wonderful organization, protecting those sea turtles. I joined a few years ago."

I shifted in my seat to look at him. "Really? I didn't know you belonged. Have you seen the hatchlings come out of the nest?"

"I have. It's pretty awesome. The incubation period is around sixty days, so if she dropped her eggs the other night, that nest will have the hatchlings heading to the water around mid-June. If you'd like to see, you can go with me."

"Oh, I'd love it," I told him. Having watched the mother work to build the nest, drop the eggs, and then return to the ocean, I felt like I had a vested interest in those hatchlings. "Yes, definitely."

He reached over and gave my hand a squeeze. "Good. It's a date."

I was glad that he'd changed the subject from my mother to other topics. I needed time to put everything I had learned aside, take a breath, and figure out exactly what I wanted. Because at the moment I wasn't at all sure if I even wanted things to change with my mother.

* * *

After we stopped for lunch off the interstate, Chadwick picked up I-75 and we continued north to Atlanta.

"A little over three hours," he said, "and we'll be there. My parents' home is just outside the city limits."

"Oh, you live on a plantation," I said, joking with him.

"Not anymore. Most of the land has been sold off over the years."

Was he serious? I had a feeling he was.

"So the homestead has been in your family for a long time?"

"Since before the Civil War, yes."

"I was only kidding with you. But you're serious. Why haven't you said anything about this?"

He seemed surprised that it appeared to bother me.

"I didn't think it was important. Does it make a difference? With us?"

"No," I hastened to say, although I wasn't really sure. "No. Of course not. It's just that . . ."

I wasn't really sure what I felt or thought. I knew Chadwick certainly hadn't had a deprived childhood, but he grew up on a plantation? Now I wished I'd taken more interest in what I packed. God, they probably dressed for dinner.

He patted my knee and left his hand there. "You have nothing to worry about. Really."

"And I imagine you have servants too?" I said, again joking.

"Only Mary. She's an all-around cook and housekeeper. She's been with us since I was small. My mother doesn't allow her to do any of the heavy cleaning anymore. Mary's in her mid-eighties now. So my mother hired a cleaning company."

This was beginning to sound like *Downton Abbey*. If I hadn't been nervous before I certainly was now.

"Here we are," he said a few hours later. "Home, sweet home."

He had pulled onto a long road covered with a canopy of live oaks, but I didn't see a house immediately. Then I saw a huge, three story, red brick structure at the end with white columns and a portico.

Okay, maybe not quite as large as Downton Abbey. But close. And he referred to it as "home, sweet home"? Clearly, I had not been prepared for this.

Chadwick parked in the circular driveway, leaned over and kissed me.

"All set?" he asked.

I nodded. "Yeah."

I almost expected liveried footmen to appear to take our luggage, but we each carried our bags to the front door, which was flung open by a tall, thin black woman wearing a black dress and white apron.

"Master Chadwick," she said and there was no denying the excitement in her voice. "It's so good to see you."

Chadwick smiled and placed a kiss on her cheek. "And Miss Mary, it's always good to see you. I want you to meet my friend, Isabelle Wainwright."

She extended her hand and I was surprised at how strong her grip was.

"Miss Isabelle, welcome."

I knew immediately that Mary was one of those people you meet and instantly know you like.

"Thank you. It's so nice to meet you."

Chadwick took my suitcase and deposited both bags at the bottom of an enormous, swirling staircase. He shook a finger at Mary.

"You leave those right there, hear? We'll bring them upstairs later."

Mary let out a burst of laughter and nodded. "If you say so. Your parents are out back on the patio."

"Thanks," he said, taking my hand. As we walked through the house I tried to take in glimpses of rooms, furniture, framed paintings, and photos on the walls.

We emerged through a set of French doors that took up an entire wall onto a huge brick patio. Big tubs of various plants and bright flowers were placed around the perimeter. The focal point was a large, pristine, aqua pool at the far end.

"Ah, you're here," I heard a deep masculine voice say and turned to see a white-haired man rise from a chair and walk toward us. Tall and fit, he wore khaki slacks, polo shirt, and deck shoes.

"Dad, how are you?"

Neither man showed embarrassment as they first clasped hands and then embraced in a bear hug.

"I'd like you to meet Isabelle."

I got the same warm hand clasp followed by a hug.

"We've heard so much about you. It's nice to finally meet you."

"Same here, Mr. Price," I said, surprised by such a warm welcome.

He shook his head. "No, no. Call me Austin."

"Oh, they're here."

Coming out of the house carrying a tray with pitcher and glasses was a tall, thin woman who appeared to be around my mother's age. Her salt-and-pepper hair was cut in a short and chic style. She wore capri pants, tunic top, and sandals. Maybe they didn't dress for dinner in this house after all.

Chadwick went to take the tray from her, kissed her cheek, and placed the tray on the large round table as she walked toward me, both hands extended.

"I'm Ginnie," she said, a huge smile covering her face as she clasped my hands. "And you're every bit as pretty as Chadwick said."

I heard a definite southern accent in his mother's voice.

"Isabelle," I said. "It's so nice to meet you, and thank you for inviting me." I could feel a blush creeping up my neck at her compliment.

"Oh, it's our pleasure. I hope you like martinis. I just made a pitcher for us. We'll have a drink before Austin grills the steaks."

"Sounds good," I replied and followed them to the table.

I was aware of how Chadwick pushed two of the chairs closer together, took my hand and indicated I should sit beside him.

"Did you have a good drive?" his father asked as he filled glasses from the pitcher.

"We did," Chadwick said and leaned forward to take a glass, which he passed to me before taking his own.

"Well, here's to good health," Austin said, raising his martini glass in my direction. "And to meeting Isabelle."

I smiled and nodded before taking a sip.

"So tell us about yourself," Ginnie said. "Chadwick tells me you have a lovely daughter. She's how old?"

I smiled and felt good that he thought enough of my daughter to mention her to his parents.

"Yes, Haley. She turns fifteen in September. She's actually up here in Atlanta for the week, visiting her father." I wasn't sure what Chadwick might have told his parents about Roger, so I refrained from mentioning the wedding.

"Oh, that's nice," Ginnie said. "After a divorce, it's important that the children stay in touch with both parents."

I thought of my own situation, but again I said nothing and only nodded.

"Chadwick told us that your mother has relocated to Ormond Beach," his father said. "Has she settled in there?"

I wasn't sure what Chadwick had told them about this situation either, so I only said, "Yes. She seems to like it a lot. She's keeping very busy with social events and making new friends."

It was becoming obvious to me that over the course of the past few months my name had been the topic of conversation a number of times in this household.

Chadwick and his father then began discussing general business matters as Ginnie and I listened. Any nervousness I might have felt earlier had quickly evaporated. Ginnie and Austin Price might be wealthy and prominent citizens of their community, but they were down to earth and lacked any pretense.

"Miss Ginnie, I'm sorry to interrupt. But do you need anything?"

We looked to where Mary was standing in the doorway.

"No," Ginnie replied, standing up. She gave the older woman a hug and I heard her say, "As a matter of fact, we'll be just fine, Mary. You take the rest of the evening off."

"If you're sure, Miss Ginnie."

"I'm positive. You go relax."

Ginnie returned to the table and shot me a smile. "Mary has been with us since my boys were little and her mother and grandmother before her were with my family."

"She seems so sweet," I said.

"Oh, she is. She's getting up there in age, though. She turns eighty-five on her next birthday."

"Gosh, she certainly doesn't look it," I said, genuinely surprised.

"I know, but she has a few health problems now and I have to force her to slow down."

"Does she live nearby?" I asked.

"Oh, she lives here with us," Austin said. "She had lived with her daughter, but she passed away about ten years ago, so we insisted she stay here. She has her own little suite of bedroom and sitting room upstairs."

"The stairs were getting difficult for her," Ginnie said. "So we had a small elevator installed."

Yup, these people were not the usual type you thought of when you heard the word *wealthy*.

Austin topped off our glasses and said, "Well, I'm going to fire up the grill. How do you like your steak, Isabelle?"

"Medium, please."

Ginnie also stood up. "Isabelle, if you wouldn't mind, could you help me set the table out here? I have scalloped potatoes in the oven and a salad in the fridge, so we can bring those out too."

"My pleasure," I said, getting up to follow her into the kitchen.

I had not given much thought beforehand to Chadwick's parents. But after spending an hour in their company, I knew they were two people I liked a lot. They were the type of people I welcomed into my life.

Chapter 33

Iawoke the next morning and saw that it was just beginning to get light outside. I lay there recalling the pleasant evening I had spent with Chadwick and his parents.

After a delicious dinner, I helped Ginnie clean up while Chadwick and his father enjoyed a cigar together. I hadn't even known that Chadwick smoked cigars, but watching father and son sharing this male ritual made me feel warm and fuzzy.

Then the four of us enjoyed coffee and delicious peach cobbler, which I was told had been made by Mary earlier in the day. And then Austin's father surprised me by asking if I enjoyed Scrabble. I hadn't played a board game since I was a child, but shortly into the game, I could see that this was a favorite family pastime in the Price household.

By the time Chadwick and I headed upstairs, it was close to midnight. Our rooms were on the second floor, at opposite ends of the hall. He walked me to my room, opened the door, gently pushed me against the wall and kissed me. One of his special long, passionate kisses. It crossed my mind that he would reach for my hand and lead me to the huge bed. But he did not.

When we stopped kissing, both of us breathing heavily, he whispered in my ear, "I really want to share that bed with you. And I really want you. But I don't want our first time to be here. I want it to be special."

At that moment I hadn't been thinking about *special*. I was thinking pure lust, but I nodded and said, "Okay," surprised by my own level of desire.

I rolled over in bed and smiled. This bed might be empty but I had a feeling it wouldn't be much longer before Chadwick satisfied that desire.

By the time I had showered, dressed, and repacked my bag, it wasn't quite seven. I wasn't sure if I should venture downstairs alone or wait to be summoned. Just then there was a soft knock on the door and Chadwick walked in.

"Good morning, beautiful," he said, pulling me into his arms. "I wasn't sure if you'd be up. Sleep okay?"

"Yes, I did. Very well."

"I smelled the aroma of coffee and cooking—are you ready for breakfast?"

"Sounds good," I said, taking his hand and walking out to the hallway.

As we descended the staircase, I paused to glance at the framed photos lining the wall.

"Your family heritage?" I asked.

Chadwick smiled. "Yeah. But I want to show you one in particular."

We walked down a few more steps and he pointed to a large professional portrait. Ginnie and Austin were sitting on a stone bench with the Price home behind them. On one side Chadwick squatted next to his mother and a very good looking fellow was in the same position next to Austin.

"That was taken a few months before my brother, Aaron, passed away," Chadwick explained.

"You said it was cancer?"

He nodded.

"Gosh, he looks so healthy here," I said. "And so young."

Chadwick nodded again. "Yes, it was very fast, which was good for Aaron but tough on the rest of us. He had just turned thirty—only two years older than I was."

"I'm sorry," I said, touching his arm.

We continued down the staircase and walked into the kitchen to find Ginnie and Austin canoodling. She was pouring juice into a glass and he stood behind her, arms around her waist, nuzzling her neck. They both looked up but didn't pull apart in embarrassment.

"Good morning," Austin said. "Did you both sleep well?"

"Very well," I said, smiling at their uninhibited display of affection.

Mary had her back to us and was busy preparing something on the stainless steel stove.

She turned around. "I have some of my famous cheese grits here. And your mother is making omelets."

"Sounds wonderful," Chadwick said, and I nodded.

He poured each of us a mug of coffee, which we took out to the patio. It was a gorgeous April morning with the scent of spring flowers in the air.

"Are you sure you don't mind staying here while I go into the office with my dad for that meeting?" he asked.

"Of course not," I assured him. "I brought my knitting and I'll just stay out here and enjoy the morning."

"We should be back by eleven and then we can leave right away so we'll be back in Ormond Beach before seven."

"That's great."

Following a delicious breakfast, Chadwick left with his father and Ginnie allowed me to assist with the cleanup. We then spent the next few hours on the patio getting to know each other. There was no doubt that Ginnie had been brought up with southern gentility and money, but I was impressed with how she had chosen to put her wealth to the advantage of others. She told me about various fundraisers held by her and Austin to support the poor, education, and the arts. I knew that Chadwick did the very same thing in our area, and he was proof that the apple had not fallen very far from the tree.

By the time Chadwick returned, I felt as if I'd known Ginnie Austin forever and I liked her a lot.

Amid hugs and good-byes and promises to visit again soon, we headed outside to Chadwick's car with his parents following.

"And next time," Austin said, "you be sure to bring your daughter with you. We'd love to meet Haley."

We were both quiet as Chadwick pulled the car onto I-75 and we headed south.

After a few minutes, he said, "So did you like them?"

"I adored them. They're both delightful and made me feel so welcome."

"Good," he said, reaching for my hand. "Because they felt the same way about you."

We made small talk during most of the drive, and as we approached Jacksonville, Chadwick said, "I want to ask you something and I will understand if you say no."

I shifted in my seat to better see his face, which looked serious. "What is it?"

"Well, I know Haley is gone until Sunday evening. So . . . I was wondering if maybe . . . you'd like to spend the next few nights at my house."

This was a definite invitation to take our relationship to the next level.

Without hesitating, I said, "I like your idea."

"So this is a yes?"

"This is a definite yes."

A huge smile covered his face. "Good. I was hoping you'd say that. Why don't we pull off the highway and grab a burger and then I'll drop you at your house so you can repack that overnight bag? I'll come back to get you in about an hour."

"Sounds like a plan," I said as butterflies fluttered in my stomach.

I walked into Koi House and smiled. In three short months my life had done a complete turnaround.

I poured myself a glass of ice water and took it with me upstairs. I emptied out the dirty clothes from my bag and placed them in the hamper and then began to open bureau drawers, refilling the bag with clean items. I spied the tissue paper–wrapped lingerie from Victoria's Secret and smiled.

"Oh, yeah," I said out loud. "I think it's time to christen you."

I made a dash to the shower and before putting on the sexy bra and panties, I smoothed a fragrant verbena-scented lotion over my body.

By the time Chadwick arrived an hour later, my hair had been restyled, makeup applied, my newly packed overnight bag filled— and my Victoria's Secret underwear was hidden beneath my sundress. Ready to make its debut.

Chapter 34

Chadwick unlocked the door and I stepped inside to hear the soft strains of Andrea Bocelli fill the air. I looked straight ahead and saw that cushions had been arranged on the floor in front of the sofa and a tripod stood nearby holding an ice bucket containing a bottle of champagne.

He took my hand and drew me into the room. In the twilight I could now see the fire pit on the patio had been lit and red rose petals covered the floor cushions.

This was pure romance and something I had never experienced before.

Chadwick led me to the cushions and pulled me into an embrace.

"We have the entire night," he whispered in my ear before kissing me.

When we broke apart, he said, "Make yourself comfortable. Champagne?"

I nodded as I sat on one of the cushions and leaned back against the sofa.

Looking up at his handsome face, I said, "Absolutely."

Chadwick popped the cork, filled two flutes, and came to join me.

Touching the rim of my glass, he said, "Here's to us, Isabelle. To all our tomorrows, and whatever they might bring."

"To us," I whispered and let out a sigh.

After taking a sip, he put his arm around me and I snuggled against his chest.

"Do you remember the day we met last summer?" he asked.

"Of course. I was with Chloe having lunch at LuLu's."

"You need to know," he said. "That moment I saw you . . . that

very first moment . . . as soon as my eyes met yours? I knew. I knew
we had something very special between us. At the time I had no idea
where it would lead. If anywhere. I knew you were returning to Atlanta and I might never see you again, but I also knew I had never
met anybody like you."

I sat up straighter to look at him. "You met me for a few minutes
and you knew all this?"

He nodded. "Yeah. I guess it's true what they say. The heart
knows. It just knows."

I thought back to that afternoon and I nodded too. "Yeah, you
could be right. I had a lot going on in my life at the time and a lot
more followed. I did think of you a few times but I wasn't even sure
we'd see each other again. But in early February when I met you in
that rainy parking lot . . . I felt something. I didn't want to admit it.
But it was there."

He leaned toward me and his lips met mine. I felt him slip the
straps of my sundress off my shoulders. He broke the kiss only long
enough to remove my dress, and somewhere in the back of my mind
I was very grateful that Petra had dragged me on that shopping spree.

I heard him whisper, "You're so beautiful," his voice husky with
desire. He reached to touch my lingerie. "Very nice."

We continued kissing and touching and I marveled at the inti-
macy we shared.

When I wasn't sure I could hold on much longer, I heard him say,
"I want you. I want you, Isabelle."

I shifted so he could position himself on top of me, looked into
his eyes, and said, "I want you too. God, I want you, Chadwick."

I woke at some point during the night curled up in Chadwick's
arms. We were still on the floor cushions. The house was silent and
the fire pit had died out. By the moonlight streaming into the room I
could see Chadwick sleeping beside me and I let out a deep sigh.

What I had shared with him I had never shared with anybody else.
Despite romance stories and films, I hadn't even been sure it was
possible to feel such a connection with another person. But Chadwick had proved to me that it was entirely possible. I had been amazed
at how knowledgeable he had been with my body. Almost as if he
knew it better than I did. The words *and they became one* floated into

my head. Because that's exactly what had happened. I felt like I was a part of Chadwick Price in every way possible.

I recalled how he had said I love you over and over and when I repeated those words back to him, they came from my soul.

I felt Chadwick stir. His eyes opened and he smiled when he saw me staring at him.

"Hey, beautiful. Have you been awake long?"

I shook my head and snuggled back into his chest. "No. Just a few minutes."

I felt his hand stroking the side of my face. "I love you, Isabelle."

"I love you too."

With his words ringing in my head and his body connected to mine, I fell back to sleep.

When I woke again, morning light was filtering into the room. I turned my head and saw that Chadwick was now staring at me, and I smiled.

"Good morning," I said.

"Good morning. Did you sleep okay?"

"The best." And I had.

And then I thought of something. "Oh, damn," I said.

Chadwick shifted and leaned on an elbow looking down at me. "What's wrong?"

"What time is it? I totally forgot that I have to do the coffee and muffin deliveries."

"Not a problem," he said, standing up and reaching down for my hand.

When I stood beside him, he nuzzled my neck and said, "You hit the shower and I'll get the coffee and breakfast going."

"I don't want to leave you." I felt a pout forming on my face.

He laughed. "And I don't want you to leave. As soon as you finish, come back here. I'll make it worth your while."

I smiled. "Promise?"

He laughed again. "Oh, yeah. I promise."

Yarrow's head shot up when I walked into the tea shop just after seven.

"You got back from Atlanta okay?" she asked.

"Yes. It was a great trip and I loved Chadwick's parents."

I saw her scrutinizing my face.

"Something wrong?" I said.

"No. You just look different. Really good. You're glowing. That must have been one special trip," she said, and I caught the wink she sent me.

"Hmm, yeah. It was." That was all I said before reaching for the basket and heading out.

Four hours later I was back at Chadwick's house and we were on the patio enjoying a late-morning cup of coffee.

I gazed out at the Halifax River and smiled. Sitting here beside him on the lounge, sipping coffee and conversing seemed so natural. As if we'd been doing this forever.

"I missed you," he said, reaching for my hand. "While you were gone."

I smiled. "I missed you too."

"I don't want to pressure you, but where do you think we'll go from here, Isabelle?"

I hadn't given that any thought. "I don't know. What do you mean?"

"At the very least . . . I'd like to know that we have a commitment to each other. But I'm not sure if you'd like to date other people."

After what we had shared last night? Was he crazy?

"Absolutely not," I said. "I love you, Chadwick. I don't want anybody else."

He stood up and pulled me up beside him. Placing his hands on my shoulders, he said, "Good. I was hoping you'd say that."

We shared a deep, passionate kiss and when he pulled away, he said, "Shall we try the bedroom this time?"

The next few days flew by in a blur. We had lengthy conversations about everything from family to books and films to politics. I loved talking with Chadwick. Not only was he interesting and well informed, but he was interested in my point of view and how I felt. We cooked together, shared meals, and made love when the mood hit us. We even had a few games of Scrabble Friday evening while we sipped wine—before we ended up back in the bedroom.

By Sunday morning I dreaded all of it coming to an end and returning to my real world. The world of raising my daughter, finding a permanent place for us to live, finding a decent job, and dealing with my mother.

I had been exceptionally quiet over breakfast, and while we were cleaning up, Chadwick came to put his arms around me and kissed the top of my head.

"What's wrong?" he said.

He had proved to me over the past few days how well he knew me. He seemed to have the uncanny ability to sense my moods and my emotions.

"I already miss you. I haven't even left yet and . . . I miss you."

He nodded. "I know the feeling."

He took my hand and led me to the sofa.

"Okay. So how can we fix this?"

I shrugged. I had never been known for my problem solving abilities.

He let out a deep sigh. "Well, I want . . . no, I *need* you to know that I would love it if you would move in here with me."

When I remained silent, he said, "Right. I'm not sure that's the wisest idea since you have a fourteen-year-old daughter."

That's what had been nagging at me. "I'm glad you understand, and yes, if not for Haley, I wouldn't hesitate. I'm not a prude, but . . . I just don't feel that's a great example to send to a teenager. If she was younger, it would be easier. But she's at a tough age."

"And I know that. So . . . here's what we're going to do. We will be together as much as our schedules allow. I think Haley likes me and I think she'll be fine with that. But we love each other and we want to share that love. So we'll just have to get creative."

"Creative?"

"Yeah, like afternoon delights when Haley is involved with other things. She sometimes spends the night at Mavis Anne's or your mother's. We can take advantage of that."

"Hmm," I said. "That'll work, I guess."

"No, it's not perfect. Far from it. You're going to be busy over the next month with Chloe's wedding, running the yarn shop while Chloe and Mavis Anne are gone, and I understand that. So how about if we plan to be together as much as we can during this time and then in about eight weeks, in mid-June, we reassess the situation?"

I felt a smile cross my face. "Yes. I like that idea. Very much. But I have a question."

"What is it?"

"Will you go with me this evening to Jacksonville to pick up Haley at the airport?"

"Only if you'll get creative with me over the next few hours," he replied.

And my smile increased.

Chapter 35

By the end of the following week I was convinced that all of my stars were in alignment. Haley had seemed happy that Chadwick was with me when we picked her up at the airport. She was overflowing with excitement about the details of her father's wedding. My mother had phoned me a few times but mostly in reference to Haley. It didn't escape me that she could have texted Haley directly, but my world was quite rosy at the moment and I overlooked it. I had had Chadwick to dinner the evening before and Haley had gone to Barnes and Noble with Tina and Brenda, so we took full advantage of our privacy.

I walked into the yarn shop Friday afternoon to find the table full of our regular knitters.

"Oh, people do crazy things when it's a full moon," I heard Louise say.

"Hey, Isabelle," Chloe said. "Come join us."

"I finished my scarf and wanted to show you guys."

I removed the scarf from my bag and held it up.

"Gorgeous," Fay said. "I have a few more rows and mine will be done."

"I love it." Mavis Anne held up the scarf she'd knitted with a variegated yarn. "I do think I prefer the solid color better, though."

"Everybody's doing a wonderful job," Chloe said. "I'm glad you're enjoying the pattern so much."

"What's this about a full moon?" I asked.

Louise laughed. "Well, it's a full moon tonight and people can really do wacky things then."

Mavis Anne shook her head. "Oh, sure, you don't believe that my house has energy and a soul, but you believe the moon affects people?"

"That's different," Louise argued.

"Not one bit different," Mavis Anne retorted.

"Girls," Chloe said, raising a hand in the air. "Play nice. We're all entitled to our own opinions and beliefs."

"Grace is arriving on Sunday, right?" I asked Chloe, making an attempt to change the subject.

"Yes." A smile crossed her face. "Gosh, I can't wait to see her and Lucas and Solange."

"Makes it nice that they're arriving a week before the wedding," Mavis Anne said. "It'll give you a chance to visit and catch up."

Chloe nodded. "I know. They're going to take two nights during the week to spend in Cedar Key so Grace can visit everybody there. I wasn't sure if we should invite all our friends there to the wedding but Grace said we had planned a small wedding and that's what we should stick to. Besides, they don't know Henry and were really more Grace's friends than mine."

"Makes sense to me," Mavis Anne said. "Where's Haley this afternoon?"

"Off with my mother. She had errands to do and Haley went with her. Any more baby news?" I asked Chloe.

"No. Treva is doing great. I told her she'd better not think about having my first grandchild until I'm back from Hawaii."

I laughed. "Oh, and I'm sure she'll comply with that."

I left the yarn shop just after five and headed back to Koi House.

I had just walked in when the phone rang. I answered to hear Brenda's voice.

"How are you?" I asked. I hadn't heard from her in a couple weeks.

"I'm really good, Isabelle. That's what I wanted to share with you. Tina and I are going to be moving."

My heart fell at the thought of my daughter losing her best friend.

"Are you leaving the area?" I asked.

I heard her laughter come across the line. "No. No. But I've managed to save enough money and I've gotten a nice raise at work. We're going to be moving into a two-bedroom, two-bath condo here in Ormond Beach."

I smiled and shared her happiness. "Oh, Brenda. That's wonderful news. I'm so happy for you and Tina."

"Thank you. We're going shopping tomorrow for furniture. Nothing elaborate, but enough to get us started. We're moving in June first."

"If there's anything I can do, please let me know. Haley and I would be more than happy to help."

Brenda laughed. "Haley already offered your services. Tina called her earlier to tell her the news. Well, I won't keep you. I just wanted you to know. When I get settled in, we'll have you over for a little impromptu house warming."

"Absolutely," I said, hanging up with a smile on my face.

Brenda Sanchez was so deserving of a break. She'd been through hell, clawed her way back, and had worked hard. It was nice to see good things happening to good people.

I had just finished putting a casserole into the oven for dinner when I heard Haley come in the back door. I turned around to see that my mother was with her. And Haley was cuddling a dog in her arms.

Of course my first words were, "What is that?" although I knew perfectly well what it was.

I heard my daughter say, "Mom, I need to talk to you," and I knew it wasn't going to be pleasant.

"Why do you have that dog?"

Haley clutched the dog in her arms. A little ball of fluff that looked like there was some terrier in its heritage.

"Nana and I stopped by the rescue place. Her owner died and they were going to put Ginger to sleep tomorrow."

I knew she was playing on my sympathy but the dog's demise did sound harsh.

"And I suppose this was your idea?" I said to my mother.

"Well . . . I had only planned to pop by there to drop off some food I was donating. And one of the assistants told us about Ginger. It's so sad to think just because her owner died she has to die too."

"So why didn't *you* take her?" I retorted.

"Because I took her brother, Fred."

"Oh." I didn't have a comeback for that.

"Can she stay, Mom? She's eight months old and housebroken. You know I'll take care of her. You won't have to do anything. We even stopped at Petco and Nana bought Ginger some dog food, a new collar and leash."

"So where's Fred?" I asked, finally getting the connection between the two names.

"I'm going back to pick him up," my mother said. "I wanted to get Haley situated first."

Sure, I thought. *Put this dog's life in my hands.* If I said no, it was as good as signing her death warrant. And if I said yes, I had the irrational feeling that my mother would have won. What exactly she had won I wasn't sure.

Refusing to commit one way or the other, I said, "Whatever."

"Does that mean I can keep her, Mom?"

I let out an exasperated sigh and shrugged. "I guess," I replied, and walked into the other room.

When I returned to the kitchen, my mother was gone and I saw Haley in the backyard with the puppy. She did look happy. Really happy. And I couldn't help but wonder if that was what pissed me off the most: the fact that my mother had upstaged me in providing that happiness. And the more I thought about it, the angrier I got.

After we finished supper, I told Haley to clean up and I'd be back shortly. She didn't question where I was going. I jumped in the car and drove to my mother's house.

She opened the door with a smile on her face, oblivious as to why I was paying her a visit.

"Come on in, Isabelle. Can I get you anything?"

"No. I just want to talk to you."

I followed her into the family room where I saw an identical replica of Ginger curled up in a soft dog bed near the sofa.

I spun around to face my mother before she could ask me to sit down.

"I'm not staying," I said. "I just want you to know . . . I don't appreciate your interfering in my daughter's life. You had no right . . . no right at all . . . allowing Haley to bring that puppy home. It wasn't up to *you* to make that decision. You forfeited your own rights as a mother thirty years ago when you walked out on me."

I saw my mother flinch and the sad expression that crossed her face, but I didn't care.

"And you can't go looking for a second chance with my daughter. It doesn't work that way. You knew I'd have to allow her to keep that dog. Otherwise, I'd be the bad guy. And I won't allow you to come between my daughter and me. So if you want to be in her life . . . and right now, I'm not so sure that's a good idea . . . you need to back off. Do you understand?"

I was ready for my mother's excuses. I was ready for her to yell and raise her voice as loudly as I had. To argue with me.

But all she did was softly say, "I'm sorry."

Without another word, I marched to the door, flung it open and headed to my car. By the time I got inside and turned the ignition key, I realized my hands were trembling.

Instead of driving home, I went to Biggby Coffee on Granada, got myself some mocha–whipped cream–flavored concoction and sat outside at one of the tables consuming calories and trying to calm down. Louise had been right—people do wacky things with a full moon.

When I felt sufficiently calm, I dialed Chadwick's number and related the episode.

"Do you want me to come and be with you?" he asked.

I didn't miss that his first concern was for me.

"No," I mumbled.

"Well, Isabelle, you were talking about getting a dog for Haley."

"Yeah, but it wasn't up to my mother to do that."

"Maybe not," he said. "But sometimes we have no control over those things. Sounds to me like it was love at first sight for your mom, Haley, and the puppies."

When I didn't respond, he said, "Maybe you need to lighten up a little with your mom. She was only trying to do the right thing."

I felt my anger flare again. "Oh? And I wasn't? So I'm the bad guy here?"

Before he had a chance to reply, I disconnected the call.

How had everything that had been going so well turned to total crap?

I sat there for at least an hour nursing the remains of my coffee and thinking.

Getting up, I tossed the container into the trash, got into my car, and headed to Petco, where I purchased a fancy pink dog bed, packets of treats, and assorted puppy toys.

Louise was definitely right. People did wacky things at a full moon.

Chapter 36

The following week flew by. Grace, Lucas, and Solange arrived from France and were staying at a nearby hotel. Chloe and Henry were busy finishing up last-minute details for the wedding, and Mavis Anne, Yarrow, and I were keeping things going at the yarn and tea shop.

I hadn't heard a word from my mother, but Mavis Anne mentioned she'd spoken to her and she was all set to work at the yarn shop the following Wednesday. I refused to think about how awkward that would be.

The only thing I cared about was that Chadwick and I were okay. I had called him back after I got home and apologized for my rudeness, and he accepted my apology.

When I had walked into the house with my offerings for Ginger, even Haley seemed to forgive my earlier words and behavior. I didn't pay much attention to the puppy but had to admit that she didn't seem to be causing any trouble. Haley assumed total responsibility for her care.

I awoke the morning of the wedding and was preparing the coffeemaker when I heard whining at my feet. Normally the puppy didn't come downstairs until Haley did. Chloe had spent the night in her old room, wanting to stick to the tradition of the bride not seeing the groom before the ceremony, so I thought maybe she was up and heading into the kitchen. I also thought she could tend to the puppy.

But the whining continued and Chloe wasn't coming.

I looked down at the pup. "You have to go out and pee, don't you?" More whining.

If she piddled on the floor it would be my own fault. So I bent down and scooped her up into my arms. I was surprised at how soft her fur was. She looked up at me with adoring eyes.

"Oh, no, you don't," I said. "I'm not won over that easily."

I carried her outside to the garden, where she promptly squatted and peed.

I was foolishly pleased that I had been correct about what she wanted. I let her sniff a little while longer and then took her back inside.

After getting my mug of coffee, I took it into the living room and settled on the sofa. Ginger had followed me and was now sitting at my feet staring at me. She let out a couple of soft woofs.

"You can't have to go back out," I said, trying to figure out what she wanted.

A minute later, she backed up, took a running leap and jumped up on the sofa, where she wasted no time curling up in my lap.

"You little stinker," I said, and felt a smile cross my face.

Again, she looked up at me with those soulful eyes. It suddenly hit me that this beautiful and sweet little puppy might not even be here if she hadn't been rescued. I felt tears stinging my eyes. I knew all too well what it felt like to be rejected. Forgotten about. And to not understand why.

I stroked the fur between her ears and then picked her up and held her close to my face.

Her tail was wagging away and her happiness was obvious.

"Okay, Ginger," I said. "I think we've bonded."

The flurry of activity continued all day at Koi House. Workmen arrived to set up a canopy in the garden area. Another crew came to arrange chairs around the pond where guests would witness the ceremony, and then the workmen put together a beautiful white trellis entwined with fresh flowers, where Chloe and Henry would stand to take their vows.

The ceremony was scheduled for five, and by late morning a catering van pulled up and the kitchen was turned over to the chef.

I walked in to hear Chloe giving them instructions.

"Everything going okay?" I asked.

"Yes, perfect. I think everything is under control. The only thing left to do is shower and dress."

"And it's too early for that. Mavis Anne just called and suggested that Haley, you, and I come over for lunch and let the workers do their thing. She said David and Clive insist."

Chloe laughed. "That might be a good idea. I'm feeling I'll only be in the way here."

We walked next door and found that lunch had been set up on the patio.

"This is so nice of you," Chloe said. "I hadn't given a thought to eating."

"Exactly," David said. "That's why Clive and I wanted to make sure all of you had lunch."

Clive came outside carrying a pitcher and began filling glasses.

"Ah, mimosas," Mavis Anne said. "The perfect late-morning beverage to toast Chloe."

When we had our glasses, she lifted hers and said, "To Chloe and Henry. I'm so very happy you found Yarrow's tea shop that afternoon. You've brought joy and happiness to all of us . . . but especially to Koi House."

Chloe nodded. "Sometimes it still seems like a dream. To think I almost didn't come to Ormond Beach at all after Gabe died. I have to feel that things really do work out exactly the way they're supposed to."

"Yeah," Haley said. "And if you hadn't come here, Mom and I wouldn't be here either."

They were both right and I was grateful that Chloe had taken that step to book Henry's condo the previous year.

"Right," Mavis Anne said. "And even though Chloe is now leaving, Koi House has the two of you to keep it filled with love."

Chloe and Henry had decided to stay at his condo for the time being. They weren't sure if they wanted to purchase a home, and the condo suited them well for space and location. As for Haley and me, I still wasn't sure where we would live permanently. And for now— Koi House was home.

Grace arrived with Solange shortly after noon to help her sister get ready.

"Okay," she said. "After you get out of the shower, I'll do your makeup and hair," she told Chloe. "It was easier for Solange and me to get ready at the hotel."

Grace looked very chic in a celery green sheath. But Solange looked like a child model out of the pages of a top fashion magazine. She wore a knee-length dress with cap sleeves. It was a shimmery gold polyester with some type of metal fiber. A slim black ribbon circled the waist and depending on how the light caught the dress, it changed from gold to black. With her chin-length dark curls, the child was absolutely stunning, and the dress made her more so.

"Oh, Solange," I said. "You look beautiful. Are you excited?"

She nodded and smiled. "Yes. Mama said I get to carry a basket of rose petals."

I laughed. I guess at five years old, one is oblivious to the allure of fashion.

Haley and I headed to my room to get ready, and an hour later we were helping each other to fasten bracelets and zip zippers.

"You look gorgeous, Mom."

"So do you," I told her.

Just thinking about the fact that it seemed like yesterday that my daughter was the age of Solange brought moisture to my eyes. The years were tumbling by much too fast.

My cell phone rang, preventing me from getting too sentimental, and I smiled to see Chadwick's name.

"Hey," I said. "Are you here?"

"Just pulled up in the driveway. How's it going?"

"Great. Haley and I are ready. I'll meet you outside."

I walked through the kitchen to see the caterers engrossed in their work.

Chadwick was on the patio waiting for me.

"You look stunning, Isabelle."

He leaned over to place a kiss on my lips.

"You look pretty handsome yourself."

And he did, wearing a light gray suit, white shirt, and charcoal gray tie.

He took my hand and led me to the pond area.

"Shall we go get seated?"

I nodded and smiled.

David and Clive had offered to seat guests and they directed us to two seats up front. A moment later I saw Chloe's son, Eli, and his wife, Treva, seated across from us and waved. From the size of her abdomen I hoped she would hold off on having the baby until Chloe returned from Hawaii.

A tall, good looking fellow was seated beside Eli. I knew this must be Chloe's other son, Mathis. Within a short time the chairs were filled with the remaining guests.

A little while later I heard strains of classical music fill the air and Solange walked toward the trellis dropping rose petals behind her. She was followed by Haley.

When they reached the end of the pond area, we turned to see Chloe enter on the arm of Henry. I don't think I'd ever seen her look as beautiful or as radiant. For a brief second I thought of my father and how odd it was to be here witnessing her marry another man. But I also knew it was right. I had no doubt that Chloe was exactly where she was supposed to be.

Chadwick reached for my hand as we sat and listened to the exchange of marriage vows.

Following the ceremony, everyone filtered out to the garden area to celebrate their union with champagne, dinner, dancing, and music.

At the end of the evening I walked Chadwick to his car.

He put his arms around me and pulled me into an embrace.

"It was a beautiful wedding," he said.

"It was. I'm so happy for Chloe."

He remained silent for a moment before whispering, "I don't want to leave you."

I nodded. "I know. I don't want you to."

He let out a deep sigh before kissing me and then saying, "I love you, Isabelle."

"I love you too," I told him.

As he pulled out of the driveway, I waved good-bye—and felt that a part of me had gone with him.

Chapter 37

By Wednesday morning things were pretty much back to normal at Koi House. No signs of the wedding remained. Chloe and Henry had flown to Hawaii on Monday and called to let me know they had arrived safely. Grace, Lucas, and Solange had flown back to France. Eli and Treva had returned to Jacksonville, and Mathis had gone back to Atlanta.

I had finished my morning deliveries and returned to the tea shop. My mother had been due to arrive about a half hour before.

I walked in to find Yarrow helping somebody in the yarn shop and another customer waiting in the tea shop to place an order.

"Where's my mother?" I called to her.

"I have no idea," she said. "But could you take that order for me?"

"Sure."

I filled the order for coffee and a muffin to go, wondering where the hell my mother was. It brought back unpleasant memories of those first few days after she left home. At first, I thought my father was joking and maybe she'd just gone away for a couple of days with a girlfriend. There had been no indication at all that my mother was planning to move out of my life.

When both customers left, I said, "Did she call you?"

Yarrow shook her head. "No. I thought maybe she'd called you."

"Not a word."

Just like thirty years before. Was this her pattern? To make a commitment and then not follow through?

"I don't know what to say." And I didn't. "I thought she wanted to help out here. That she was even looking forward to it."

Just then my cell phone rang, and I saw Florida Hospital on my caller ID. I felt my hand tremble as I touched the phone to answer.

"Yes?" I said in a voice that didn't sound like me.

"Is this Isabelle Wainwright?"

I nodded and then realized the person on the other end couldn't see me.

"Yes," I said again.

"This is the nurse in the ER at Florida Hospital. We have Iris Brunell here. Is she your mother?"

"Yes, she is. What happened?"

"I'm afraid she's been involved in a motor vehicle accident. We need you to come here as soon as possible."

When I remained silent, she said, "Do you understand?"

I answered with another question, "Is she okay?"

"You just need to get here. You were listed as next of kin. We're located on Williamson Boulevard. Do you know where that is?"

"Yes. I'm on my way."

I hung up, feeling like I was in a trance.

"My mother's been in a car accident. I have to go," I said as I headed to the door.

"Isabelle, wait," Yarrow said, grabbing my arm. "I'll take you. You shouldn't be driving."

"No. I'm fine. I'll call you."

I flew out the door to my car and headed up Granada Boulevard.

Why wouldn't the nurse tell me how my mother was? Was she dead? Years of guilt, anger, sadness, and regret washed over me. Was it too late? Was it too late to tell her that I *did* love her? That although I didn't agree with what she had done, I understood? A million thoughts raced through my mind as I speeded to the hospital, half expecting to get pulled over by a cop.

In what felt like hours, I managed to get to the hospital, found a parking spot outside of the emergency room and raced inside. I ran to the information desk.

"Iris Brunell," I said. "I'm her daughter. Where is she?"

The woman behind the window nodded. "One minute," she said, holding up a finger and picking up the phone. "A nurse will be right out," she told me when she hung up. "You can have a seat over there."

I wanted to scream. I could barely breathe, never mind sitting down and acting calm.

A few minutes later, a nurse called out, "Isabelle Wainwright?"

"Right here," I said, running over to her. "My mother. Is she . . ."

She took my arm and led me down a corridor. "She's having a CAT scan done right now. She was unconscious on arrival. Let's go in here," she said, leading me into a small office.

Relief washed over me. She was alive. "Is she going to be okay?"

"It's too soon to tell the extent of her injuries. Have a seat," she said, and looked down at the clipboard in her hand. "She has a fractured right arm and various lacerations. The doctor is most concerned with possible head injuries. But we'll know more after the scan is finished. Do you have any questions?"

Before I could even stop myself, I blurted out, "Had she been drinking?"

She glanced down at the papers in her hand. "Had she been drinking? No. We did a tox screen. However, the fellow that hit her was intoxicated."

I almost burst out laughing. How ironic! She had given up alcohol thirty years before, only to be hit now by a drunk driver.

"Does your mother have a drinking problem?" she asked.

I shook my head emphatically and felt a huge sense of remorse. "No. She's a recovering alcoholic and has been in AA for thirty years."

"Good for her. Okay. Well, you can come down to the ER waiting area. As soon as we hear anything, we'll let you know."

All of it suddenly came crashing down on me—the guilt, the anger, but most of all, the fear of losing my mother yet again. I began sobbing and felt the nurse's arm go around me. She reached for a tissue from the box on the table and passed it to me. Years of sadness poured out of my eyes and I wasn't sure I'd ever stop crying.

The door opened and I heard Chadwick's voice. "Isabelle?"

I jumped up and went into his arms.

"My mother . . . she . . ."

I felt him patting my head. "Shh, I know. I know. Yarrow called me."

The comfort and safety of his arms allowed my sobs to subside.

"Is she okay?" he asked.

"I don't know. They're doing a scan right now. She was unconscious when they brought her in."

"Okay," he said. "So we'll wait. Together."

I sat beside Chadwick in the waiting area, my hand clutched in his. Neither one of us spoke. We didn't have to.

About an hour later a doctor called, "Isabelle Wainwright?"

I jumped up. "Here," I said.

He walked toward me, extending his hand. "Dr. Brewster. I'm the neurologist looking after your mother."

"How is she?"

"Well, the scan results show she has a mild concussion. She hasn't woken up yet so it's a matter of waiting."

I felt Chadwick come up behind me. "Is that normal? Not waking up?"

The doctor nodded. "Yes. Actually, she is beginning to stir a bit. So it probably won't be too much longer."

"Can I see her?"

"Yes. She's in a room down here. Now don't be alarmed. We have her hooked up to IVs and various monitors and it can be a bit overwhelming."

I nodded and grasped Chadwick's hand as we followed the doctor into a small room.

I felt my heart drop when I saw my mother in the bed. She looked so small and frail. And vulnerable. Gone was her perky smile and upbeat energy. They had been replaced with pale white skin, smeared makeup, a bandage on her forehead, and various cuts on her face. This woman did not resemble my mother.

"Oh, my God," I whispered as my hands flew to my face. I felt Chadwick's arm go around me.

A nurse had been hovering near the bedside. "Are you her daughter?"

I nodded.

"It oftentimes looks worse than it is. Actually, her vital signs are very good and she's beginning to stir a little bit. You can come closer," she assured me.

I walked to the bed and reached for my mother's hand. It was then that I noticed her right arm was in a sling. I gave her left hand a little squeeze.

"Can she hear me?" I asked the nurse.

"We're never certain, but yes, we always think so. I'll be right outside at the desk. If you need anything, just come to get me. My name is Rachel and I'm your mother's nurse."

"Okay. Thank you," I said and turned back to my mother as I felt the tears coursing down my face once again.

Chadwick came to stand behind me and just feeling his closeness gave me some reassurance.

"Mom?" I whispered. "It's me. Isabelle."

No response.

After a few minutes, Chadwick said, "I'm going to get us some coffee, okay? That'll give you some time alone with your mom."

"Thanks," I said.

I stood there with my mother's hand in mine and stared at her. I was shocked at how much she seemed to have aged in the blink of an eye. And I recalled so many good moments I'd spent with my mother. Like a kaleidoscope, they went flashing through my brain. Until I'd met Petra, she had been my best friend. We had been so close. Maybe that's why it hurt so much when she left. But for the first time, I was able to put that aside. This time—she had not left me. This time—she was right here. With me. With her hand in mine.

"Mom," I whispered again. "It's Isabelle. You were in a car accident and you're in the hospital, but you're going to be okay. I'm right here with you. And I'm not leaving. And . . . I love you, Mom." Tears blurred my vision as I continued to stare at my mother. "I've always loved you. And I always will. I need you to know this. I'm glad you didn't give up and that you came here to find me."

I saw her eyelids flutter, and a sound came from her lips.

"Isabelle?" she whispered.

"Yes. It's me. I'm right here."

She slowly nodded her head. "I know you are. I knew you would be . . . because a mother knows those things."

She opened her eyes and gave me a weak smile.

"How do you feel?" I asked.

"Sore. And tired."

"Mrs. Brunell, you're awake," Rachel said, walking into the room with a smile covering her face. "We'll let Dr. Brewster know right away. Do you need anything?"

"Just my daughter right here by my side."

Chapter 38

Chadwick had insisted that he be at Koi House when Haley returned home from school so he could explain about her grandmother and bring her to the hospital. My mother was getting her fractured arm set and I was waiting for an update from the doctor.

My cell rang, and I smiled when I saw Petra's name.

"Oh, God, Isabelle. Yarrow called me. How's your mother?"

"Considering what she's been through, she's doing surprisingly well. Fractured arm, a mild concussion, and cuts and bruises. She's getting her arm set now."

"You must be a wreck. Do you want me to come down there? Because I will."

I smiled. "I know you would, but no. I'm doing much better now and Chadwick has been here with me."

I heard a chuckle come across the line. "Aha. I can see I'm being replaced. But that's a very good thing. Okay, if you're sure. Call me tomorrow with an update. I love you."

"Will do, and I love you back."

A year ago I wouldn't have hesitated to tell Petra to come. She would always be my rock, but I knew that Chadwick was now my mountain.

He returned with Haley, and the three of us waited together until my mother was settled in a room on the medical floor.

Haley rushed to her bedside and gently leaned over to place a kiss on her cheek. "Nana, I was so worried about you."

My mother reached out for her granddaughter's hand and the first words out of her mouth were, "Fred."

"What?" I said, and walked to the bedside.

"Poor little Fred has been alone in his crate since I left this morning. Somebody has to go get him."

I hadn't even thought about him—or Ginger, for that matter. But I realized that Chadwick and Haley must have tended to her at the house.

"Okay," I said.

"Oh, I forgot to tell you, Mom. Yarrow said I could spend the night at her house and that I can bring both Fred and Ginger. Is that okay?"

"That would be great, because I want to stay here with your grandmother."

"When you're ready to leave, I'll drive you to get Fred," Chadwick said. "You can wait with him at your house until Yarrow closes the shop."

It was then that I realized Chadwick and my mother had never met, and I couldn't suppress a giggle.

"I know you always want to look your best," I told my mother. "And this is far from the best of times, but . . ." I turned around and reached for Chadwick's hand to draw him closer. "I want you to meet . . ." I wasn't sure what title to assign him. "A very special person in my life, Chadwick Price."

My mother smiled and nodded. "No. Not the best time, but, Chadwick, it's such a pleasure to meet you, despite the circumstances."

"Same here. And I'm very glad you're going to be okay. It's a pleasure to meet Isabelle's mother."

An hour later when they left, I pulled a chair beside my mother's bed. She had been drifting in and out of sleep; the nurse said that was natural with the pain meds. The doctor had come in and said all the lab and scan results looked good, but they wanted to keep my mother for a couple of nights to be sure.

I sat there quietly watching her as she slept and remembered the time I was nine and had contracted a severe case of measles. With such a high fever, I had been having nightmares, but each time I opened my eyes, my mother was sitting there to assure me it only had been a dream.

After a little while she opened her eyes again and smiled.

"Are you having much pain?" I asked.

"No. I'm fine. Thank you for being here, Isabelle. But when Chadwick gets back, I want you to go. It has to be late and I know you haven't even eaten."

I glanced at my watch and was shocked to see it was a little after seven.

"Okay. Now that I know you're going to be all right, I am feeling a little hungry."

"Isabelle, I like him. I like Chadwick a lot, and I couldn't be happier for you. He seems like such a nice fellow."

"He is."

"You know, and I probably shouldn't say this, but when I met Roger for the first time, I just didn't think he was right for you. I couldn't explain it. Just a mother's intuition, I guess."

"Hmm. And you were right." I wasn't sure exactly how to tell her except to blurt it out. "Roger is gay."

She nodded. "I knew that."

"What? How on earth could you possibly know that? *I* didn't even know."

"Well, I didn't know for sure back then. I only suspected, but Haley told me when she found out, and I wasn't all that surprised." She reached over to take my hand. "How are *you* with this news?"

I let out a deep sigh. "At first . . . I was a mess."

"That's understandable. I'm so sorry you had to go through something like that. I wish I'd been there to try to help."

"To be honest, I'm not sure you could have. I think it was something I needed to get through on my own."

"And now?"

"I'm fine with it. Then you must know Roger and Gordon were married a few weeks ago and Haley attended the wedding?"

She nodded.

"I'm happy for him. I really am. Roger isn't a bad person and he's always been a very good father to Haley."

As soon as I said the words I saw the similarity with my own parents. Neither one of them were bad people. They were simply human. And as such, each one had their own flaws.

My mother gripped my hand. "I might not have had much to do with your upbringing, but I have to say again, I'm so proud of the woman you've become, Isabelle."

"I need to tell you something. First of all, you had *everything* to do with my upbringing. Up until the time I was fifteen, everything I had learned was from you. The important things in life—like kindness and understanding, but most of all about love. Because of you, I knew how to be a mother to my own daughter. I'm just so sorry that you missed out on so many of those years. But that's the past . . . and I want to start over. I want for *us* to start over as mother and daughter."

I saw the tears streaming down my mother's face and I passed her a tissue.

"You have no idea how many times I've wished for this. I'm not under any delusion that we won't have our ups and downs. Of course we will. It goes with the territory." She grinned. "But hopefully, we have many years ahead to share. And Isabelle, I couldn't be any happier."

Since Haley wouldn't be spending the night at Koi House, I extended an invitation to Chadwick. He didn't hesitate to accept. We had opted for a light supper there rather than going out to a restaurant.

"Mother-daughter relationships are way more complex than I ever thought," Chadwick said, as he stood near the stove keeping an eye on the omelets he was making for us. "But I'm so happy that you've finally resolved this, Isabelle."

I nodded. "What surprises me is that I didn't just say those words to her because I felt I *should*. It was because I truly felt them and want for us to have a relationship. For the first time, I can finally see that it was every bit as hard for my mother as it was for me."

Chadwick placed an omelet on each plate and then spooned fried potatoes beside them.

I took the plates and brought them to the counter.

He joined me and lifted his wineglass. "Here's to you and your mother. Both of you are very strong women and there's no doubt that's in your genes."

I smiled. "You know . . . I am strong. I never thought I was but looking back, I can see I've worked through some major issues."

"And at the end of the day, most people hope to be able to say that. Hey, life isn't easy. So taking those punches and getting back up? That's what counts."

After we ate and cleaned the dishes, I curled up next to Chadwick on the sofa.

"This is nice," I murmured, a drowsy contentment coming over me.

He kissed the side of my head. "Very nice. I could get used to this every night."

"You wouldn't get tired of me?"

"You're kidding, right? Nope. Never."

I felt the smile that crossed my face at the same time I felt Chadwick's hand on my thigh.

"Hmm, good," I said.

"Since you invited me to spend the night, I assume you want me to sleep in your bed."

"Your assumption would be correct, yes."

"I know it's only just after nine, but it's been a long day for you. How about if we shut off the lights and go upstairs?"

"To sleep?" I asked.

"Eventually, yes. But oh, no, beautiful. I have some enticing ideas in mind first."

I stood up and reached for his hand. "I always welcome your ideas."

Chapter 39

Mavis Anne had returned from her cruise the following week and my mother was recuperating at home.

I walked into the yarn shop one afternoon to find the table filled with the regular knitters. I had been so busy making my deliveries in the morning and spending time with my mother in the afternoon and evening that except for Mavis Anne, I hadn't seen any of them since before my mother's accident.

"Isabelle," they called out when I walked in, and I had to admit that it felt nice to be welcomed.

"How's your mother doing? We were so sorry to hear about her accident," Fay said.

"Yeah, Mavis Anne and I leave on a cruise and all hell breaks loose," Louise told me.

I laughed and sat down. "She's doing pretty well. She went home last Friday and the doctor arranged for her to have home health care, which is a godsend. The aide comes to help her shower and the nurse comes to check her out medically. I think she rather likes the attention," I said and smiled.

"Oh, but, geez, she can't knit, can she?" Maddie asked.

I shook my head. "No, not with that right arm in a cast. The doctor said it'll be about five more weeks with that and then she'll probably have to have some physical therapy."

"Gosh, what a shame, but she was so lucky." Maddie shook her head. "Why the hell was that kid that hit her drunk at nine in the morning?"

I shrugged. "I just hope he gets some help before he kills somebody."

I reached into my tote bag and removed a cable pullover sweater I was making for Chadwick for the coming winter.

"Oh, that's gorgeous," Maddie said, leaning over for a better look. "For Chadwick?"

I nodded. I was making it with a worsted weight gray tweed and I was pleased with the results. "I hope he'll like it."

"Oh, please," Maddie said. "That guy is totally besotted with you. It wouldn't matter what you made him. He'd love it."

I laughed and heard Louise say, "Oh, is there another wedding on the horizon?"

I could feel the heat radiating up my neck. Why did people put other people on the spot like that?

"Oh . . . I . . . no," I stammered. "I don't think so."

"Right," I heard Maddie mumble.

Two hours later I packed up my knitting. "Well, I have to get to my mother's. I told her I'd be over tonight to cook dinner."

"Well, the four of us had a discussion before you got here," Mavis Anne said. "And we decided that you're going to wear yourself to a frazzle trying to care for your mother twenty-four-seven. So we're going to take turns making her dinners. Each of us will go over and cook dinner for her one night a week and visit with her, but we'll also bring a dish we cooked at home. Something she can just reheat in the microwave. So this way, you won't need to be cooking every night."

I seemed to be exceptionally weepy lately because I felt my eyes getting moist.

"That's so nice of you. And it will be a huge help. Thank you."

"Hey," Maddie said. "That's what friends are for."

And if I hadn't considered it before, that's exactly what these women had become. My friends.

"We all chipped in," Yarrow said, walking toward me from the tea shop carrying a large basket covered with plastic wrap and a huge bow. "And we did up a basket for you to take to your mother from us."

"Oh, wow," I said, genuinely moved. "She will absolutely love that."

"Well, we know she's going to be limited in what she can do with that arm in a cast," Fay said. "So we thought chocolate, some good books and magazines to read, and flavored coffee might help."

* * *

My mother opened the door with Fred at her heels and smiled when she saw the basket.

"From the women at the yarn shop," I said, placing it on her dining room table.

"Oh, my goodness. That was thoughtful of them. How nice."

"And they've arranged to provide your dinners each night by coming to cook and spend some time with you."

"Are you kidding? Now that's extremely thoughtful. Plus, it will give you a break. Even though I've told you I'd be fine making myself a sandwich."

"You never fed me sandwiches for dinner when I was a kid," I said. "Coffee?"

"That would be great," my mother said, going to sit in the family room while I prepared the coffeemaker.

Over the past week I was coming to feel at home in her kitchen. Much the way being in her life was beginning to feel.

When the coffee was ready, I brought her a mug and sat down to join her. It felt like old times, like those lost years were a distant memory and all that counted was right now.

"You know, Isabelle, you made a very wise choice when you moved here."

"I think you're right," I agreed.

"Isn't it strange that when you think about it, all of it had to do with your father."

"What do you mean?"

"Well, if he hadn't initially gone to Cedar Key, he never would have met Chloe. And if he hadn't met Chloe, maybe she wouldn't have relocated here and then invited you to come visit last year."

"Hmm, true. And maybe you wouldn't have sought me out and wanted to move here."

She smiled. "Oh, no. That's where you're wrong. As soon as I found out your father had died and was no longer in the picture—I would have gone to the ends of the earth to find you. The location didn't matter to me. Being with you and trying to rebuild what we'd lost was all that mattered."

"I'm glad," I said.

"So in a roundabout way, your father might have played a major role in keeping us apart, but in the end he also played a major part in your finding happiness. I was thinking about Chadwick. By moving here, you met him."

A smile crossed my face and I nodded. "That's very true. And I actually met him last summer when I came to visit Chloe. Then shortly after I moved here I met him again and we began dating."

"Is it serious?" she asked.

Without hesitating I said, "Yes. Yes, it is."

"Good. I hope you know how happy I am for you."

"How about you?" I said, and I realized there was a whole chunk of my mother's life that I knew nothing about. "I know now you didn't have a guy in your life when you left, but thirty years is a long time. Has there ever been anybody else?"

"Oh, yeah. There was. Once. His name was Patrick. I met him at one of my AA meetings about a year after I'd gotten sober. He had about ten years in the program."

"What happened?"

"We were together for five years. Actually, we lived together. And then one day I began to suspect that his demons had returned. That he was drinking again. I confronted him. He denied it, of course."

I took a sip of coffee and waited for what I knew was not going to be a happy ending.

"After a few months and discussing it with my sponsor, I knew I had to do what was best for me. Even though I truly didn't want to. I had to move out and hold on to my own sobriety. I knew I couldn't fix him. Only he could do that."

I waited for her to continue. I could tell even all these years later, it still bothered her.

"About six months after I left, he was killed in a car crash. He was driving drunk and plowed into a guardrail."

"God, I'm so sorry, Mom."

She nodded. "I had a hard time dealing with all of it. I loved him. A lot. And we were good together—except when we weren't. When he began drinking again. So I had to choose between him and my own survival." She paused before saying, "I chose to survive."

Chadwick had been correct. I did come from a gene pool of strong women.

Chapter 40

By the time mid-June arrived, many changes had taken place. Brenda and Tina had moved into their new condo and invited Haley and me for a delicious Mexican dinner. Chloe and Henry returned from Hawaii ready to begin their married life together. And three days later Chloe's new granddaughter, Elizabeth Chloe, arrived. She would be called Eliza.

My mother's cast had been removed a few days earlier and each day we forged more of a bond. I had come to see that the past thirty years had been no easier on my mother than they had been on me. Her life seemed to consist of teaching art at the university, occasional social events with colleagues, and that was about it. She had never traveled and she had never fallen in love again. Although she probably wouldn't admit it and certainly would not complain about it—it was obvious that her life had been very lonely. I almost got the feeling she felt she had been doing penance over those thirty years. And that made me very sad.

I was sitting on the patio knitting and thinking about what Chadwick had asked me the evening before. Betty was retiring in September and he very much wanted me to be her replacement. I hated to leave Yarrow in the lurch, but I'd certainly be giving her plenty of time to find somebody new. Not only would I be able to see a lot more of Chadwick, but I thought I'd truly enjoy learning the real estate business. After discussing it, I told him I'd make a decision soon and I was now convinced I wanted to do this.

I glanced at my watch and saw it was almost six. Chadwick was picking me up shortly for dinner at his house. Haley was spending the night at Tina's, providing us with another opportunity to be creative.

I walked into the house to bring my knitting inside and check on things before I left for the night. The house seemed empty without Haley and Ginger here. She had brought the puppy to stay with her at Tina's. Both girls adored the dog and not for the first time I silently thanked my mother for rescuing both Fred and Ginger. Fred was very good for my mother while she was recuperating and I knew she welcomed his constant company.

I saw Chadwick pull up in the driveway and walked to the door, a smile covering my face.

"You look gorgeous," he said, coming inside and pulling me into an embrace.

Rather than my usual shorts or capris, I'd decided to wear a sundress.

"Thanks," I said, after he kissed me.

He reached for my hand. "All set to get creative?" he teased me.

"More than ready," I assured him.

When we got to his house, he led me outside, and I was surprised to see the lower patio area had been set up with an ice bucket holding champagne, flutes, and a bouquet of red roses in the center of the table.

"I thought we'd sit down there overlooking the river," he said. "It's such a beautiful evening. Dinner won't be ready for a while."

"Sounds good." I followed him down the terraced steps.

It was a gorgeous June evening. Not too much humidity and the perfect time to be sitting outside. After he opened the champagne, he passed me a flute and sat beside me.

"It's beautiful out here," I said, letting out a sigh of contentment. "Oh, I've made a decision."

"About us?" he asked, reaching for my hand.

I smiled. "No, about replacing Betty in September. I think I'd like to do that. I think it would be good for me to learn something new. You won't be too tough of a taskmaster, though, will you?"

He threw his head back, laughing, and squeezed my hand. "No, I can assure you I will be most fair. Have you told Yarrow she'll be losing her delivery person?"

I shook my head. "No. I wanted to tell you first. And besides, I'm giving her three months to find somebody else."

"Well, I couldn't be happier. I think we'll work very well together."

I saw something flittering in my peripheral vision and turned to see what it was.

"Oh, look! Dragonflies."

A swarm of dragonflies hovered over the water.

We both stood up and walked to the railing for a better look.

"They come here certain times of the year," Chadwick said. "Did you know they represent renewal and living in the moment?"

I nodded. "I do. They're so fragile and teach us how important every moment is."

Chadwick took my hand and turned me to face him.

"Have you thought about that other decision? About us? We said we'd discuss it and try to come up with a solution."

I shook my head. "No. I'm not sure what we should do about being together more and . . ."

Before I could complete my sentence, Chadwick was kneeling on one knee and had produced a small velvet box from his pocket. He flipped it open and a stunning marquise-cut diamond ring was staring up at me. The football shape was surrounded by other diamonds.

My hand flew to my mouth and I gasped. Although I'd thought perhaps we would end up together, I certainly was not expecting a proposal tonight.

"I love you, Isabelle. I've loved you from the first moment I saw you. I want to be with you forever and I think that's what you want too. Will you marry me?"

He slipped the ring on my finger without waiting for my response and stood up.

I looked at the ring. I looked at him. And I knew without a doubt this was one of the happiest moments in my life.

I nodded as I stared into his handsome face. And then I nodded more emphatically before I said, "Yes. Yes, I'll marry you."

He pulled me into an embrace and then held me at arm's length as the huge smile on his face reflected our joy.

"I was hoping that would be your answer. I know it might seem a bit soon but I don't think that time has a thing to do with happiness or love."

I knew he was right. Love is love no matter how short or how long.

He placed a kiss on my lips and in that moment I felt like time was standing still and I was embarking on a journey that I had always been meant to take. Each step, each disappointment, and each loss had led me right here, to this moment in time.

"I love you, Isabelle. I'll love you forever."

He took my hand and brought it to his lips to kiss.

"I love you too," I said and felt moisture stinging my eyes with emotion.

He topped off our flutes and raised his. "Here's to spending eternity with you."

"To us," I said.

"And now we have to choose a wedding date. When do you think?"

"I don't know," I said, sitting down. "I wasn't expecting this. What do you think?"

"Next week?" he said.

Surely he was joking but the expression on his face looked serious.

"Next week?" I repeated.

He reached for my hand and gave it a squeeze as a smile crossed his face.

"In truth, yes, I'd love for us to be married next week. But I want you to have the kind of wedding you'd like."

I hadn't given any thought to this either and remained silent.

"Big? Small? Huge? Over the top?" he asked. "Whatever type of wedding you'd like is what we'll have."

"I think I need a little time to think about it."

"Okay," he said, standing up and leaning down to kiss me. "You give it some thought. Come on, we'll have dinner. Will you have an answer by the time we have coffee?"

I saw the smile on his face but wasn't certain he'd been joking.

We were sitting on the patio sofa enjoying coffee and cognac.

"I don't want to pressure you, Isabelle, about a wedding date. But it just seems really silly to wait too long. There's no reason to."

He was absolutely right. I nodded.

"But depending on what type of wedding you'd like will determine when it can happen."

"Gosh, I'm really not sure, but I know I don't want over the top. Maybe something along the lines of what Chloe and Henry had. Small but tasteful and elegant. How does that sound?"

He smiled and gave my hand a squeeze. "Perfect. I was hoping you'd say that. But I do want to throw out another possibility. My parents would be more than happy to host a grand scale wedding at their home. If you think you might like that."

"Would you?"

"No," he said, without hesitating.

Now I squeezed his hand. "Good, because neither would I."

"How about here?" he said. "We could have the ceremony down there on the patio overlooking the river and there's plenty of room up here for a reception with about a hundred guests. I've done fund-raisers here before and it's a nice setting."

I laughed. "A hundred guests? That's not too small."

He grinned. "I know. But I have to be realistic. This will be a first for my parents. A son getting married. And I know they're going to want to invite many of their friends and my dad's business associates."

I thought of my mother and how she had missed the opportunity to be mother of the bride my first time around. "I love it," I said. "I love the idea of having it here."

"Great," he said. "Now all we need is a date."

"September. Late September. That'll give us a little over three months to plan and get everything done. What do you think?"

"I wish it were tomorrow, but yes, September sounds great. Maybe we'll be so busy with all the planning the days will fly by."

I stood up and reached for his hand. "And now it's time to enjoy that creativity we do so well together."

He laughed and stood up to pull me into an embrace.

"Just what I'm going to love. A wife who knows her mind and can make a good decision."

Chapter 41

I hated to leave Chadwick the following morning, but I had my deliveries to make and Haley was due home from Tina's by eleven. When I went into the tea shop to get the coffee and muffins, I was happy that Yarrow was busy with a customer, because I wanted Haley to be the first to see my engagement ring.

I went directly home after my deliveries and waited for my daughter.

I picked up the phone and dialed Petra's number. When she answered, I said, "Save the date: September twenty-fourth," I told her. "Because I need you to be my maid of honor."

I heard the gasp that came across the line and smiled.

"No! Really? You and Chadwick are getting married? When did this happen? Oh, my God, Isabelle, I'm so happy for you."

I laughed. "We are—he proposed last night. Very romantic, by the way. Complete with a swarm of dragonflies and a ring that took my breath away."

"I just knew it the moment I met him. I knew you two were destined to be together. This is so exciting. What did Haley and your mother say?"

"You're the first to know. I'm waiting for Haley to get home from Tina's. And I plan to visit my mother later."

"I hope you know that I couldn't be happier for you. Have you made any plans for the wedding?"

"Well, not too many yet. But we have decided that it will be held at Chadwick's house. We'll have the ceremony overlooking the river and the reception at the house."

"Perfect. And you know if there's anything I can do to help, I'll be there."

"I do know that. Thanks. Oh, have to go," I said as I heard the front door close. "Haley's home."

"Okay. Love you. Call me when you get a chance with more details."

I hung up as Haley walked into the kitchen with Ginger at her heels.

"Hey," she said. "You finished your deliveries?"

"I did, and there's something I want to talk to you about."

"Okay," she said, reaching for a banana from the fruit bowl and perching on a stool at the counter. "What is it?"

I stood across the counter from her, keeping my left hand out of sight.

"Well . . . Chadwick proposed to me last night."

Her head shot up. "Really? You're getting married?"

"We are. September twenty-fourth."

"Oh, wow. I'm so happy for you, Mom. I like Chadwick a lot."

"I was hoping that would be your reaction," I said as I placed my hand on the counter in front of her.

She leaned over to touch the ring and then jumped up to give me a hug.

"Wow, that is some ring, Mom. Oh, my gosh, this will be my third wedding this year."

I laughed as Ginger danced in circles with excitement.

"Where will we live?" she asked. "Will we be moving into Chadwick's house?"

I nodded. "Yes, we discussed that last night. Is that okay with you?"

"Sure. It's just down the street. I won't have to change schools when we go back in the fall. I love his house. Who else knows? Did you tell Nana?"

"Not yet. I only called Petra, and you're the first to see the ring."

I didn't miss the look of pride that crossed her face.

"Wait till Chloe and Mavis Anne and everybody at the yarn shop find out. They'll be so excited for you."

I smiled. "Okay. Let's have lunch and then I'm going over to Nana's to tell her. Do you want to come?"

"No. I think this should be a special time for you and Nana. You know?"

I did know, and once again I marveled at the insight my daughter possessed.

* * *

I hadn't called beforehand, so I hoped that my mother was home. I rang the bell and was happy when she opened the door.

"Isabelle," she said, and there was no doubt she was happy to see me. "What a nice surprise. Come on in."

Even before I stepped over the threshold I flung out my left hand. "I'm getting married. I need *you* to help me plan my wedding."

Her gaze flew from the ring, up to my face, and down to the ring again. I saw the tears that filled her eyes as she pulled me into an embrace.

"Oh, Isabelle. How wonderful!"

I followed her inside and sat beside her on the sofa.

"My gosh, when did this happen?"

"Last night," I said, and shared the details.

"September twenty-fourth. That doesn't give you a whole lot of time, does it? Have you decided on any of the plans yet?"

"Only the date and that we're holding the ceremony and reception at Chadwick's house."

She nodded. "Oh, that's good. That will eliminate trying to get a venue in just a few months. Will it be a large wedding?"

"Moderate size. Just around a hundred people, and that's because Chadwick said his parents will want to invite a lot of old friends and business colleagues."

"Yes, of course. Well, how about invitations? That will really be the first thing to get done. They have to be printed and mailed out so people can respond. You'll need a pretty firm count when you get in touch with the caterer. Are you having a sit-down dinner or a buffet?"

I could see there was going to be a lot more to planning this wedding than I was aware of. When I'd married Roger, we had a civil ceremony and a dinner at a local restaurant afterward with about ten people.

"Gosh, I don't know. Hold on," I said, reaching for my phone. "Let me give Chadwick a call. He's at the office today."

He must have seen my name on his caller ID because he answered by saying, "I love you, Isabelle, and I miss you."

I smiled. "I love you too, but sit-down dinner or buffet for the wedding?"

I heard him laugh. "I take it you're at your mother's?"

"Yeah, and I think there's going to be a lot more to planning this wedding than I realized."

"Whatever you'd like, but I was thinking we could get married around five and then have a hot buffet dinner. I have a caterer I've used a number of times and they do a really nice job. I'll get the company I use to set up a few tents in the garden area and that will give us plenty of room for people to mingle and then sit down to eat."

I was beginning to feel grateful for the expertise of both my mother and Chadwick.

"That sounds perfect. Okay. Oh, and my mother said we have to do the invitations first so they can be mailed out."

"Right. Why don't you go to a printer with her and bring home a couple of books? We can sit down together this evening and choose what we'd like."

"Okay."

"As a matter of fact, plan to bring your mom and Haley and come for dinner at my place this evening. Is it possible to get to a printer this afternoon?"

I looked over at my mother, who had been listening. "Do you have plans this afternoon? Or could you go with me to a printer to get a couple books to look at?"

"I'm your wedding assistant. Of course I can go."

"She said . . ."

"I heard her. Great. Okay. So get the books and come over to the house around five. I'll leave here early. I love you."

"I love you too," I said, hanging up and letting out a whoosh of air. "Wow. This is going to be a lot of work."

My mother waved a hand in the air and laughed. "This is going to be a labor of love. Trust me. Okay, how about if we have some coffee while we look through the phone book for some printers."

We pulled up in the driveway of Chadwick's house shortly after five.

"Oh, Isabelle, what a beautiful house," my mother said, leaning forward in the passenger seat. I realized she had not been here before.

"It is," I said.

Chadwick had given me a key so I rang the bell to let him know we were there, unlocked the door, and we walked inside.

"Hey, beautiful," he said, coming from the kitchen with a towel over his shoulder.

He kissed me and then gave Haley and my mother each a hug.

"Come on in. Soft drink, coffee, ice water? What can I get you?"

"Ice water would be great," my mother said. "What a beautiful home you have."

"Coke, please," Haley said before heading out to the patio area.

"Thanks. Isabelle, why don't you show your mother around and I'll get the drinks."

I placed the wedding invitation books on the kitchen counter and proceeded to give my mother a tour of the house.

We returned to the kitchen to find Chadwick putting a casserole dish into the oven.

He turned around and smiled. "I hope you like country casserole. It's a southern favorite in my house that Mary has been making for years. Pasta, chicken, cream of chicken soup, veggies, and cheese."

"Sounds wonderful," my mother said, taking the glass of water he passed her.

"It does," I agreed. "You'll have to share that recipe with me when we get married. On second thought, never mind. I'll just let you make it."

My mother and Chadwick laughed.

"Sounds like some pre-wedding cooking lessons might be in order," my mother joked.

Chadwick passed me a glass of wine.

"Why don't we take these books out to the patio table?"

By the time dinner was over, we had made our decision about the wedding invitation.

"Oh, we'll need a count," my mother said. "Do you have any idea how many we'll need?"

Chadwick nodded. "I spoke to my mother earlier. She's over the moon, by the way, and said she'll call you tomorrow, Isabelle. She would also love for us to go up there and stay a few days so she can meet you, Iris, before the wedding."

"How thoughtful," my mother said. "Yes, of course. I'd love to go. You just tell me when."

I smiled. Something so simple and yet I knew it meant the world to my mother.

"My mother said her part of the guest list will be about sixty with friends and family," he said. "And I have about twenty-five friends and colleagues. Have you made a list?"

"I'd like to invite Charlotte, my sponsor," my mother said. "And maybe a few others from my salsa class."

"And I want to invite all the regular knitters," I said. "But that's less than ten. And David and Clive, of course."

"That's fine. Okay, why don't we order a hundred and ten invitations? That'll give us some extra in case we think of somebody else before we mail them out."

I nodded. "My mother and I will return the books tomorrow and get them ordered."

"Oh, did you ask Petra to be your maid of honor?" Chadwick asked.

"I did. Of course, she accepted. Do you have a best man?"

"Yes, I'm going to give my good friend Drew a call. We've known each other since we were kids and went to college together. You'll meet him when we go up to Atlanta."

For the girl who had always felt isolated when it came to family, I was beginning to feel that my world was about to expand in a huge and wonderful way.

Chapter 42

A t the end of July, Chadwick and I drove to his parents' home with my mother and daughter. His proposal had been a surprise, but unbeknownst to me I had two more surprises coming before my wedding day.

Ginnie had called my mother to personally invite her, but this was their first time meeting in person. By the time we finished dinner on the patio, I could tell they had hit it off.

Chadwick's parents seemed to adore Haley and she was having a great time in the pool. I watched as she did laps back and forth and smiled.

"That was a wonderful dinner, Ginnie. Thank you so much," my mother said.

She was sipping iced tea, and if they thought it odd that she had refused their offer of wine, they never said a word. I was happy to see that my mother had had a good recovery from her car accident. Her arm had healed well and her bruises had disappeared. She looked happy and vibrant again—minus the blue streak in her hair.

"I'm glad you enjoyed it." Ginnie took a sip of wine. "I thought tomorrow we girls could hit the mall and do a bit of shopping. What do you think, Isabelle?"

"Sure. That would be fun."

I was probably wrong, but I thought I saw a look exchanged between my mother and Chadwick's mother.

The following morning Chadwick and his father headed out for a game of golf at the country club and the four of us left about ten for our shopping.

Haley enjoyed checking out new shops. My mother insisted on

buying her some new clothes for the coming school year. Ginnie and I browsed, and when she suggested we stop for lunch I was ready.

It seemed we lingered over lunch longer than necessary, but the conversation flowed and it was fun getting to know Ginnie better.

We arrived back at the house shortly after two. When I walked out to the patio, I suddenly understood the reason for the shopping and the lengthy lunch, because a group of about thirty women yelled, "Surprise!"

I began laughing as my hands flew to my face and I saw the colored balloons floating above the pool, streamers and white wedding bells dangling above the table overflowing with beautifully wrapped packages. I was forty-five years old, this was my second marriage, and I hadn't given a thought to a bridal shower.

I looked at my mother and Haley. "You knew," I accused them, and they both laughed and nodded.

"Over here," Ginnie said, leading me to a black velvet chair with a huge white bow.

"How on earth did you get this all put together?" I asked as I sat down and somebody draped a silver boa around my neck.

A woman about Ginnie's age began laughing. "With the help of her best friend and a few others. It was a scramble, but we managed."

I now saw that platters and bowls of food were arranged on a long table. They really had done an admirable job in just four hours.

It was such a fun afternoon, opening gifts, sipping wine, eating and getting to know Chadwick's aunts, cousins, and women who had married into the family.

After the gifts were opened, I walked over to my mother, who was standing beside Haley.

"I can't believe you guys knew about this and never said a word."

Haley laughed. "It was a *secret*, Mom."

"Ginnie called me last month and told me what she had planned and wanted to know what I thought. I said it was a wonderful idea."

"It was," I said, pulling my mother into an embrace. "It was so much fun but . . . the best part? That you could be here with me to share it."

"I think I enjoyed it as much as you did. You got some lovely gifts."

I nodded just as I heard Chadwick say, "Hey, beautiful," and I turned around to see him walk onto the patio with his father.

I laughed and pointed at him. "*You* knew too, of course."

He was grinning as he hugged me and brushed his lips over mine. "Of course I did. I was worried I'd slip and say something, but I was careful."

"Ginnie wanted to do this for the two of you," Austin said. "So I'm glad you enjoyed it."

I took Chadwick's hand. "Come look at the lovely gifts we got."

I pointed out southern cookbooks, scented candles, a couple of framed paintings, coffee mugs, and various items that were all practical. Not the usual gifts that got hidden away or never used.

"Your mother said she told everybody that you already had a fully furnished home so to give us things that would be useful."

"Leave it to my mother," he said, reaching for a gorgeous blue-and-white cut glass fragrance diffuser. "What's this?"

"Aromatherapy. That's from your aunt Ceil. You fill it with this liquid," I said, holding up a bottle of French lavender. "And the scent fills the air."

"Hmm," he said, putting an arm around me and pulling me close. "I know exactly which room that will go in."

A month later there seemed to be a breather from wedding plans. Petra was coming to visit for a long weekend. She arrived with Lotte on Thursday afternoon. I had only seen her once since the engagement, so I was looking forward to four days with her.

After she got settled in her room, I opened a bottle of wine and we were relaxing on the patio.

"It's been quite the whirlwind for you the past couple of months," she said.

"I know. I can hardly believe the wedding is in four weeks. Oh, did you bring your dress?"

"Yup. It's in the garment bag. I'll show it to you later. I think it's such a great idea that you're going to wear Emmalyn's dress."

I smiled. "It just seems so appropriate. I wore that on my first date with Chadwick and he loved it. I do too."

"Does he know you're wearing it?"

I shook my head. "No. I want to surprise him. I asked Mavis Anne if it would be okay and of course she was thrilled. She said Emmalyn would be so happy. It's very dressy and formal, so it's perfect."

That was when I remembered my most recent dream about Emmalyn.

"I had another dream about her the other night," I said.

I had told Petra about my dreams, but she had never commented very much.

"Oh?"

I nodded. "I never believed in them too much before."

"But now?"

I let out a sigh. "I don't know. I'm beginning to think there might be something to them. And I think this one . . . I think it might be the final one I have of Emmalyn. In this one she was out by the pond and when I walked out, she was excited and happy. And she held up an incredibly stunning lace shawl."

"Did she say anything?" Petra asked.

I nodded. "Yeah. She said, 'See, the stitches are all together now.' And that was it. But I also felt so happy in the dream, and when I woke up, the first thought in my head was that Emmalyn's job was finished. Silly, right?"

Petra shrugged. "Who knows. Didn't Chloe have dreams about Emmalyn when she lived here too?"

"Yup."

We had decided to spend a few hours on the beach the next day. It was hot, humid, and sunny. Petra and I chatted for a while as we lounged in our chairs with feet in the water.

"This is nice," I heard her say.

"Hmm," I mumbled drowsily.

"I never go to the beach up my way. I don't know why that is."

I must have dozed off because when I woke the tide had gone out and Petra was sitting beside me reading.

I stretched my arms up. "What time is it?"

"Close to five. We're due at your mom's for dinner shortly."

"Yeah, we'd better get going. Haley said she'd meet us there."

We stayed at my mother's house till almost seven and headed back to Koi House. Haley was staying the night at my mom's.

Petra and I had been home about twenty minutes when Chloe called.

"Isabelle, could you do me a favor? I'm here at the yarn shop working late to unpack a lot of deliveries we got today. Any chance you could pop over and help me? It won't take very long with both of us."

"Sure," I said. "I'll bring Petra and she can help too. We'll be over in a few minutes."

I explained the call to Petra. "Yeah, let's go."

We walked over, and the moment I opened the door and flipped the light switch, I heard "Surprise!"

I jumped and began laughing. I spied my mother and Haley and shook my head. Gathered around the table were Mavis Anne, Yarrow, Louise, Fay, and Maddie. Chloe came to hug me.

"You honestly didn't think we'd let you get married without a lingerie shower, did you?"

I groaned and knew this one wasn't going to be PG-rated like the shower at Chadwick's house.

And it wasn't. All of them had given me gorgeous and risqué panties, bras, nighties, and even a garter belt and silk stockings. These were from Mavis Anne. All I could do was shake my head and laugh.

After the gifts were opened, we sat around enjoying cake and beverages: wine for some of us and coffee for others.

"This was so much fun," I said. "You guys are just the best. Thank you so much."

"Well, honey, a woman has to have those sexy items to keep the spice in her marriage," Mavis Anne said. "Although with you and Chadwick, it'll probably be a long time before you'll be thinking of diversions."

I laughed again. Mavis Anne Overby never had been shy.

"A woman has to have those things for the honeymoon," Maddie said. "Oh, where *are* you going for your honeymoon?"

"I don't know. That's a surprise too. Chadwick said he'll announce it the night of our wedding reception."

"Gosh, how will you know what kind of clothes to pack?" Louise asked.

Mavis Anne gave her a jab on the arm. "Oh, Louise, honestly. It's a honeymoon. How important do you really think clothes are?"

Once again the yarn shop filled with laughter.

"So you'll be moving out of Koi House, won't you?" Fay asked.

I nodded. "Yes. Haley and I will be living at Chadwick's house. I'm glad it's just up the street, but . . . I feel bad about deserting Koi House and leaving it empty again."

Mavis Anne waved a hand in the air. "Oh, well, that's not necessarily true." I saw the glance she shot in Petra's direction. "Do you want to tell her?"

"I have another surprise for you. I've decided to come down here for an extended stay. So Mavis Anne and I have been talking the past couple of months, and she's graciously insisted that I stay at Koi House until I decide what I'm doing."

I jumped up to give her a hug. "You had hinted you might think about moving down here. Oh, Petra, you know I couldn't be happier. This is wonderful news! When are you coming?"

"Well, I have some loose ends to tie up and I'm hiring somebody to look after my house. So I'm thinking I'll be down right after Thanksgiving."

"Three months from now and you'll be here to celebrate Christmas with us. That's the best gift I could get."

"Hey, best friends forever, we always said. And besides, somebody has to keep you straight."

This brought forth a round of clapping and more laughter in the yarn shop.

Chapter 43

I awoke at Koi House shortly after seven the morning of my wedding. I thought back to the previous September and how my life had been spiraling out of control. Filled with anger, drinking way too much, no direction, and very little self-esteem.

I'd had a lot of help, but I knew it was true that I had been the one to take that first step. By agreeing to relocate to Ormond Beach I had ultimately turned my life around. And when I made the decision to do that, everything else fell into place.

A ten o'clock appointment had been booked at the spa for my mother, Chadwick's mother, Petra, Haley, and me. This had been Ginnie's idea, and she insisted on the works. Manicure, pedicure, hair, makeup, and massage. She was staying at a nearby hotel with Austin, as were many of their friends and relatives.

After showering and dressing, I headed downstairs and found Petra and Haley already in the kitchen. Ginger and Lotte were playing tug with a toy. The aroma of coffee filled the air.

"Good morning," I said, going to fill a mug.

"You must be so excited." Haley came to give me a hug.

I nodded. "I am. I was thinking back to a year ago and I can't believe how much my life has changed."

"All for the good," Petra said. "You *have* had an amazing year."

"Are you nervous?" Haley asked.

"I don't think so. Should I be?"

She laughed. "No. I just wanted to make sure."

"The weather looks perfect," I said, walking to the French doors. "When we planned the ceremony for outside, I was a little worried, but the backup plan was to have it on the sheltered patio."

"I checked the forecast," Haley said. "Sunny all day, low eighties by this evening and no chance of rain."

"Does anybody want breakfast?" I asked.

"No, I don't. Nana texted me and she's taking the five of us to lunch after the spa. It's her treat and she already spoke to Ginnie about it."

"Oh, that's nice of her," I said. "Where are we going?"

Haley smiled. "To LuLu's, of course."

I sat in the spa chair and smiled as the tech worked on my pedicure. Haley had her eyes closed and was listening to music coming through her earbuds. My mother was knitting. Ginnie was reading. I could have been mistaken, but I thought Petra was lightly snoring.

The four most important women in my life and I was thrilled to be sharing my special day with them. I knew that my mother had savored these past few months. Having a meaningful relationship with me meant everything to her—but being able to share in all the special moments leading up to my wedding had filled her heart with joy. And I felt the same way.

By letting go of past hurts, I had been able to open a whole new life for both of us. I came to realize that while it's never easy letting go of the anger, the only way to move forward is by doing exactly that.

Petra stirred next to me.

"God, was I snoring?" she asked.

"Yes, terribly. They had to turn up the radio speakers to drown you out."

She gave me a playful jab on the arm.

"Oh, stop." She let out a yawn and stretched her arms above her. "No matter what's going on in a woman's life, a pedicure makes everything better. I'm glad Ginnie came up with this idea."

"Me too. I think I lucked out in the mother-in-law department."

"My BFF, you have now lucked out in many areas. I was pretty worried about you for a while, but you found your footing. With Chadwick by your side, even the bad days will be easier to take. Because you'll be together."

I smiled. "He *is* pretty special, isn't he?"

Petra nodded. "He's that one special person who crossed your path and is meant to stay forever."

I knew she was right.

"And so are you," I said. "I'm so excited that you'll be moving down here."

"Well, I didn't exactly say *moving*. I'm coming for an undetermined amount of time. I can work from anywhere, so that makes it possible. And . . . well, we'll see what happens."

"Any further luck on locating your father?"

She shook her head. "Not yet, but I've only started searching. I just have a gut feeling that I'll locate him. He might not even be in this country and he might not even be alive . . . but somehow I believe I'll find him."

I reached for her hand and gave it a squeeze. "And I'll be right by your side when you do."

It had been decided that I would get dressed for my wedding at Koi House along with my mother, Petra, and Haley. Clive would be driving us to Chadwick's home for the ceremony. I had asked David to escort me down to the patio area where Chadwick would be waiting with his best man, Drew.

My mother assisted with slipping Emmalyn's stunning black dress over my head and zipped the back.

"Oh, Isabelle, you're beautiful. That dress was made for you."

I saw the tears in her eyes as I turned toward the mirror and nodded. It looked every bit as gorgeous as it had when I'd worn it on my first date with Chadwick seven months before.

"And the finishing touch," I said, walking to the vanity and sitting down. I reached for the black headband. "Could you fasten this around my forehead?"

My mother tied the beaded accessory and I was happy that I'd chosen the French twist hairstyle again.

"You're the most beautiful bride I've ever seen," she said.

I laughed. "And you might be just a little biased. You look pretty gorgeous yourself, mother of the bride."

And she did. She was wearing an ice blue cocktail dress that fit her perfectly and made her look both classy and stylish.

She reached into the tote bag she'd brought with her and passed me a small package wrapped in silver paper.

"A little something for you."

I unwrapped it and my breath caught in my throat. A bottle of Chanel No. 5 perfume—Emmalyn's favorite scent. But my mother could have no way of knowing that.

"That was my favorite perfume in college. I thought a few sprays might be appropriate for you today."

I pulled her into a tight embrace. "You have no idea," I said. "And Mom, I want you to know something. Remember you had said that you were an average mother? You weren't. You were the *best*. Always. And you still are. I love you."

"And how I love you."

Petra walked into the room and stopped short when she saw me.

"Oh, Isabelle. No wonder you loved that dress so much. You look absolutely stunning! What a great choice."

I smiled. "And my maid of honor is going to have heads turning. I *love* your dress."

She had chosen a shimmery, cream-colored dress that fell to her knees in points. Rhinestone spaghetti straps added to the allure, and the finishing touch was her dark hair. With it parted in the middle and pulled away from her face to a knot at the base of her neck, she oozed sex appeal.

"Thanks. Well, I haven't met the best man yet but just in case he might be available, I wanted to be sure I'm looking my best."

My mother and I laughed as Haley walked into the room. She had chosen to wear the mint green dress she'd bought for Chloe's wedding. Having just turned fifteen a few weeks before, my daughter was growing into a beautiful young woman.

We complimented Haley and then my mother said, "Ready? Clive will be here shortly to drive us."

"Yeah. You guys go downstairs. I'll be right along."

When they left the room, I looked around and smiled. I had spent my final night at Koi House and a whole new life was opening up for me. Maybe Mavis Anne had been right. Maybe the house did have energy and enveloped its inhabitants with love.

I walked to the door, turned around, and whispered, "Thank you, Emmalyn. Thank you for whatever you might have done."

We pulled up to Chadwick's house and all of a sudden I had butter-flies in my stomach. Clive assisted me out of the car while my mother and Haley went inside.

Petra stood beside me. "I guess I have to go find my best man. I'll see you shortly." She leaned over to place a kiss on my cheek.

A few minutes later, David came outside.

"Okay," he said. "Everything is ready. All set?"

I blew out a breath of air and nodded. "Yes."

With my hand on David's arm, we walked inside and I heard the strains of classical music coming from violins and a flute. Walking to the edge of the covered patio, I saw two men and a woman playing the instruments, while my gaze took in a crowd of chairs along the terraced area. And there at the bottom on the patio overlooking the river was Chadwick, looking up at me with a huge smile on his face. He looked incredibly handsome wearing a charcoal gray suit, white shirt, and light gray tie.

Holding tightly to David's arm, I descended the steps down to Chadwick, never once taking my eyes from his.

I had chosen to carry three calla lilies tied with a cream ribbon, and I now passed these to Petra. I saw the tall man standing beside Chadwick. He nodded and gave me a smile. And then I turned to Chadwick as he took both of my hands in his.

We had decided to exchange traditional wedding vows, minus the *obey* phrase, and as we said the words I knew that all of it, everything that had happened in my life, had brought me to this moment in time. To uniting with the love of my life and becoming Isabelle Price.

When we were officially pronounced husband and wife, Chadwick leaned over and kissed me, to the applause of the crowd. And then, turning, he said, "Drew, I want you to meet my wife, Isabelle."

The word *wife* took on a very special meaning for me.

"I'm so happy to meet you," he said, smiling. "And let me be the first to wish you a lifetime of happiness."

Petra leaned forward to return my flowers and kiss my cheek. "I love you both," she said. "May your life be filled with all good things."

"You look ravishing," Chadwick whispered in my ear as we ascended the stairs to the reception area.

The next few hours were a blur. Shaking hands and exchanging hugs with family and friends. Dancing, grabbing a few bites of the hors d'oeuvres, and sipping champagne.

It had been arranged that Drew would drive us to the Orlando airport around nine. We were booked for our wedding night at a hotel before taking off the next day for my secret honeymoon destination.

Petra came over to me. "Hey," she said. "You wouldn't mind if I came along for the drive to the airport, would you? Drew has invited me to come with him."

"Oh, really?" I said and felt a grin cross my face. "Interesting. And of course not, we'd love for you to come."

"I knew you'd say that," she said, before we heard Chadwick at the microphone asking for attention.

He motioned for me to join him and slipped an arm around my waist.

"The honeymoon destination has been a surprise for Isabelle," he said. Reaching into his jacket pocket, he removed a packet and waved it in the air. "So the time has come to let her know where we're going." He leaned over and placed a kiss on my lips. "My beautiful wife and I will be leaving tomorrow night on a flight to Paris, where we'll spend a few days. And then we will be leaving on a fourteen-day Viking cruise to Germany, Vienna, and Prague."

I gasped as the crowd cheered and clapped.

"Oh, my, God, Chadwick! I can't believe you remembered I wanted to go there."

I recalled that a few months ago he had insisted I apply for a passport. Without giving anything away, he explained that he wanted us to travel a lot after we got married and that at age forty-five, it was time I finally had a passport. That's when I realized that I hadn't even packed it.

"I don't have my . . ." I started to say and he laughed.

"Passport? Not to worry. Haley took care of that for us. She has it for you."

I shook my head. This man had thought of everything.

After dinner had been served and guests were dancing and mingling, Chadwick took my hand to walk down to the patio where we had exchanged vows a few hours before. The sun had just set and the river was tranquil and serene.

I let out a contented sigh as we stood there in comfortable silence.

"Happy?" he asked.

"I know I've never been happier. I love you, Chadwick, and I look forward to spending the rest of my life with you."

He kissed me and then said, "I love you too, and I have a little something for you."

He reached into his jacket pocket and passed something wrapped in tissue to me.

I removed the tissue paper and saw a gorgeous blue-and-white glass dragonfly.

"Oh, it's beautiful. I love it."

"The night that I proposed to you right here in this spot the dragonflies appeared. I felt it was significant to our love and our life together."

And I knew he was right. Like the dragonfly, life was fragile and required change and renewal. The past year had proved to me that when we allow love to direct us, we are transformed and end up exactly where we're supposed to be.

Author's Note

The scarf pattern mentioned in my story, Isabelle's Challenge, was designed by April Reis. If you would like a hard copy of the pattern or any of April's other lovely designs, please visit her page on Ravelry at http://www.ravelry.com/designers/april-reis.

Isabelle's Challenge Scarf

Designed by April Reis

Materials

Yarn: Universal Bamboo Pop, 292 yards (1 ball)

Needles: US-6

Miscellaneous: Waste yarn for provisional cast on, stitch markers, tapestry needle

Optional: 64 qty. beads (to fit on desired yarn)

Gauge: 6.5 stitches per inch in stockinette

Final Measurements: 5" wide x 54" long

Basic Stitches

K – Knit

P – Purl

K2TOG – Knit 2 stitches together

P2TOG – Purl 2 stitches together

PFB – Purl into the front and back of the stitch

YO – Yarn over

SL1 – Stitch one stitch, Knitwise on the RS rows and Purlwise on the WS rows unless otherwise noted

PSSO – Pass the slipped stitch over the stitch you just knit

PM – Place marker

SM – Slip marker

Special Stitch

Star – Purl 3 stitches together, leave the 3 purled together stitches on the left needle, YO around the right needle, purl the 3 stitches together again, drop stitches off left needle.

Notes

- The first stitch of every row is slipped; knit-wise on right side rows and purl-wise on wrong side rows, unless otherwise specifically stated.

Bead Placement - Optional

- Beads are only used on horseshoe lace parts of the pattern (the ends).
- To place bead, after you pass the slipped stitch over the K2TOG, add bead to the K2TOG stitch.
- There will be four beads placed on each RS row for a total of 32 beads per end.

Pattern

Using waste yarn, provisional cast on 40 stitches. Begin with Star Lace Pattern.

Star Lace Pattern

Row 1 (RS): SL1, K1, PM, K37, PM, K2
Row 2 (WS): SL1 purlwise, K1, SM, (Star, P1) to marker, SM, K1, P1
Row 3: Repeat Row 1, slipping markers as you come to them
Row 4: SL1 purlwise, K1, SM, (P1, Star) to marker, SM, K1, P1

Repeat Star Lace Pattern, Rows 1 – 4, for a total of 58 repeats.

Repeat Row 1 one more time, removing markers as you come to them.

Part Two

Row 1 (WS): SL1 as if to purl, K to last stitch, P1
Row 2 (RS): SL1 as if to knit, P to last stitch, K1, increasing one stitch by PFB in the center
Row 3: SL1, P to end

Row 4: SL1, K to end
Row 5: SL1, P to end
Row 6: SL1, K to end

Horseshoe Lace Pattern

Row 1 and all WS rows: SL1, P9, K1, P9, K1, P9, K1, P10

Row 2 (RS):   SL1, (YO, K3, SL1, K2TOG, PSSO, K3, YO, P1) x3, YO, K3, SL1, K2TOG, PSSO, K3, YO, K1

Row 4: SL1, (K1, YO, K2, SL1, K2TOG, PSSO, K2, YO, K1, P1) x3, K1, YO, K2, SL1, K2TOG, PSSO, K2, YO, K2

Row 6: SL1, (K2, YO, K1, SL1, K2TOG, PSSO, K1, YO, K2, P1) x3, K2, YO, K1, SL1, K2TOG, PSSO, K1, YO, K3

Row 8: SL1, (K3, YO, SL1, K2TOG, PSSO, YO, K3, P1) x3, K3, YO, SL1, K2TOG, PSSO, YO, K4

Row 9 – 16:   Repeat rows 1 – 8

Next...

Row 1: Purl all

Row 2: Knit all

Row 3: Slip 1st stitch purl-wise, K to last stitch, P last stitch

Row 4: Slip 1st stitch knit-wise, P to last stitch, K last stitch

Bind off loosely.

Turn work and remove your provisional cast on, pick up 40 stitches. Start at Part Two and work the remainder of the pattern.

Bind off loosely.

Did you miss the first of Terri DuLong's Ormond Beach series?
PATTERNS OF CHANGE is available now in either ebook or print
on demand format!

PATTERNS OF CHANGE
An Ormond Beach Novel

"DuLong reminds me of a Southern Debbie Macomber but
with a flair all her own."
—Karin Gillespie

New York Times *bestselling author Terri DuLong turns a new
page in breezy Ormond Beach, Florida, where a woman looking
for a fresh start discovers her dreams coming true in ways
she never imagined . . .*

Chloe Radcliffe was ready to shake the dust of Cedar Key off her
feet and sink her toes into the warm sands of Ormond Beach with
her soon-to-be husband. But when tragedy struck, she found herself
alone, unraveled—and unsure where she belonged . . .

A series of vivid dreams of a Victorian house with a beautiful
fishpond convince Chloe to take a leap of faith and rent a condo in
Ormond Beach. There, she makes fast friends with a group of
knitters and the owner of a tea shop, who also happens to have a
house nearly identical to the one in Chloe's dreams—and she's
willing to rent her the property. Just as Chloe begins casting on her
grand plans for the home, her tangled past comes back to haunt
her—but her dreams and newfound friends just might point her
toward the love she's been missing all along . . .

INCLUDES AN ORIGINAL KNITTING PATTERN!

TERRI DuLong

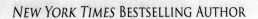

PATTERNS OF CHANGE

An Ormond Beach
Novel

"DuLong reminds me of a
Southern Debbie Macomber
but with a flair all her own."
–Karin Gillespie

Chapter 1

Sitting on Aunt Maude's porch watching the April sun brighten the sky wasn't where I thought I'd be ten months ago. Having experienced two major losses, I found myself still in the small fishing village of Cedar Key . . . and like the boats in the gulf, I was drifting with no sense of purpose or direction.

Life had proved to me once again that it can change in the blink of an eye. I certainly found that out four years ago when my husband, Parker, left me for a trophy wife. But eventually I pulled myself together and made my way from Savannah to this small town on the west coast of Florida. Straight to the shelter and love of my aunt. At the time, I'd been estranged from my sister, Grace, for many years, but eventually Grace and I renewed our bond and now we were closer than we'd ever been.

The ring tone on my cell phone began playing and I knew without looking at the caller ID that it was Gabe's daughter, Isabelle—she was the only person who called me before eight in the morning.

"Hey," I said. "How're you doing?"

A deep sigh came across the line. "Okay. I just had another battle with Haley about going to school, but I managed to get her out the door. How about you?"

"Yeah, okay here too. Just finishing up my coffee and then I'll be heading to the yarn shop to help out."

I wasn't even gainfully employed anymore because I'd given up my partnership with Dora in the local yarn shop when I thought I was relocating to the east coast of Florida . . . with Gabe. And now Gabe was gone.

Another sigh came across the line. "It's funny. I didn't see Dad all that much, but I knew he was *there*. Do you know what I mean?"

"I do. Sometimes I think we just take it for granted that those we love will always be with us."

Losing Gabe in the blink of an eye was a heartbreaking reminder of the fact that life was indeed fragile. We had made great plans for a bright new future together. When he arrived in Cedar Key to spend the winter months, he had signed up to take some men's knitting classes at the yarn shop. I knew immediately that I liked him, and the feeling was mutual. Eight months later we'd made a commitment to relocate together to Ormond Beach on the east coast. Gabe was also an expert knitter and we had put a deposit on a lovely home just outside the city limits, where he would tend to the alpacas we'd raise and we'd both run a yarn shop downtown. But that wasn't to be.

"Exactly," Isabelle said. "And poor Dad didn't even make it to Philly to sell his condo. This might sound selfish, but if I had to lose him, I'm glad it happened right here at my house." I heard a sniffle across the phone line. "At least I was with him at the end."

We both were. Gabe had wanted to make a stop outside Atlanta on our way to Philly to visit his daughter and granddaughter. But on the third day of our stay, sitting on Isabelle's patio after dinner, a grimace covered Gabe's face, he clutched his chest and he was gone. I jumped up to perform CPR while Isabelle called 911 but by the time the paramedics arrived, it was too late. A massive coronary had claimed his life. Just like that.

"No, it's not selfish at all," I said. "I'm glad I was with him too."

"We've both had a time of it, haven't we? I lose Dad and then two months later, Roger decides he doesn't love me anymore."

It was actually the breakup of Isabelle's marriage that had brought the two of us closer. While she had been civil to me when we'd first met the previous June, she had been a bit cool. I remembered how she had emphatically informed me that she wasn't called Izzy or Belle. "It's *Isabelle*," she'd said.

I chalked it up to father-daughter jealousy on her part. Although she wasn't at all close to her mother, who had taken off to Oregon years ago after her divorce from Gabe, I had a feeling that Isabelle didn't want another woman in her father's life. But when her husband up and left her, I was the first person she called. Sobbing on the phone, she related that she was experiencing the same thing that had happened to me—her husband had fallen out of love with her. Common troubles have a way of uniting women.

"Any further word on the divorce settlement?" I asked.

"Yes, that's why I'm calling. It's been decided that I will get the house. At least until Haley is eighteen, so that gives me five years to figure out what I'm doing. And when we sell it, we each get half."

"That sounds fair enough."

"Yeah, except that Haley is so unhappy here. Between the loss of her grandfather and her father leaving, it's been a difficult time for her. And to make matters worse, things at school aren't going well either."

I knew Haley was a bright girl and a good student, so I was surprised to hear this. "What's going on?"

"Well," she said, and I heard hesitation in her tone. "In the ten months since you've seen her, Haley has really packed on some pounds. Unfortunately, I think she's taking comfort in food. And you know how cruel kids can be. Especially thirteen-year-old girls."

"Oh, no." I didn't know Haley well, but when I met her for the first time we immediately clicked. Unlike her mother, she didn't display any frostiness toward me. Quite the opposite. She seemed to genuinely like me and I liked her. "What a shame. Gosh, I know kids have always been mean but today, from what I hear, they seem to have taken it to a new level."

"You have no idea. Hey, how's Basil doing?"

I smiled and glanced down at the twenty-pound dog sleeping inches from my foot. I guess you could say that Basil was my legacy from Gabe. I had gotten to know the dog well during the months that Gabe was on the island, and we had taken an instant liking to each other. When Gabe passed away, there was the question of what to do with Basil. Although I know that Haley would have loved to keep him, Isabelle had insisted that wasn't possible and even hinted that perhaps he should go to the pound. That was when I stepped in and offered to give Basil a home. I think gratefulness has a lot to do with loyalty, because Basil hasn't left my side since we flew back to Florida from Atlanta. Basil in his carrier, in the cabin with me, of course.

"Oh, he's great. I'm so glad I took him. He's a great little dog and sure keeps me company."

"That's good. Well, give him a pat from Haley and me. Any decision yet on what you're doing? Do you think you'll stay in Cedar Key?"

"I honestly don't know, Isabelle. I'm no closer to a decision now than I was after Aunt Maude died two months ago. And Grace has been hinting that she and Lucas might want to move to Paris permanently."

My sister had married a wonderful fellow four years before. Lucas owned the book café in town, but he was originally from Paris, and it was beginning to sound like he wanted to bring his family back to his roots in France. Which included my sister and three-year-old niece, Solange.

"Oh, gee, and where would that leave you? Would you put your aunt's house up for sale?"

"I just don't know. I think Grace is trying to go easy with me right now. She doesn't want to add any more pressure, but it's not fair of me to hold them back if that's what they want. Besides, in this economy, property just isn't selling on the island. My building downtown has been on the market for ten months."

"Yeah, true. Well, listen, Chloe, I need to get going here. You take care and keep in touch."

"Will do, and give Haley a hug from me."

I disconnected and looked down at Basil, who had his head on his paws but was looking up at me with his sweet brown eyes.

"Well, fellow, time for us to get moving too."

He jumped up, tail wagging, ready for whatever I suggested.

I headed into the house for a shower and breakfast before we opened the yarn shop at ten.

Dora and I took turns opening the shop, and today she wouldn't be in till noon.

"Come on, Basil. Time for coffee first," I said, unclipping his leash and heading to the coffeemaker.

Dora had her own dog, Oliver, who was now elderly and didn't come to the shop with her anymore, so she was more than happy to have Basil with us during work hours. He was a good boy and enjoyed greeting customers, and I think he was a hit with them as well.

Very well mannered, he had just turned two years old. Gabe had gotten him as a puppy from a rescue group. His ancestry was of unknown origin, but he strongly resembled a cross between a Scottish terrier and a poodle. When designer dogs became popular and Gabe was questioned on Basil's breed, he'd jokingly refer to him as a Scottiepoo.

I had just poured the water into the coffeemaker when the door chimes tinkled and I turned around to see Shelby Sullivan enter the shop.

"Hey, Shelby. Just in time for coffee. It'll be ready shortly."

"Great. I found a nice pattern to make Orli a sweater, so I need to get some yarn."

Shelby Sullivan was a best-selling romance author, born and raised on Cedar Key, and an addicted knitter, especially when she was between novels.

"How're Josie and Orli doing? I imagine they appreciate the sweaters to keep them warm in the Boston area."

Shelby laughed as she fingered some yummy lavender alpaca yarn. "They're doing great and they seem to have survived their first winter up there and all the snow. Although I'm told it's not unusual to get some even in April."

Shelby's daughter, Josie Sullivan Cooper, had married the love of her life and the father of her daughter, Orli, the previous October. The wedding had been the event of the year on the island and thanks to Shelby's expert guidance, it had been on par with many celebrity weddings. Josie's husband, Grant, was an attorney in Boston and the three of them resided on the North Shore of the city.

"I saw on the national weather that the temps are still pretty chilly up there," I said, handing her a mug of coffee. "I'm sure it's quite a change from the tropical climate they're used to."

Shelby nodded. "Thanks. Yeah, but they both seem to love being in Boston and that's what matters."

I smiled as I recalled the control freak that Shelby used to be. But a scare with uterine cancer the year before had put life in perspective for her. She truly did seem to be less stressed and more understanding of Josie, allowing their mother-daughter relationship to strengthen.

"How about you?" she asked. "How are *you* doing?"

I let out a sigh. "I'm doing okay. As well as can be expected, I guess, but I'm beginning to feel like my life is on hold. In limbo."

"Two major losses in your life within eight months will certainly do that. When the time is right, you'll know which direction to take."

"I hope so," I said and took a sip of coffee. "I feel fortunate that we had Aunt Maude these extra years. We knew her heart was bad. The house is just so empty without her around."

Shelby placed eight skeins of alpaca on the counter and patted my arm. "I'm sure it is. Maybe you should still consider going over to Ormond Beach. You know . . . something different. New beginnings and all that."

"It just wouldn't be the same without Gabe. All of our plans are gone."

"Yes, they are, but that's part of life. It constantly changes whether we want it to or not. Believe me, I found that out last year. But, Chloe, that doesn't have to be a bad thing. Life is always full of surprises, and some of them can be quite wonderful. If we pay attention. Maybe you should go over there for a visit. Allow yourself to chill out and renew your energy."

"Alone? You mean go to Ormond Beach alone?"

Shelby laughed. "First of all, you wouldn't be alone. You'd have Basil with you. But yeah, find a nice place to stay for a while. No pressure. No commitments. I don't think women do this nearly enough. It's good to be alone sometimes. It allows us to reconnect with ourselves. Especially during times of change or confusion."

"Hmm," I said, slowly beginning to warm to the idea. "Maybe you're right. Maybe a change is what I need for a while."

"Give it some thought, Chloe. We just never know what's around that next corner," she said, passing me her credit card to pay for her purchase.

Born and raised north of Boston, **Terri DuLong** was previously a resident of Cedar Key, Florida. She now resides on the east coast of the state in Ormond Beach with her husband, three dogs, and two cats. A retired registered nurse, she began her writing career as a contributing writer for *Bonjour Paris*, where she shared her travel experiences in France in more than forty articles with a fictional canine narrator. Terri's love of knitting provides quiet time to develop her characters and plots as she works on her new Ormond Beach novels. You can visit her website at www.terridulong.com or at her Facebook fan page, www.facebook.com/TerriDuLongAuthor

CPSIA information can be obtained
at www.ICGtesting.com
Printed in the USA
LVOW07s1935140917
548743LV00002B/250/P